KISSED BY THE DRAGON'S BREATH

KISSED BY THE DRAGON'S BREATH

Caron Harrison

Copyright © 2011 by Caron Harrison

Caron Harrison asserts the moral right to be identified as the author of this work.

All rights reserved.

No part of this book may be reproduced, transmitted or stored in an information retrieval system in any form or by any means, electronic, graphic, photocopying, recording or otherwise, without prior written permission from the author.

This novel is a work of fiction. All characters portrayed in it are fictitious. Any resemblance to actual persons, living or dead is purely coincidental. Any references in the novel to herbal preparations and nutritional supplements should not be taken as medical advice. Readers with health concerns should consult their own qualified medical practitioner.

ISBN 978-1-4476-4631-0

Front cover image by Bryony Harrison
Back cover image by Nigel Harrison

KISSED BY THE DRAGON'S BREATH

Born Caron Wagner in 1957 in Epsom, Surrey Caron never had any intention of becoming a writer. After gaining a degree in geography at Durham University in 1978, she married Nigel Harrison, a doctor in the Royal Air Force. Caron's decision to be a full-time mother to their two daughters was the catalyst to her writing career.

In 1987 she began writing the *Cider and Schnapps* series. The four novels took eighteen years to complete and self-publish, in between moves around the UK, to Germany, Cyprus and to the Isle of Man.

A settled period of ten years on the Isle of Man followed, but in 2006 she and Nigel moved to Whangarei, New Zealand, leaving both daughters on the Isle of Man.

Caron spends her time teaching adult literacy, choral singing, gardening and trying out a wide variety of artistic endeavours. She can be contacted via her website: www.caronharrison.co.nz.

Other books by Caron Harrison

The *Cider and Schnapps* Series:

Shades of Grey
Divided Loyalties
Eclipse of the Son
Hunting Season

ACKNOWLEDGEMENTS

I would like to express my thanks to all my old friends at the Manx Wildlife Trust with whose roles I have taken such liberties, especially Duncan Bridges the current Director. My grateful thanks go to Andree Dubbeldam, whose beautiful book *Wildflowers of Mann* I have found most useful. I must also thank Felicity Cain, Sales Director of Wildlife Ltd, the MWT shop where I spent many a happy Tuesday morning as a volunteer sales assistant between 1996 and 2006.

There were many synchronicities, coincidences and serendipitous happenings leading up to and during the writing of this book. The right books seemed to cross my path at exactly the right moments, and I have listed the most influential in the bibliography.

Above all I thank my friends and family, especially my husband, Nigel, for their unfailing support, help and encouragement over the years.

Finally I wish to voice my heartfelt sorrow and support for the people of Christchurch and Canterbury, New Zealand and for the people of Japan, who have been so afflicted by the devastating earthquakes, which occurred in the final stages of preparation of this book.

NEW ZEALAND'S SOUTH ISLAND

CHAPTER ONE

The fairy face smiled at Kara from the wooded shoreline. It certainly looked like a face, being roughly of human size as far as she could tell, but somehow strangely not human. Despite the misty gloom surrounding the precipitous Fiordland slopes of Doubtful Sound, the face seemed to glow.

It was a trick of the light, Kara reasoned. Possibly just the pale under side of the mountain beech leaves. Or it could even be the white flowers of a manuka tree or some New Zealand bush unknown to her. She knew that the human brain will always try to manufacture a face from seemingly random blobs of vegetation or cloud, and Kara was certain that her brain worked perfectly.

As she watched, the sun broke briefly through the mist-shrouded peaks and a ray of light passed over the face. She followed the ray's path down through the bush and onto the surface of the water. As the cloud passed overhead, the ray of light skipped across the rippled water directly towards her until she felt it touch her face with a tingling fizz of radiation. The warmth lingered on her cheeks even after the cloud cover swallowed up the sun. Kara put her hand up to her face and smiled, mystified by how intensely happy she now felt after the fairy's touch.

As the glow on her face began to fade she looked towards the shore again, but the light pattern had changed and the face was no longer apparent amongst the impenetrable forest of mountain beech and the tall black tree fern. For an instant she felt a sense of loss, as though some connection had been severed. It was that same feeling of connection she always felt at the ancient Iron Age-Viking settlement at the Braaid, near her home on the Isle of Man. Nowhere so far in her grand tour of New Zealand had she felt that sense of antiquity she was used to at home. Until now.

It was strange, she thought, because Doubtful Sound and almost all of Fiordland National Park were virtually uninhabited. It was for that reason that the captain of the tour boat had stopped the boat's engines in the sheltered bay, and told them all to listen to the silence of the Sound. There were no jet planes, no roar of traffic, just the rustling beeches, occasional birdsong and the lapping of the water against the hull. Even the few children on board were engulfed by the silence. But in that silence Kara had felt a subtle contact with antiquity.

Their five minutes of silence over, the engines started up and the tourist boat cruised gently out of the bay, rapidly picking up speed to return up the sea fiord that was Doubtful Sound – so named, the boat tour guide told them, because Captain Cook was doubtful they would be able to sail out of it once in. As Kara disembarked the boat at the head of the fiord she looked back down the silver waters towards the bay with the fairy face. Overhead a patch of blue sky allowed sunshine to pour down again onto that spot where she had felt touched by magic.

'This way, Kara.' The voice was Robin's, the guide for her 'Mostly Wildlife' tour of New Zealand. 'We're all waiting for you.'

Startled, Kara turned back to the land. Everyone else on the excursion was already seated on the coach waiting to take them over the divide to Lake Manapouri, where another boat awaited them.

'Sorry,' she mumbled to the ever-patient Robin as she climbed aboard the coach. 'It's just so beautiful. I can't bear to leave.'

'A lot of people feel like that after they've been here,' he acknowledged with a reassuring smile.

Kara sat down next to him, and couldn't help gazing back again to the silver waters of Doubtful Sound as the coach began its return journey.

*

Kara was part of a tour group discovering the wildlife of New Zealand. There were only twenty of them on the tour, which was aimed at the 'more mature' traveller. When booking, Kara had rather surprised herself when she decided upon this more sedate tour, being quite happy roughing it normally, but she was having a particularly tiring week at work, and in the end she was pleased with her choice. She had to accept that middle age had well and truly come, and she was appreciating the chance to relax and indulge herself for once. The majority of her companions were of a similar age or older, although she had not really got to know any of them yet.

She had flown in to Christchurch, joined the tour with their appropriately named guide Robin, and so far had thoroughly enjoyed the experience. They had seen royal albatross, yellow-eyed penguins and fur seals on the Otago Peninsula, near Dunedin. Today on Doubtful Sound the calm weather conditions had allowed them to sail further out and see more fur seals in the Tasman Sea, and she could even tick off on her list the small pod of bottlenose dolphins that inhabited Doubtful Sound. So far she was very impressed with the youthful Robin's enthusiasm and expertise, as he had been able to answer every question she had put to him. She had been less attentive, however, to her fellow travellers, and had scarcely exchanged more than a few words with most of them.

Shyness had always been a big problem for her. Since her schooldays she had lived with her nose in books and never learnt the art of social conversation. She knew she came across as aloof and an intellectual snob to many people, but she was quite happy with her own company and the few like-minded friends she had managed to glean during her fifty-two years of existence.

That evening at their hotel in Te Anau she was the first of the 'Mostly Wildlife' group into dinner. As she sat at one of the two designated tables studying the menu, trying to decide between lamb shanks and cashew couscous, a couple from her tour group approached the table.

'May we sit next to you?' the woman asked in a barely noticeable Norwegian accent. Her gesture included her husband standing next to her.

Kara looked up. It was churlish to refuse, of course, but the couple had seemed pleasant enough so far on the trip, and were obviously bored with their own company or else thought she looked lonely. Perhaps she was at last. She smiled and waved to the empty seats. 'Please.'

'I'm Julia Korsvik and this is my husband Henrik. We're from Norway.'

Kara was glad to be reminded. Everyone had been introduced at the beginning of the tour, but Kara was hopeless at remembering names. They looked to be about Kara's own age, with nothing remarkable about them, just like herself.

'I'm Kara from the Isle of Man. Not Kelly but Kara.' The joke was lost on them of course. Who knew that old song these days, even in Britain? She always did this sort of thing when talking to people, making a fool of herself or gabbling irrelevancies. She found conversation so difficult. Fortunately the Korsviks helped her out in their excellent English.

'We know the Isle of Man. We were there in 2002 for your Tynwald Day when our King and Queen were the guests of honour.'

'Really? I remember that year, as I was invited to the official banquet at Castletown Golf Club in my capacity as Director of the Manx Wildlife Trust.' Kara stopped abruptly, fearing she was sounding pompous.

'Well, then we may have seen each other!' Henrik exclaimed. 'It's a small world, isn't it?'

The table was beginning to fill by now with other tour members, but they got into conversations of their own and Kara was left talking to the Korsviks. Kara found herself warming to the jolly couple over their starter of avocado and walnut salad, and began confiding things she normally kept to herself back home in the goldfish bowl that was the Isle of Man.

'I never got married as I always had some next project in line and couldn't make the commitment to anybody else,' she heard herself explaining after their enquiry about her family. 'I moved on between various conservation jobs after my degree, had a few boyfriends, only one of them serious. Now I find myself aged fifty-two, "of a certain age" as they say, with a house, an interesting job, a few friends, but suddenly wondering what it's all about.' Her new companions nodded as if they understood her predicament. 'When my father died last year he left me a little money. I knew he'd always wanted to visit New Zealand but had never got around to it, so I thought I'd use his money and travel for him. Perhaps if he's up there he's travelling with me!' She grinned to indicate her lack of belief in such things, and Julia and Henrik politely smiled back.

As the next course arrived, cashew couscous for Kara and lamb shanks for the Korsviks, Julia asked: 'Are you vegetarian?'

'No, although with my interest in wildlife conservation I suppose it might be logical. No, I just fancied a change from meat and fish today. I'm trying to eat more healthily these days, as we all are, and I try to buy organic food when I can find it and afford it. Ah, that reminds me.' She reached into her battered but capacious handbag and pulled out a lidded tub containing an assortment of capsules and tablets. 'My supplements,' she explained rattling the tub. 'I always take them with my evening meal. I've read that modern food can be deficient in many vitamins and minerals. The soils have been depleted of minerals, and fresh food often travels too far and is stored too long so the vitamins decay. You Norwegians probably eat enough oily fish for your omega 3, but I take these high-strength fish-oil capsules.'

She knew she was pontificating again on her latest pet subject of nutrition and soil mineral depletion. She either preached or was tongue-tied. There was no middle ground, but the couple seemed receptive and she might be helping them with her advice. 'You Norwegians, with your dark winters, certainly need these', she said holding up a small golden capsule towards the window. It took on a warm amber glow from the still high sun. 'Vitamin D. Liquid light!' she laughed and swallowed it down.

*

The next morning she felt embarrassed walking into breakfast. The Korsviks were already seated at a table with one of the Australian couples, she realised with relief. She filled her glass with orange juice then sat at the other table reserved for their group, her back to the Norwegians. They must have thought her a right old bore. After a whole evening spent with them, she realised she had learnt next to nothing about them or Norway. After she had dominated the conversation with her new knowledge about the importance of nutrition to general health and fighting disease, they had only spoken about places of interest on the Isle of Man. She knew she was obsessed with the place, having arrived on the island from mainland Britain ten years previously, knowing next to nothing about it, but now waxing lyrical to all and sundry ever since.

There was truly something magical and mysterious about the place, with its mist- and heather-clad hills, hidden waterfalls in bluebell-wooded glens, its rugged coastline and, above all, its ancient places and real sense of history. She had happily taken up the Manx custom of greeting the fairies when driving over the Fairy Bridge on the road from Douglas to Castletown, although she would never tie a message to the rowan tree there, as some locals and visitors did. She had sat many times on the stone wishing chair in Glen Helen and, as sincerely as a child blowing out its birthday candles, made a wish. It was the closest she ever got to praying, but sat there under the massive beech trees she felt at peace like nowhere else on earth, and it had become her place of solace.

It was something of that same cathedral-like majesty that she had felt yesterday at Doubtful Sound, she realised as she sipped her juice.

Surrounded by the waterfall-streaked, near-vertical fiord sides, only boats or planes could access the area, and there were few places where anybody could possibly climb ashore. But she knew she had felt antiquity, or a presence of some kind.

'I'm going daft!' she muttered into her orange juice. 'I'll believe in fairies next.'

*

Their day in Queenstown was one of the few free days of the tour when wildlife took a back seat and Robin had a break from nannying. For those not interested in the thrills and spills of high-octane Queenstown or even a wine-tasting tour round some of the numerous vineyards, Robin recommended something a bit quieter: the picturesque and historic gold-panning town of Arrowtown. Kara, along with a few others in the group, Julia and Henrik included, all made the short journey by local bus to wander leisurely through the little town amongst the hordes of other tourists.

The sun shone brilliantly over the forested mountains onto the Wild West style shops and gold stores. Tired and hot after scrambling around the restored hovels of the old Chinese encampment just upriver from the main town, Kara sought refuge in an ice cream parlour in a shady arcade. She tried the Kiwis' favourite Hokey Pokey flavour ice cream, deciding it was like crunchy caramel, then feeling refreshed she wandered back down the arcade to a little shop at its riverside end, which had dragons in the window among many other assorted New Age items.

As a very small child two of her favourite television programmes had been Oliver Postgate and Peter Firmin's animations, *Ivor the Engine* and *Noggin the Nog*. Ivor had a friend who was a red Welsh Dragon called Idris, and Noggin encountered a very large, sad ice dragon, which had occupied the Northlands. Kara had taken the side of the dragon against St George and started a collection of dragons large and small, which later in life included a green spotted gurgling Soup Dragon from yet another favourite children's programme, *The Clangers*. Indeed, such was her penchant for dragons, that when she had first arrived on the Isle of Man and seen the famous tiered Tynwald Hill, where the government and dignitaries gathered on July the fifth each year to promulgate the new laws of the island, she had immediately been reminded of one of the books she had kept from childhood: *Borrobil* by William Croft Dickinson. The book's cover featured a huge, bright-yellow dragon breathing luminescent-green smoke at a knight charging towards it with a flaming lance. The dragon had its tail wrapped tightly around the background hill, squeezing it into visible layers. Now when all the dignitaries and members of the House of Keys gathered on Tynwald Hill each Tynwald Day, Kara saw in her fertile mind's eye the golden dragon's tail holding them all firmly down on each tier.

It was one of the things she had found herself telling Julia and Henrik the previous evening, that King Harald V and Queen Sonja of Norway had sat on the top level, safe from the encompassing dragon's tail. She had also told them about greeting the fairies, never, ever saying the word r...a...t out loud (she couldn't even think it without spelling it now) and of the Manx custom of leaving a ruined cottage, or *tholtan*, for the fairy folk to inhabit. They had been amazed just how many Manx superstitions still held sway in the modern era.

'I see dragons!' It was Henrik's voice. They were standing right beside her, inspecting the shop window display.

'Oh. Yes.' She smiled warmly at them, ashamed to have turned her back on them at breakfast. 'I was just thinking about you both, remembering our conversation last night. I was hoping I hadn't bored you too much.'

'Not at all,' Henrik replied courteously. 'We both found it fascinating, and I'll never forget what a close escape our King had from that dragon on Tynwald Hill. I shall tell him when I next see him.'

Kara could tell he meant it, and was amused to think that her fantasy would be related to the King of Norway.

'Will you buy one?' Julia asked, nodding towards the dragons.

'If I find one that speaks to me,' Kara told her. 'I've got so many now that they have to be special in some way.'

'Exactly,' Julia agreed. 'I'm the same with sheep, but I'm finding so many new ones here in New Zealand, my suitcase will be full of them. Here, look.' She held up a carrier bag and pulled out a tissue-wrapped item. It was a beautifully carved merino ram, showing off its magnificent horns.

'He's gorgeous. Very masculine,' Kara said admiringly, running her fingers over the polished body.

'Isn't he,' Julia sighed.

The two women shared glances and laughed.

'Come on, wife!' Henrik said with a mock-Viking snarl. 'I'm hot. I need a drink of beer.' Turning to Kara he became the diplomat again. 'We'll leave you to select your dragon in peace. Goodbye for now.' So saying he took his wife gently by the arm, stepped out from the arcade into the fierce sun and wandered off in search of beer.

Glad to be staying in the shade, Kara stepped into the shop. Inside were displays of stones and crystals, dream-catchers and all the usual paraphernalia of the New Age. Buddhas sat by unicorns, Feng Shui fountains bubbled in a corner. At the back of the shop one whole display was dedicated to model fairies, while dragons perched upon a neighbouring shelf, their gaze drawing her in. But it was the bookshelf beside the fairies that Kara studied first. Even before dragons, books were her passion, and her taste in reading matter had recently changed to more esoteric matters after years of studying and working in the field of ecology. Her more recent interest in nutrition had diverted her to complementary therapies, homeopathy, acupuncture and the concept of the energy force Chi, Qi or Ki, depending on whether you were a Mandarin, Cantonese or Japanese speaker. Although Western thought had no satisfactory scientific explanation for any of these therapies, they had apparently worked for hundreds, if not thousands, of years, and Kara found herself intrigued and wanting to learn more.

Her eyes wandered across the shelves of alternative healing therapies, sayings of the Dalai Lama and books about angels. A book with a deep-red cover attracted her, and she drew it out. It was entitled *Fairy Folk Tales of the Maori*, written by a man with a Manx-sounding name, James Cowan. It seemed rather old and, on checking the date, she found it was published in 1925. She turned to the first page of text and her eye was immediately caught by a reference to the 'fairy-ridden' Isle of Man. How extraordinary to come across a reference to the Isle of Man in a book about New Zealand, she thought.

Skim-reading the first chapter, Kara read of a forest-dwelling, fair-skinned race of people, the Patu-paiarehe, whom the Maori came across when they first arrived in New Zealand and deemed to be sprites of the woods or supernatural beings. A few pages flicked over by themselves, and suddenly she was reading about how the Patu-paiarehe were pursued into the wilderness beyond Lake Te Anau.

Kara stood there quite stunned. Had she seen one of them two days ago on the slopes of Doubtful Sound? She grinned at her foolishness. What she had seen was a trick of the light, exactly the sort of thing that creates myth and legend. Nevertheless, the book's curious conjunction of New Zealand with the Isle of Man made her decide to buy it for further reading. Casting a quick eye over the dragons she decided that none of them was sufficiently appealing, so she strolled over to the counter to pay for the book.

The young woman serving had dyed purple hair, black nail varnish and wore a fluorescent-green cheesecloth top. Dragon's breath, Kara immediately thought, remembering the cover of *Borrobil*.

'How're you today?' the young woman greeted her cheerily in the manner of most Kiwi shop assistants.

'Good, thank you.' It had taken a few days for Kara to switch to answering 'good' instead of her usual 'fine' to this greeting. 'And you?'

'Good. Enjoying the hot weather at last.' The assistant took the book and wrote down the title and author in a notebook. 'Excuse our old-fashioned book-sales system,' she apologised. 'But we find it works and never seems to go wrong, unlike modern technology.' She looked again at the book's cover. 'That's a strange coincidence. I've just been reading about the New Zealand fairies in this magazine.' She pointed down to the counter where pages full of tightly packed print with a black- and-white photo showed an in-depth article on something. 'It's all very political here, you know.'

'What is?' Kara asked, handing over her credit card.

'Fairies. Or rather the fair people.' She pointed again to the magazine article. 'It says here that Maori legend tells of the fairies as a fair-skinned race who looked and behaved much like ordinary humans, and occupied the land before the Maori came to New Zealand. But since the 1970s, when politics and the issue of Maori land rights came to the fore, the government refuses to grant access to archaeologists to the areas where they've found strange, old, stone ruins in the past. It's all gone very hush-hush, apparently, and very contentious.'

The young woman concentrated on the credit card transaction for a moment. As she handed back Kara's card, she glanced at the name on the bottom and raised her plucked eyebrows. 'Did you know your name has a meaning in ancient Egyptian?'

'No. I thought it was just my parents being Anglo-Saxon in their spelling of the Italian word for "dear".'

The young woman shook her head then shrugged her shoulders in a 'could be' gesture. Turning round she picked up a hardback book from the floor beside her and flicked through the early chapters until she found the page she was looking for. 'I only remember this because my name, Sharon, is sort of mentioned too, so I took note of it. Ah, here it is. It says "Ka" is the life spirit or soul and "Ra" is of course the sun god. My name occurs in "The Plane of Shar-On", meaning the Realm of the Orbit of Light, according to Laurence Gardner, the author. So you're the Spirit of the Sun and I'm the Orbit of Light. Cool, huh?'

Kara nodded, intrigued by the information. 'What is that book?'

'It's called *Lost Secrets of the Sacred Ark*. It's brilliant. Absolutely mind-blowing,' Sharon said, handing her the heavy book to look at. 'I can't begin to tell you what's in it because it's so complex and so weird. But the more you read the more amazing it gets, but it all seems so totally logical and explains so many things. You really ought to read it, if you can get hold of it. I'm reading it for the second time now.'

The book was still open at the page Sharon had found. 'How strange,' Kara remarked. 'Page fifty-two. That's my age. Life is full of coincidences, isn't it?'

Sharon gave her a curious look. 'Serendipity,' she replied meaningfully. 'You were obviously meant to see that now.'

Kara could barely suppress her smile of amusement, not wanting to offend Sharon, who clearly believed in such things.

Another customer had approached the counter wanting serving, so Kara handed back the book, having noted the title and author. She would certainly look out for it and read it just to see if she was as bowled over by it as Sharon obviously was.

'Well, it was very interesting meeting you, Orbit of Light,' she told Sharon.

'You too, Spirit of the Sun. Don't forget your book. Oh, and you can have this magazine. I think you'll find it all fascinating, not just the fairy article. It's a bit different from most, and I'm keen to spread the word on the things they write about. Take it back to the UK and show your friends.' So saying, Sharon popped the magazine in the paper bag with the book and handed it to Kara.

What a fascinating woman, Kara thought as she left the shop. And so easy to talk to.

By now she was thirsty and ready for some food. She strolled in the direction that the Korsviks had taken, following the River Arrow downstream. As the riverside road turned back up to rejoin the main street, she saw a beer garden where Julia and Henrik were sitting under a sunshade. They spotted her and beckoned her to join them, as the tables were by now all full.

Pausing first to order a cold beer and a salad inside at the bar, Kara then made her way to the garden and sat on the chair next to Julia, trying to keep in the shade.

'You didn't buy one?' Julia asked with a nod at the bag that was too flat to hold a dragon.

'No. Just a book.' Kara found herself reluctant to tell her new friends about her strange series of coincidences in the shop: that the book she had just happened to pull out had turned out to be so relevant, even mentioning the Isle of Man and Te Anau; that Sharon had been reading an article on the very same subject; that both their names were given ancient Egyptian meanings in the Laurence Gardner book on the page that was her age. She had the sudden feeling the magazine would turn up more surprises.

CHAPTER TWO

During the course of that evening Kara sat on the hotel's terrace, enjoying a glass or two of the local Chard Farm Pinot Gris, and read both the magazine article and part of the book. It was intriguing that James Cowan had observed many apparent parallels in the folk beliefs of the Maori and Celtic peoples, notably the fairy folks' avoidance of daylight and fire, and their ability to conjure up mists to hide in. She recalled that the Manx called a rapidly rolling in sea mist 'Manannan's cloak', by which means the Celtic sea-god would protect his island when undesirable visitors were approaching by sea.

It was while reading this section that Kara was brought up sharply by a parallel with yet another culture. The sun was referred to as *Tama-nui-te-Ra*. Kara put the book down on the table in front of her. Was Ra part of the name for the Maori sun god, just like the Egyptian god? Or was it even the word for the sun? She would have to check it out and find a Maori language book. In the meantime the magazine article had stimulated her curiosity to want to look at the referenced website, which contentiously implied the original settlers were of Celtic origin. She could certainly see why the Maori people might be upset by that theory, as their claims to first land occupation rights would be invalidated.

She had deliberately not brought a laptop with her on her holiday, not wanting to be even remotely tempted to catch up with what was going on at work. She had her cheap and cheerful mobile phone, and her colleagues at the Manx Wildlife Trust could text her if there was anything important, but it meant she had no easy access to the Internet. Her research would have to wait until she returned home.

Quaffing the last of her wine she picked up the book and magazine then stood up to leave the terraced bar. The sand flies had got to her, despite her long trousers and sleeves, and she needed to find her tube of antihistamine cream urgently before she scratched herself raw.

They were due to have an early start next morning, as it was a long drive from Queenstown, past Wanaka to Haast and onwards up the West Coast to the Franz Josef Glacier. Kara had initially meant to read her books on the flora and fauna of New Zealand in preparation for the next part of the tour, but the fairy book and magazine had distracted her. Now the wine and the heat of the day had got to her and she decided on an early night.

Settling down to sleep she recalled one of the photos in the magazine, this one in colour, of an artist's impression on a New Zealand stamp of one of the fairy folk. He was strangely reminiscent of the tall elves in *The Lord of the Rings* films, with their long blond hair, and she remembered James Cowen writing about two different sets of fairy folk in New Zealand, the redheads and the golden heads. It was all getting very complicated.

*

'Life is khaki,' the brown-cloaked figure told her. He was standing in a circle of standing stones on a cliff top. Behind him the sun was setting over the sea, its rays shining through the white hair on his head like a halo, leaving his face in shadow. In his right hand he held a staff, and as she watched he turned towards the sun, raised his staff in greeting towards it then carefully positioned the staff back on the ground in the centre of the circle. The long shadows of man and staff streamed towards her, touching the stone by which she stood. She felt a tingling vibration like an electric shock.

*

The glowing red numbers of the bedside clock said two in the morning, but Kara felt wide awake, the dream as sharp as crystal in her mind. The white-haired, bearded man had looked just like the cloaked figure of Manannan in the guiding videos around the House of Manannan Museum in Peel, on the west coast of the Isle of Man. The cliffs could have been Peel Hill or one of the many hilltops along that western coast. But what on earth had he meant by the words 'life is khaki'? What jumbled message was her brain manufacturing while she slept?

Kara couldn't work it out. As far as she knew, khaki was Urdu for 'dusty', and the only standing stones on Peel Hill were the comparatively recent Corrin's Tower. It had been built at the beginning of the nineteenth century, she vaguely recalled, by Thomas Corrin, who was eventually buried there with his family, as he did not want them to be buried in church consecrated ground. Perhaps the tower had been built over the site of some old standing stones? The hill was a prominent landmark and just the sort of place where Neolithic people might have wanted to erect some kind of monument. South Barrule, just inland from there, had a massive ancient hill fort on its summit, and there were many other stone circles and ancient sites dotted around the island. Perhaps it was worth looking up in the old records to see if there was anything on the hill before Thomas Corrin built his tower there.

She sat up in bed and switched on the light. When she was this awake she knew she wouldn't fall asleep again for ages, so she got up to make herself a cup of tea. As the kettle began to boil she remembered that Peel's nickname was 'Sunset City', and from South Barrule she wondered whether the sun would set in line with Peel Hill on either a solstice or equinox. Summer solstice if anything, she reckoned, conjuring up a mental map of the Isle of Man. South Barrule was a bit south-east of Peel Hill, so the sun setting in the north-west might line up with it. She was probably just being fanciful after her strange dream, but it would be a good excuse for a pleasant evening's wander up South Barrule at the next summer solstice to test out her theory, or see how far wrong she was.

Bringing her cup of tea back to bed she reached for Sharon's magazine to read. The articles in it ranged from the latest conspiracy theories, as she would have called them until she actually read the articles and was quite persuaded by the arguments, to lost civilisations and alternative archaeology, to suppressed findings in medical research. A lot of it was a bit heavy going for this time of night and she began to flip through the pages to the end section where she found some interesting book reviews.

'Good heavens!' she gasped out loud, putting down her teacup with a crash onto its saucer. The theme tune of the TV series *The Twilight Zone* coursed through her mind as she saw the words 'Isle of Man' for the second time in twenty-four hours written on a page in New Zealand.

'This is getting weird,' she muttered to herself, as she began to read the review of *The Sacred Center: The Ancient Art of Locating Sanctuaries* by John Michell. The photograph of the recently deceased author reminded her instantly of Gandalf, with his wise and wizardly eyes. He seemed to have studied geomancy and was credited for the popular interest in leylines. In the book he showed how to apply sacred geometry and some divination to establish the locations of ancient sacred sites. Tynwald on the Isle of Man was such a site, apparently, as was the more famous Delphi. The reviewer had found the book fascinating and thoroughly researched.

Kara studied the picture of the cover, which depicted the white pyramidal shape of Mount Kailas, sacred to Buddhists and Hindus as the mountain at the centre of the earth, which Michael Palin had found so fascinating during his televised journey through the Himalayas. The magazine's photo reproduction was rather small but despite the dim light of the bedside lamp she spotted something else on the cover, above the mountain's peak. Peering closely, she could just make out a faint map showing the outlines of the British Isles with the Isle of Man targeted dead centre. Kara knew she would have to order the book, and it had to be done online.

She could not explain the sense of excitement she felt on discovering this book and the urgent need she had to read it. She wondered why her dream woke her up so she would remember it, and why she had read this article on such a similar theme as her dream immediately afterwards. Her brain began feverishly to ask all kinds of questions. What exactly were leylines and did New Zealand have any? If there were people here before the Maori, could they have left any signs such as stone circles or standing stones? The magazine article had certainly reported beehive-shaped stone huts being found in the ancient forests of Northland, and that the Maori had referred to these fair-skinned people as the ancient stone-builders. It was not inconceivable they had left their mark elsewhere on the landscape, as yet unrealised or unacknowledged by the current archaeologists.

Suddenly her eyelids began to feel heavy again. Letting the magazine slip from her grasp onto the bedcovers, Kara turned out the light and settled back down to sleep.

*

She was late for breakfast. The others in her tour group were already vacating their tables by the time she hurried into the hotel's breakfast room. She grabbed a glass of orange juice, a bread roll and an individual portion pack of Vegemite, which was the best substitute for the usual Bovril on toast she had at home. Gulping them down, she then hurried back to her room to get ready for departure.

She had thought she might doze on the coach after her disturbed night's sleep, but the scenery was simply too breathtaking to miss and she kept her eyes glued to the coach window. From Queenstown State Highway 6 passed the craggy tussock- grassed mountains of the now deserted ski fields, was constricted through the Kawarau River Gorge and passed the famous Kawarau Bridge bungy jump. Kara shuddered at the sight of it but was quickly diverted from thoughts of such madness by the numerous vineyards that dotted the banks of the river. Chard Farm, which had supplied her previous night's wine, flitted past her window, and she rapidly recognised a few more names from her recent evenings in New Zealand.

At the confluence with the Clutha River they turned north towards Wanaka, following the tumbling waters of the Clutha upstream past an open-air gold-panning museum. Robin gave them a running commentary on the history of the area as the Clutha's glacial outwash valley opened out on the approach to Wanaka, filling with cherry orchards and yet more vineyards.

Following their route on her map, Kara leaned forward to the front seat and asked Robin if they were stopping in Wanaka.

'No, it's too early yet. We've a five hour journey to Franz Josef,' he replied. 'We turn off before it, anyway. Our first stop is in Makarora. You'll like it there. Very peaceful.'

Kara looked on her map and located it on the Makarora River, which flowed into the northern end of the massive Lake Wanaka. They drove alongside Lake Hawea for quite some way, with its blue waters and impressive mountain backdrop, before crossing the small divide to Lake Wanaka itself. The coach was silent as everybody took in the majesty of the mountains. Not a boat or farm was to be seen, with only the road clinging on to the glacially eroded slopes of the lakeside as the only obvious sign of civilisation. Once they reached the Makarora River, however, there was more flat land, and farm buildings appeared. The hamlet of Makarora boasted a small café and store for travellers heading for the Haast Pass, and it was here they made a stop for coffee.

Robin was right, Kara thought as she sipped her flat white, looking out over meadows to the braided river channel a few hundred metres away. It is peaceful here. She sat listening to the strikingly clear birdsong, which Robin identified for them as a bellbird's, emanating from a nearby copse of southern beech. Breathing in the crystal clear mountain air she felt she hadn't a care in the world. Her mind emptied of its chatter and she just sat there, conscious only of peace and tranquillity.

All too soon they were back on the coach entering a different landscape of lush beech rainforest clothing the valley. After about half an hour they made a brief stop to see the Blue Pools. Robin took them for the short walk through the open forest on a well gravelled path, pointing out the spindly, juvenile lancewood trees with their strange saw-tooth-sharp long leaves growing under the beech canopy.

'Once the lancewood trees grow taller than a feeding moa they change their leaf-shape and look more like a regular tree,' Robin told the group. 'Or so the theory goes. But now, of course, there aren't any more moa. They were hunted to extinction.'

A small bird twittered from a branch nearby. 'Fantail,' Robin said. 'They hang around waiting for insects to be stirred up when we walk.'

They continued walking slowly through the beech trees, listening to the bird song as Robin identified them and the other trees around. Kara took photos of a totara tree covered in what looked like long wisps of silvery moss then stopped short as she saw a tree to the left of the path with a face on it. This time she could see it clearly as hollows and mossy ridges on the trunk, but it looked uncannily like the profile of the Ent in *The Lord of the Rings* films. She took a photo, as did others in the group who noticed her activity and were likewise tickled by the features of the beech tree.

They soon reached the tumbling river, which they had to cross over on a narrow suspension bridge with a maximum of ten at a time. It swayed slightly as they walked over it, such that Kara had to catch hold of Loris, a rather frail American lady in their group, who nearly fell over. Her robust husband, Wayne, who was trying to photograph the river from the swaying bridge, gave up, offering Loris his arm instead to accompany her the rest of the way over. Little and Large. Kara smiled wistfully to herself.

The Blue Pools themselves were viewed from another suspension bridge, which again made photography tricky. Two large trout were visible in the deep ice-blue water against the pale underlying rock, causing some excitement among the fishing fraternity, Wayne amongst them. Kara could hear Robin explaining there was strictly no fishing allowed in the Blue Pools themselves, as she waited for a brief lull of people on the bridge before managing to snap a couple of photos. She then hurried to catch up with Robin to ask him some questions about the trout, leaving Wayne and Loris struggling to negotiate the swaying bridge.

The road through the Haast Pass wound round the river valleys, crossing numerous streams on single-track bridges, and eventually descended steeply to the Gates of Haast, an impressive gorge under the narrow road bridge. After that, the valley slowly began to widen into the gentle river flats of the coast and the road straightened out, much to Loris's very vocal relief.

They ate lunch at Haast township, which Kara expected from the map to be a moderate sized town, but which seemed to be just a few motels, a backpackers hostel, a possum fur and merino shop, a gemstone shop and the café opposite the public toilets. Knowing that Loris was feeling queasy both from the suspension bridges and the very windy road, Kara chatted to the Americans to try to help Loris keep her mind from her stomach.

It was another two-hour's drive up the isolated West Coast to Franz Josef village where they finally stopped for three nights at the Scenic Hotel. The twenty members of the tour group gathered in reception awaiting their room allocations. Kara flicked through the rack of tourist pamphlets as she waited her turn. There seemed so much to do, like everywhere else they had been so far, she could have stayed here a week. There were eco tours, native bird-watching trips, a visit to the nearby white heron colony which they were doing tomorrow, a Department of Conservation Visitor Centre to browse around, as well as the more activity-based entertainments such as horse riding and tramping, as they called hiking here. She was very tempted by the Glacier Hot Pools and picked up the information leaflet.

When it was her turn at the reception desk she found that they all had rooms in the superior 'Douglas' wing of the two-wing hotel. The other was called the 'Graham' wing, and Kara couldn't help but smile at the appropriateness of the allocation, as she lived in Douglas on the Isle of Man. Another coincidence, she thought. A minor one for sure, but coupled with all the others recently it became more noteworthy.

CHAPTER THREE

Their first full day at Franz Josef had them divided up into two separate groups to visit the white heron sanctuary up the coast at Whataroa. It involved a sedate jet-boat ride up the Waitangi Roto River, followed by a guided boardwalk around the swamp and rainforest, which was New Zealand's only nesting site of the Kotuku, or white heron.

Kara was scheduled for the morning tour, and took so many photos of the platform nests with their bundles of heron chicks and brilliant white parents, and of a few even rarer royal spoonbills, that she had to go to a local store to buy more batteries for her camera. There she met up with Julia and Henrik, who found themselves in a similar predicament.

'What are you doing this afternoon after our glacier trip briefing?' Julia asked her as they pondered the array of batteries. 'You are going on the half-day glacier trip, aren't you? I know not everybody has the energy.'

'I wouldn't miss it!' Kara exclaimed. 'But I know Wayne and Loris are taking a scenic flight instead. Poor Loris suffers with her balance, hence her trouble with the bridge yesterday. She said she's fine in a plane though.'

'I was talking to Karl and Silke – the German couple,' Julia explained on seeing Kara's lack of recognition of the names. 'They're also flying. Poor Karl wanted to walk up to the glacier, but Silke wouldn't let him. Wise of her really, considering his age, as even the easiest valley walk takes about three hours. I think they're taking the helicopter and landing up there, so at least he'll get to see it close up. You haven't spoken to them yet?' Julia probed.

'No, not really. Remiss of me, I know,' Kara admitted with a tinge of guilt. 'I'm a bit of a loner, really, although they all seem a nice bunch on our tour.' She remembered her plans for the afternoon and quite spontaneously added: 'I was thinking of relaxing in the Glacier Hot Pools later on today. Would you care to join me?'

Kara had no idea why she asked the Norwegian couple, but suddenly it seemed nicer to have someone else to talk to, and she realised she was quite getting to like them.

Julia looked at Henrik. 'What do you think? Should we escort this lady to the baths?'

Kara hadn't thought of it like that, and hoped they didn't think she was angling for a chaperone. She was quite capable of looking after herself at her age. Then she realised by Julia's expression that she was only teasing.

'That sounds splendid!' Henrik replied eagerly. 'Although I think Robin said our glacier trip has been upgraded to include entry to the pools. But I certainly don't mind going twice.' He looked at his watch. 'We'd better get these batteries paid for and head off for our glacier briefing, then we can meet up to enjoy a good soak amongst the rainforest.'

*

The next day Kara prepared herself for the trek up to the Franz Josef Glacier, loading her camera with the fresh batteries. She had several layers of clothing available, two of which were in her rucksack for the moment, along with a tube of sun-cream and her sunglasses. Donning her white Manx Wildlife Trust cap, with its flying tern logo, and her walking boots, she left her room and headed outside. The day was overcast and windy, and Kara was looking forward to the exercise now after the somewhat sedentary pace so far. She was hoping they would get to see a kea, a large greenish-brown scavenging parrot, which Robin warned them was now something of a nuisance to unwary travellers.

Outside the hotel she met up with Robin and the dozen members of their tour going on the glacier trip. Their local guide, a very tanned and experienced-looking young man, arrived soon after, dressed in the company shorts and polo shirt.

'Morning everybody. My name's Hamish,' he announced in a broad Scots accent. 'It's my pleasure to take you all up onto the glacier today. The weather looks reasonable so far and is supposed to brighten up a bit later, but I hope you all have spare warm clothing you were advised you to bring with you?' There were murmurs all round the group then Hamish handed out bags containing crampons, which they tied round their waists.

As they started out on the walk up to the glacier through the rainforest, Kara chatted to Julia and Henrik, but she soon resorted to being her normal solitary self, as she stopped too often to take photographs for most people's liking. Gazing up through the rainforest to the nearby glacier and the snowy peaks of the Southern Alps, she was once again awestruck by the remoteness of them and how incredibly difficult the early explorers must have found travelling here. The whole of the south-west corner of New Zealand was a vast wilderness, and it was no wonder that a bird thought extinct, the dodo-like blue takahe, had suddenly turned up again in 1948 in the Murchison Mountains west of Lake Te Anau. She had also read that a lost herd of buffalo was reputed to exist somewhere in the wilds. Who was to say there weren't any fairies hiding out still in the dense mountain forests, chased there by New Zealand's later immigrants?

Kara wondered whether to ask Hamish whether there was any local folk-lore, but as she caught up with him he was busy pointing out hanging valleys and regaling his eager listeners with geographical information about other glacial features of the landscape, and she didn't want to interrupt him with trivia. He didn't look the sort who would know anything about fairies anyway. Just then Robin pointed out a kea perched up on a rocky outcrop, much to everyone's delight, and Kara's thoughts of fairies evaporated.

When they reached the terminal face of the glacier they strapped on their crampons. Hamish led them onto the convoluted surface by means of pre-cut steps and portable metal bridges. Kara made sure she was at the front near Hamish to hear what he was saying, glad now of her extra layers, as the wind blowing down the ice was quite cool.

When he took them into an ice tunnel carved by melt-water inside the glacier, Kara held her breath, overwhelmed by the tunnel's translucent turquoise colour. It was like being in the blue veins of some living and breathing ice monster, or in the home of Noggin the Nog's ice dragon. Sounds resonated around the ice so it was hard to locate their source, while the eerie light seemed almost tangible in the chilled air of the void. When she finally let it go, her breath hung blue in front of her.

I want to capture this moment, she thought, feeling the strange vibrations circulating through the ice tunnel around her and up through the crampons into her boots. It was like the energy of the ice, flowing over the decades and centuries, absorbing time as it travelled, capturing the memory of all the visitors who had stood here, like her, and wondered at the beauty of it.

'You look like you feel at home here,' Henrik said, disturbing her reverie.

'Oh! Um...' Kara noticed him crouched in the low tunnel in front of her with his camera poised, having just taken her picture. 'Yes, I do. It feels friendly, like being in the womb of the earth, or something fanciful like that.' She handed him her camera. 'Would you mind?'

The moment had passed, and Kara knew the photo wouldn't reflect her emotions any more as she posed with a standard cheesy grin on her face. She noticed the Japanese couple from the tour with their heads bent in the low tunnel and their eyes closed as if in prayer, as though they too were connecting with the spiritual power of the place.

On the return trek she fell into step with Julia and Henrik, obviously accomplished hill walkers with their well-worn hiking boots and stout sticks they'd picked up in the forest below. With them was the other solo traveller of their party, a young man in his late twenties, who looked to be partly of Native American descent with his black hair and high cheekbones. Apart from his name, given at their initial meeting as Martin Whitestar, she knew nothing about him except his penchant for wearing T-shirts from the exotic locations he had visited, and that he was often to be seen of an evening sitting in a corner of that day's hotel bar tapping away at his laptop.

Laptop. The wheels turned in Kara's brain and she positioned herself just behind Henrik and initiated a conversation, hoping Martin would join in.

'Pretty impressive, wasn't it? Although I suppose you're used to glaciers and such-like in Norway,' she said to Henrik.

'Not in Oslo,' he replied. 'But yes, I've seen a few. It's the noise they make I find so fascinating.'

'Yeah,' Martin agreed, looking over his shoulder to smile a greeting to her. 'All that creaking and groaning. It's like they're alive. I've cruised round the Alaskan glaciers and heard them from a long way off. Quite an eerie sound.'

'You seem to travel a lot, judging by your T-shirts,' Kara commented.

'Yup. I'm a freelance travel writer. I write about the country that I think will be or should be flavour of the month. New Zealand's still very much in vogue and I thought it was about time I visited before travel becomes too expensive… or dangerous,' he added.

'But New Zealand is always potentially dangerous,' she remarked. 'Earthquakes, volcanic eruptions, flash floods. The world is never safe. You can't always stay at home and never venture out.'

'It's all a matter of perception and relativity,' Julia pointed out, hanging back a fraction so she could walk alongside Kara.

'Relativity?' Kara queried.

'The relative time-scales involved: geological or historical. How often do volcanoes erupt? I don't suppose the ones near Rotorua will blow their tops while we're visiting. I hope not, anyway!'

Martin took up the theme. 'That's true. The threat of terrorism is perceived as an ongoing danger, whereas geological events usually aren't. Until the 2004 tsunami, that is. I think we're all more aware of that problem now. But apart from tsunamis, we all seem to think humanity poses the greater danger these days, not Mother Nature.'

'What about global warming?' Kara pointed out.

'I've noticed they call it 'climate change' now,' Henrik remarked casually. 'Perhaps they're becoming more cautious in their predictions in case the next Ice Age is just around the corner.'

'Whatever makes you say that?' Kara asked. 'I thought they were all agreed it's getting warmer.'

Henrik shrugged. 'There are questions about the accuracy and interpretation of certain data. Besides, it was even warmer in the early Middle Ages and they didn't use oil then,' he pointed out, quickening his pace towards the still distant village as though reluctant to enlarge upon his comments.

Kara sensed her opportunity to ask Martin if she might access the Internet using his laptop disappearing with each step nearer the hotel. Surprising herself, she touched him boldly on the shoulder. He slowed his pace and turned to her while Julia joined up with her husband.

'Martin,' Kara began a little tentatively now she had his attention. 'I don't suppose I might borrow your laptop this evening very briefly? I just want to order a book rather urgently over the Internet.'

He looked momentarily surprised at her request, but his good nature won him over. 'Surely. It must be an important book!'

'Well, it's not the sort of book I normally buy, but recently I've found my interests… branching out, and now I keep coming across references to things all the time. It's like there was a whole world out there I knew nothing about, but now I can see it, it's all around me and I need to find out more.'

'Oh?'

The silence that followed his simple question drew out more explanation from her. 'Since we visited Doubtful Sound, I've had strange experiences... coincidences, synchronicities or whatever you want to call them. I keep coming across references to fairies both here and on the Isle of Man where I live.' She found herself blushing now. 'You see, I fancied I saw a fairy at Doubtful Sound, and then all this started happening. And then this woman in the fairy and dragon shop in Arrowtown lent me this magazine, and last night I woke up after a strange dream and couldn't sleep, so I carried on reading the magazine and straightaway came across a book review which mentioned how important the Isle of Man was as a sacred place, and so I just had to –'

'Whoa! Hold on there!' Martin stopped dead in his tracks, holding both his palms up to quell the flow of words pouring from her. 'Easy does it. How about starting at the beginning, or even earlier. Where the heck is the Isle of Man?'

She smiled an apology and they resumed walking. 'It's in the middle of the Irish Sea, between Liverpool and Belfast. But I'd have thought you as a travel writer would have heard of it?'

'No, but then I specialise in rather more exotic locations than the UK.'

'You don't know what you're missing,' she told him earnestly. 'I suppose I'm like the newly converted, as I've only lived there a few years, but to me it's a truly magical place, with such a deep sense of history and ancient culture still prevalent even now. And beside all that, the scenery is so beautiful and varied for such a small island.' Embarrassed she stopped herself before she launched into one of her full-blown promotional speeches she was in the habit of giving whenever she spoke to other delegates at Wildlife Trust conferences. 'There I go again,' she grinned. 'I'm not normally so talkative except about the place. I just love it.'

'I can see that. Perhaps I ought to visit it and try a change from my normal writing.'

'Oh you should! You'd find so much to write about. Oh, and it's not part of the UK.'

'Pardon me?'

'It's part of the British Isles but not the UK. It has its own government called Tynwald: the longest continuous government in the world, so they say. In fact,' she added in surprise at the way the conversation had turned itself, 'that's why I want the book. It seems to highlight the Isle of Man's ancient meeting site where the open-air parliament is held once a year. And the book reviewer hinted at rather mystical reasons why the site was chosen. I've got this strange compulsion now that I've got to get the book and find out more.'

'Well, I'm only too glad to help out a lady with her strange compulsions. And now you've got me intrigued too. What say you we sit together for dinner tonight, and you can tell me more about the Isle of Man and the fairy you saw in Doubtful Sound?'

He was serious, with no hint of mockery in his tone, Kara realised. And it was good to have someone she felt so comfortable talking to. She nodded her agreement. 'I'll have you saying hello to the fairies in no time,' she laughed. 'But I only *thought* I saw it.'

'Ah, but the thinking of it creates the reality. Look at Tinkerbell in *Peter Pan*. She only existed when people believed in her. Perhaps you have to meet the fairies half way.'

Now she wasn't sure if he was mocking her, but only last week she would have been mocking too. She had changed. New Zealand had changed her. Somehow.

*

Back at the hotel after another satisfying soak in the Glacier Hot Pools, Kara wondered what Martin would make of her strange experiences; whether he would find them as intriguing a set of coincidences as she did, or whether he would laugh it all off as the fanciful notions of a lonely woman 'of a certain age'.

They had arranged to meet at seven in the bar, which was advertised as having wireless Internet. As she walked in she noticed him sitting at a table, writing up the day's activities on his laptop, his dark head bent over the screen in rapt concentration. She approached the bar first and ordered a West Coast draught beer to try out, feeling too thirsty after the day's exertions to want a wine just yet, then ambled over to where Martin was still working.

'Been here long?' she asked, noting the half-consumed glass of beer in front of him as she sat down opposite him.

Startled by her voice he looked up. 'Oh, sorry. I didn't notice you come in.' He raised his glass. 'Cheers!' He took a swift gulp then put it back down on the table. 'To answer your question, about half an hour.

I wanted to get as much of this report done as I could, while it's all still fresh in my mind. It's amazing how quickly you can forget first impressions and little details that readers find so important. But I'm just about finished.' So saying he tapped out the last few words, saved the work and logged off. 'Now I can concentrate on you,' he smiled warmly, showing off the perfect teeth Americans were so famous for.

If Kara had been thirty years younger she would have felt a flutter of excitement at his attention, but she was too old for him and all that nonsense now.

He was obviously one of those men who naturally flattered any woman, whether seventeen or seventy. Charming and heart-warming as it was to be on the receiving end, Kara had no illusions it meant anything more.

'Where shall I begin?' she said more to herself than him, as she collected her thoughts.

Martin took her question literally. 'How's about a bit about your background, what took you to the Isle of Man and so forth, just so I know what sort of a person you really are, before you start telling me about the weirder side of you.'

Kara could understand that. In fact she was glad of the opportunity to present herself to him as a serious student of science, who had never questioned the accepted rules and regulations of the middle-class world she had grown up in. She had conformed to the accepted norm in every possible way as a sober and conscientious citizen, obedient to authority and what she had been taught. 'Very boring, really,' she admitted after relating her life history so far, including her recent ten years of happiness on the Isle of Man. 'The only area where I didn't conform was marriage. But we single, career women aren't such a rare breed these days.'

'No, that's true. I've met plenty like you.' He drained his glass. 'Well, I don't know about you but I'm starving. Let's go in to eat then you can tell me more about this Tynwald thing on the Isle of Man.'

Kara smiled at his enthusiasm. 'You're right. It is a "Thing" with a capital T. But I'll explain over dinner. I'm famished too.'

They sat at their table in the Glasshouse Restaurant, the nearby mountains and forest looming close through the large windows, the western sun lighting up their flanks in bright gold. They spent the next few minutes studying the menu and discussing the day with their immediate neighbours. Martin eventually chose the local delicacy, whitebait, followed by venison cutlets, while Kara ordered the manuka-smoked chicken Caesar salad followed by 'Catch of the Coast'. Choosing a glass of decent red wine for him and white for her then took a few minutes as there were so many on the list to tempt them, but finally they settled back on their chairs and Martin looked expectantly at Kara.

'So. Enlighten me about this Tynwald "Thing".'

She took a sip of the Pinot Gris the waitress had just put in front of her, and considered where to start. 'You must realise how proud the island is of its heritage,' she began. 'First Celtic then Viking. The Vikings arrived and settled in with the original Celts so that both cultures mingled. But the Vikings brought their system of parliament based on open-air meetings or *"Things"*. Iceland's government is supposed to have been established earlier, but they had a spell when it didn't function, apparently, so that the Isle of Man's government is said to be the oldest continuous government in the world. The meeting is the *"Thing"* but the place where they meet is the Thing Field, or Tynwald. There's a proper building in Douglas, the capital, where the government does its stuff now, of course, but they still meet ceremonially at Tynwald Hill in the open air on July the fifth, just as it was always done. They often invite some Scandinavian bigwig to help with the Viking connection, and sometimes a member of the British Royal family will attend. The Queen was there in 2003.' She took another sip of her wine and smiled. 'It's funny. Her title is Lord of Man when she's there, not Lady.'

Martin swirled the Pinot Noir round in his glass as he mulled over what she had said. 'Why July the fifth?' he asked abruptly.

'Ah. Let me see if I remember this correctly.' Kara paused a moment to think her explanation through. 'The old Christian midsummer date is June the twenty-fourth, the feast of St John, but when they changed from the Julian calendar to the Gregorian in the seventeen hundreds, there was an eleven day shift. June the twenty-fourth became July the fifth, if you follow me, and for some reason they decided to stick with the Julian calendar to work out the date of Tynwald Day. Does that make sense?'

'Not really, but surely the Vikings weren't Christian? At least not to start with,' Martin pointed out.

'No, you're right. But it's based around midsummer, anyway. I read about it all some time ago in the little museum of Tynwald at St John's. I probably need to go back in there sometime and have another look.'

The young waitress brought their first course and they tucked in eagerly, conversation pending for the few minutes it took them to eat and take the edge off their appetites. As he put down his fork, Martin posed his next question.

'What is it with fairies then? Is the Isle of Man like Ireland, full of the Little People?'

'Exactly!' Kara beamed. 'The Celtic tradition is still very strong there, like in Ireland. The Manx are a very superstitious lot, although obviously not so much nowadays, but we always greet the fairies when we cross the Fairy Bridge. Even I do it and you can't get any less superstitious than me.'

'So why do you do it?'

She reflected a moment, staring into the pale liquid in her wine glass as though scrying into a crystal ball. 'I suppose when I first arrived I read all the information leaflets and books on the place, and they just said it was customary to do this to keep on good terms with "Themselves". The first time I drove over the bridge I greeted them just for fun, obeying the book, as it were.' She laughed. 'I always like to obey the rules!' She grew serious again. 'I guess the second time I drove over it, I had the strange feeling that having greeted them the first time they would be offended if I didn't greet them this time. Not a serious feeling, you understand. Just a jokey thought. So I greeted them again. And then each time I did it, it became more important to always do it, so that the odd time I did forget, I felt quite bad about it.'

'I can see that,' Martin said. 'It becomes a necessary habit.'

'I suppose... But now after ten years of living there, I think I have grown into being kind of superstitious. I've never prayed in my life, but I make serious wishes now on the wishing chair in Glen Helen.'

'So do you think you're acquiring a sense that there's more to life than meets the eye?' he asked intently.

'Possibly,' she said hesitantly then frowned. 'The way you ask that sounds like you've got a hidden agenda. You're not one of these evangelical Christians are you?'

He looked shocked. 'No way! Quite the opposite. I have a Navajo heritage of respecting nature, not lording over it.' He leaned closer. 'But haven't you noticed how everyone is talking about such things now? It's the *Zeitgeist* or spirit of the era – the Age of Aquarius, no less. Things that were taboo twenty years ago are openly discussed now. The bookshelves are full of weird and wonderful theories. And since the translations of the Dead Sea Scrolls finally were released to the world at large, Christianity has been turned inside out.' Leaning back in his chair again, satisfied she was with him still, he pursued his argument further. 'Quantum physics also says anything goes now, and we're all studying the latest crop circles, trying to work out what the messages are and who or what's making them. I was always a total sceptic, but I've started reading some of these books and I've become hooked. Now I question everything I was taught, and there seems to be so much more to the universe than we'd thought.'

'And with the Internet we're now all connecting into the universal consciousness.'

He looked at her admiringly. 'Jung and your dragons have been dropping their pearls of wisdom at your feet.'

'How do you know about my dragons?'

'I was sitting at the next table to you in The Tap Beer Garden in Arrowtown.'

The waitress arrived with their main courses, and Martin took the opportunity to order another glass of wine each.

After a few mouthfuls of his venison cutlets Martin asked: 'So to get back to your story, what about the fairy in Doubtful Sound?'

'Ah yes,' Kara said, attacking her own monstrous portion of Blue Cod fillet. 'It was only a trick of the light, of course. The sun was going in and out of the clouds, and there must have been a pale bush or leaves catching the light that looked like a person's face. You know how it is with clouds and things?'

Martin nodded.

'But ever since then, all sorts of strange coincidences have started happening, some big, some not so big, but taken all together they add up to more than the sum of the parts, if you follow me?'

'I certainly do.'

She told him all about the dragon shop, the book she had found about New Zealand fairy-folk that had mentioned the Isle of Man, about Sharon and the article on the same subject she was reading in a magazine, of the explanation of their names in ancient Egyptian and that Sharon had insisted on giving her the magazine to read. 'The strangest thing, though,' she went on, 'was the dream I had, followed by reading the magazine's book review, which again mentioned the Isle of Man and Tynwald. That's two entirely separate references to the Isle of Man in one day! And what on earth do you think 'life is khaki' means?'

'Where did you hear that?'

'It was Manannan, the Celtic sea-god in my dream. At least he looked like an image I've seen of Manannan in the museum. It was the only thing he did say. He just pointed with his staff to the setting sun then his shadow and his staff fell on the stone I was near, like a marker or gnomon on a sundial. The next thing I was awake and reading the book review about finding sacred places, particularly on the Isle of Man. It's all rather weird.'

Martin was silent a moment and she wondered whether he thought she was totally batty, but his next question proved very profound.

'Do you know anything about chakras?'

'Chakras? Well, a little from my alternative therapy reading. They're sort of energy centres or levels up the body, aren't they? Why do you ask?'

Martin pushed aside his empty plate and leant forward again, his elbows on the table. 'As part of my travels I've been to India and Nepal. Fascinating countries, full of ancient wisdom lost to the west and only just being rediscovered by us. I always like to immerse myself in the culture of the place I'm visiting and do my research, so I've read quite a bit about Vedic traditions and the Tantric philosophy of light. Now, each of the seven chakra levels in the body is associated with a different colour: red is the lowest at the sacrum, rising up the spine through the rainbow colours to violet on the crown of the head. However, some systems have another major chakra in the hypothalamus part of the brain that has to do with spiritual perception. Its colour is said to be brown or olive green, you could say a kind of khaki. So in other words, your dream might have told you that life is spiritual perception.'

'But how was my brain supposed to know that?' Kara objected. 'I'm sure I've never read about that.'

'You may have done and just not remembered it, but your brain had it lurking in its depths somewhere.'

'Hmm. I'm not convinced. It doesn't feel like the right answer somehow.'

'How would you know whether it was right or not?'

'Intuition. It just doesn't feel quite right. Maybe it's partly there, but I feel there's something missing.'

Martin looked at her oddly. 'You really are getting tuned in, aren't you?'

'How do you mean?'

'Relying on intuition.'

'Women's intuition, they call it. I guess we're more used to it than you men.'

'Sophia, wisdom, call it what you will. It's always been associated with women and serpents or dragons. That's why Eve and the snake were made out to be so bad, as they represented ancient wisdom that the powers-that- be wanted to control. I've just been reading Dan Brown's *The Lost Symbol*, and he says pretty much the same thing, how ancient wisdom has been lost except by a very select few.'

The word 'lost' mentioned twice by Martin struck a chord within her memory and she struggled to pin it down. Suddenly she had it.

'That book Sharon showed me, the one which explained our names in ancient Egyptian,' she began hesitantly.

'Yes?'

'It was called *Lost Secrets of the Sacred Ark*. She said it was mind-blowing in its revelations. It sounds worth reading.'

'It was non-fiction, I take it?'

'Yes, I'm pretty sure it was. By a chap called Laurence Gardner.'

'No! Really? I've read one of his already, one of his holy bloodline books – that's what I mean about me definitely not being an evangelical Christian. I like reading these alternative interpretations of the Bible. They make far more sense to me than taking it literally. But this Gardner's writing seems to come out with information hitherto kept secret, like it's being deliberately released now, when the time is ready for it. Hidden wisdom,' he added pointedly.

'So we need to seek out this wisdom,' Kara said excitedly, getting caught up by his enthusiasm, like a child on a treasure hunt.

'We do indeed.'

*

By the time they finished eating and discussing the mysteries of the universe there were few people left in the restaurant. As they stood to leave, Martin picked up his laptop from the adjacent chair.

'Ah, that book you wanted to order,' Martin said. 'I nearly forgot about it.'

'Oh my gosh! I had completely,' Kara laughed.

Retiring once again to the bar, she pulled out the magazine from her handbag and found the website for book orders. The connection was very slow but eventually Kara had typed in the order for John Michell's book, her credit card details and address for delivery on the Isle of Man. She wasn't unduly concerned that the book would be coming from Australia, so might take some time to arrive.

Martin read the review while Kara was busy at the laptop. 'I see what you mean,' he said when she was about to close the website. 'I might order a copy for myself. This John Michell seems to have been quite the authority on such things. And look here,' he said, turning over the page and showing it to her. 'They've also got some of Laurence Gardner's books you can order, but strangely not the one you mentioned.'

'Really?' Kara moved away from the laptop, allowing Martin to enter his own order for the book. She looked at the booklist Martin had showed her then rifled through the magazine to find the article on the pre-Maori population that had possibly become known as fairies in Maori legend. 'Here,' she said to Martin when he had finished. 'Have a look at this. It's all very politically incorrect here in New Zealand, apparently.'

Martin skimmed through the article and found the reference to the website the article was based on. 'Let's take a look, shall we?'

Kara found herself yawning. 'I think I'll away to my bed since we've another early start in the morning.'

'Oh, sure thing. But may I borrow this just to read in bed?' Martin asked her, waving the magazine.

'Of course. I'll see you in the morning. Thanks for letting me use your laptop and for your company this evening. It was very interesting.'

'The pleasure was all mine,' he replied gallantly. 'It's you who's the interesting one. Goodnight and sleep well. I hope your dreams are interesting.'

'Perhaps Manannan will tell me what he meant by 'life is khaki'.'

'Let's hope so.'

*

Kara lay in bed musing over their conversation. Like Martin, Kara had read Dan Brown's book over the Christmas period before setting off on this holiday. She knew the author tapped into the psyche of the time and that the whole 2012-and-beyond thing and humanity's supposed changing consciousness was extremely marketable at the moment. She was a relative latecomer to the 2012 phenomenon it seemed, only very recently having heard of it because of the number of books appearing on the bookshelves featuring that year in their titles. She had glanced at some of the blurbs, but they all seemed to have different ideas as to what it was all about. There were as many doom and gloom, end of the world scenarios as there were changing consciousness themes, but Dan Brown had gone for the forgotten wisdom theme, and she found that reassuring. Whatever it was all about she was getting sucked into it, whether she liked it or not.

CHAPTER FOUR

The alarm woke her up with a start just as she was having one of those disaster-type dreams where everything was going wrong. She knew she had to get to an urgent appointment but had lost her car keys and was looking for them everywhere in her house, turning drawers upside down and looking under the sofa cushions. Then she was in her office at Tynwald Mills, still searching for her keys, asking everyone if they'd seen them, which of course they hadn't.

She sat up in bed, stretched her stiff muscles and joints ready for action then got up, trying to fathom out her dream. It came to her as she was tying the laces on her trainers. The Manx Wildlife Trust was in the process of trying to move its offices and shop from the Tynwald Mills shopping complex near St John's to the centre of Peel. Her holiday had originally been planned for the quieter winter spell before the actual move was supposed to begin, but planning hold-ups had now seriously delayed the process. New premises obviously meant new keys, but why had she dreamt about car keys?

She drew back the curtains and groaned. Thick cloud shrouded the mountains and a heavy rain was falling. Oh well, it was only a travelling day, but not so good for their scenic route to Christchurch on the TranzAlpine railway that afternoon.

The mood in the Glasshouse Restaurant seemed brighter than the weather, with everyone determined not to let it blight the day. Julia and Henrik greeted her with a wave from across the room and she joined them.

'Did you enjoy your conversation with Martin last night?' Julia asked meaningfully, once Kara was settled down with her bowl of fresh fruit.

'Yes, it was very interesting. We talked about books mostly,' Kara added, wanting to dispel any notions Julia might be entertaining about holiday romances. 'He's travelled all over the world and seems to know such a lot. His articles must be very interesting to read. I'll have to get hold of this one about New Zealand and see if my perspective on it all is the same as his.'

'Yes, that would be interesting,' Henrik agreed. 'No doubt he looks for unusual things to write about that I'm sure you and I would never notice.' Henrik cast his eyes around the room. 'I can't see him here yet. He's usually one of the first ones in to breakfast. I hope he's not overslept.'

'He was probably up reading too late,' Kara suggested. 'I lent him an interesting magazine.'

'Oh well, they won't let us go without him,' Julia observed. 'Perhaps you ought to make a sandwich or something for him, in case he's too late for breakfast.'

Kara looked up just as Martin hurried in to the restaurant. 'Speak of the devil! He's made it in time.'

Julia promptly called to him to join them at their table, apparently determined to strengthen the bonds of friendship on this holiday.

'Morning, folks,' he called out cheerily, helping himself to the full cooked breakfast. Sitting down next to Kara, he jokingly reprimanded her as he ate. 'It's your fault I'm late this morning, you know? That damned magazine kept me up half the night. But gee it's got some fascinating stuff in it! I couldn't put it down. As soon as we get to Christchurch I'll be onto half a dozen different websites, I reckon.' Henrik smiled. 'That's just it, isn't it? You have to check references out, and even then, how do you know who wrote it and what their agenda is, who's paying for their research, and where they sourced their information? That's the trouble now. There's too much information out there and you can't believe the half of it.'

'Especially on global warming,' Martin steamed ahead, shovelling up a forkful of scrambled eggs. 'A computer prediction is only as good as the data you put in. What if you completely ignore a major input, such as increasing or even decreasing solar radiation? Some writers are saying we could just as well be headed for the next Ice Age!'

'Who knows?' Henrik said enigmatically, folding his napkin. He turned to his wife. 'Well, my dear, it's time we got back to our packing and let Martin eat his breakfast in peace.'

'He seems a bit touchy about that subject,' Kara commented once the Norwegian couple had left the restaurant. 'Did you notice yesterday, on the walk back from the glacier, that he said something about the Ice Age then walked away as though he knew something but didn't want to talk about it? And now he's done the same thing again.'

'Oh, some folks are a bit touchy about arguing with comparative strangers. And he's a diplomat, I think.'

'He seemed to agree with you, though.'

'Yeah, you're right.' He shrugged, put down his fork and slugged back his coffee. 'That's me done. I'm all ready for the choo-choo, but I think we're in for a disappointing ride.'

*

The coach driver deposited them in the small coastal town of Greymouth where they all bade him farewell after almost two weeks with him. From now on they were using the railways for the remainder of the South Island section of their tour. They had time for a short wander round the town and some lunch while their luggage was held at the station for them. There was not a lot to see apart from the harbour with its large piece of artwork consisting of vertical mining drills, and the solid drizzle deterred all but the most intrepid from seeing even that. As they boarded their compartment on the TranzAlpine diesel train, the windows rapidly steamed up from wet clothing. Not that there was much to see, once they had passed Lake Brunner and got into the mountains proper, except acres of tussock grass. Low cloud blanketed the slopes of the mountains and it was only when they crossed over river gorges that they had much of a view. Kara was sitting with Julia, Henrik and Martin as seemed to be the pattern now, but Martin was busy on his laptop while Julia read a novel and Henrik caught up on some sleep. It was a four and a half-hour journey to Christchurch, so Kara pulled out James Cowan's New Zealand fairies book from her rucksack and found where she had left off reading previously.

The train stopped in the middle of the mountain range at a small hamlet. An announcement by the train's conductor said that there was a slight problem with the ventilation system and that they would be there for a few minutes while it was fixed. Kara and Martin joined the brave souls who got off the train there to stretch their legs or indulge their nicotine cravings. The hamlet, called Otira according to the small station building and platform sign, consisted of the station, a small hotel and a collection of very small houses. It was quite eerily silent outside, apart from the train's twin engines sitting humming to themselves like two giant beasts. Wisps of cloud swirled around like steam or smoke from their breath. While Martin wandered down to look at the diesel engines, Kara found herself a sheltered spot away from the other passengers to gaze into the hidden depths of the clouds and try to imagine the peaks hidden from view. It was no worse up here than on Snaefell's mountain road, and she felt quite at home.

She felt her eyes drawn to an unknown spot in the mist and a tingle went up her spine, followed by gooseflesh down her arms. It was as though the 'fairy' folk were out there, behind the mist they had called down to protect them from prying eyes, and she found herself straining to catch a glimpse of them through the clouds before she realised what she was doing and grinned at her foolishness. That book was getting to her! Nevertheless, it had made her think about those people who were possibly of Celtic origin, as the magazine article suggested, who had somehow come to New Zealand however many hundreds or thousands of years ago and made it their home. It occurred to her now that with their fair-skins they would burn in the fierce New Zealand sun. They wouldn't be out roaming on a bright sunny day, as they would have to avoid bright light, just as the fairy tales told. They needed the mists or dull weather to get about during the day, or they would travel by night, whereas the darker-skinned Maori arriving from Polynesia had no such problems. Kara had fair skin herself and had already fallen foul of just how strong the sun's rays were here.

There was a lot of logic at the bottom of many myths, Kara realised, as she watched a particularly large swirl of mist float by the station towards the tunnel the train would soon enter. Closer to, she could see the train driver and conductor standing talking to each other, with Martin nearby listening in. There seemed to be some kind of a problem, and the conductor soon boarded the train again as Martin walked up to where she stood.

'It looks like we're stuck here for a while,' he told her. 'Now there's a power fault in the tunnel and the ventilation's not working. They're not allowed to drive through until it's fixed.'

'How long is that likely to take?'

'I don't know. There's a maintenance crew on its way. I think this sort of thing happens sometimes, from the way they were talking.'

'Oh.'

She could hear an announcement being made by the conductor over the train's PA system saying what Martin had just told her. More people began to get off the train now the drizzle seemed to be easing, and soon the platform was quite crowded. Kara was glad she had had the peaceful time to herself earlier. Martin wandered off again and found a group of Japanese girls to chat to, so Kara walked up to the end of the platform near the engines and studied the tunnel entrance, wondering what kind of wildlife inhabited it, whether any bats had made it their domain.

She had always found caves and tunnels interesting places. As a child she had stood with her brothers in a short tunnel under the local railway near her home, hooting and calling to make echoes. Her parents had taken them to caves cut into the chalk at Chislehurst in Surrey, which had been used as air-raid shelters during the war, and the feeling of being safely entombed had made a big impression on her. As an adult she had visited the Hellfire Club cavern at High Wycombe in Buckinghamshire, where mystical rites were supposed to have been held. Now dark, enclosed spaces with their strange acoustic affects held a fascination for her. The nearest she had ever come to a mystical experience was while sitting in Durham Cathedral as a student on a dark winter's afternoon, listening to an organ concert. At one point in the music a certain chord seemed to resonate within her, such that the cross over the rood screen glowed golden for a few moments, and she felt mentally transported heavenwards. And again, singing the Verdi Requiem with the university choir standing in the crossing under the soaring cathedral tower, she had felt that buzz, that oneness with the fabric of the building as voices and stone merged. Sound waves transported man.

The thought glowed in her mind, like the rood screen cross. Puzzled by where her train of thought had taken her she became aware again of the humming of the diesel engines and of a voice calling her name.

'Kara! We're supposed to be getting back on board now.' Martin sounded puffed and she turned round to see him trotting down the now nearly empty platform towards her. 'Didn't you hear?'

'Have they fixed it already?' she asked in surprise. 'That was quick.' She caught up with him and they hurried back to their carriage.

'I wouldn't exactly call an hour and a half quick, but in such a remote place it could be considered quick, I suppose.'

'An hour and a half, did you say? Goodness. I must have been away with the fairies! It only felt like half an hour to me.' She climbed up the steps into the carriage and found her seat, the red cover of the fairy book open on the table where she had left it.

*

'Here we are,' Martin announced as the Celtic New Zealand website they had been waiting for since Franz Josef downloaded onto his laptop.

It was the day after their prolonged train journey, and he and Kara had retired after dinner to the bar of their Christchurch hotel. It had been another free day to explore Christchurch, which, although perfectly charming along its tiny river Avon, couldn't compete with most other cathedral cities in Britain and Europe. It wasn't really surprising that a New World city couldn't deliver the same architectural impact, she had told Martin over dinner.

As a New Worlder himself, he had disagreed. 'Have you ever visited Washington DC?' he asked.

'No, but after reading Dan Brown perhaps I ought to,' she had replied, bringing the conversation irretrievably back to things mystical. 'We mustn't forget to check out that website.'

Now in the bar Martin was scrolling down the homepage. He clicked on the heading 'Articles'.

Two hours later he and Kara were rubbing their tired eyes.

'Well, he's pretty damning in his remarks about governmental hush-ups,' Kara remarked. 'Do you think they really destroyed those skeletons they found before they could be carbon-dated?'

'I sincerely hope not. All this talk of "The Surveyors" and their hilltop stones and solar marking points is interesting, although it's a shame we can't check it out. I think I'm actually starting to believe in your fairies.'

'Well, it's certainly starting to look like the ancient Celts and Egyptians may have travelled the world, if those websites are to be believed. Who would have thought they'd find Egyptian hieroglyphics in Australia! Thor Heyerdahl was right all along: ancient civilisations probably did navigate the oceans. I wonder how much more we'll be changing our ideas by the end of this trip.'

'Come down under to have your beliefs turned upside down!' Martin joked, logging off and closing up his laptop. 'Well, we've got an early start again to see the whales tomorrow. Robin said the train leaves at seven, so I'm away to my bed. Let me know if you discover the secret of the khaki car keys in your dreams.'

'The what?'

'Those two dreams you told me about. Khaki, car key, it's the same sounds. I thought you'd already made the connection.'

A bolt of lightning flashed through Kara's brain. 'Ka and qi! That's it! Ka meaning spirit and qi meaning energy. Ka-qi!' She thumped her head with the palm of her hand. 'That was Manannan's message to me! "Life is spirit energy" in Ancient Egyptian and Chinese,' Kara burst out loudly. 'How obscure can you get?' Realising she was getting too noisy for a public area she sat back in her chair and looked at Martin, shaking her head in bemusement. 'How on earth did my brain come up with that?'

'Perhaps it really was a message,' he suggested.

'Who from?' she asked scornfully. 'And why me? Why now?'

'Because you're starting to ask the right questions, perhaps?'

'But so are you, surely?'

'They obviously can't connect with me.'

'And who are "they" supposed to be? And just listen to me!' Kara suddenly said more quietly. 'If my friends and colleagues could hear me now, talking about having messages in my dreams, they'd think I was a complete and utter fruit cake!'

'Possibly not. I think more and more people are opening up to the idea that telepathy, or whatever you like to call it, is a possibility at least. Take that experiment with the quartz and glass we just read about,' he added, pointing at his laptop.

'You mean where they had better telepathic success through a quartz screen than a glass one?'

'That's it. And where does that start to take you?' Now it was Martin's turn to get over-excited. 'What about these crystal skulls, or crystal ball gazing? Does quartz crystal have some special property for connecting with the universal consciousness? Does it hold information like a microchip?'

Kara chuckled in bewilderment. 'Oh, this is all getting way too much for me! You're right. It's bedtime.' She picked up her handbag from the floor and stood up. 'Sleep well.'

'You too. Sweet dreams.'

*

Kara stood on the shore and looked out to the moonlit sea. She was alone. A stiff breeze tugged at her hair and flapped at her jacket but she didn't feel cold. Barefoot she stepped into the cool water and stood while the waves rose and fell in a gentle rhythm at her knees. Watching and waiting. She was confident they would come.

*

'Have you seen the film *Whale Rider*?' Pat, a rather chatty fellow Brit, asked Kara on the train from Christchurch up to Kaikoura, the whale-watching centre. Pat's long-suffering husband, Owen, had sought solace in a Sudoku puzzle, and Pat was obviously in need of some conversation.

'No, but I've heard of it,' Kara replied, glad that Pat had chosen a reasonable topic of conversation. 'It's a Kiwi film, isn't it?'

'Yes. I saw it on the plane coming over. It's all about a Maori girl who's destined to lead her people, some of whom have rather forgotten the old ways. She seems to have a special calling to the whales and ends up riding one. It's a lovely film.'

'Ah.' Kara was immediately back in her dream of the previous night. Was that what she had been doing? Calling to the whales?

'I said,' Pat repeated with a degree of irritation in her voice at Kara's lack of attention, 'do you think we'll see any sperm whales?'

'Oh yes,' Kara replied confidently. 'They'll be there.' She felt suddenly reckless and decided to tease the poor woman to test her reaction. 'I called to them last night.'

Pat blinked. 'Sorry?'

Kara smiled, having fun at Pat's expense. 'I called to them in my dreams last night. I know they'll come.' Seeing the look of horror coming over Pat's face, Kara relented. 'Only joking! I'm not the Whale Rider. But I think the whales are often there. The chances are good that we'll see some.'

Pat's relief that she wasn't sitting opposite some crackpot was evident. 'Perhaps we should call to them anyway,' she joined in the joke. 'You never know. It might work.'

'Go ahead and try,' Kara encouraged her.

'How *do* you call to whales, though?' Pat pondered, gazing out at the flat coastal plains of Canterbury, as the daily diesel service from Christchurch to Picton rumbled on its way northwards.

'With your thoughts,' Kara told her. 'Connect with them.'

'Right,' Pat replied dubiously, but made a show of closing her eyes and thinking deeply.

Kara had a few minutes' peace while Pat did her thinking until she opened her eyes triumphantly. 'There! I've called them. That should do it.' She tapped her husband on the elbow. 'I've just called to the whales, dear, at Kara's suggestion. She says we'll definitely see them now.'

Owen removed his reading glasses and looked across at Kara, seeing the corners of her mouth twitching as she tried to control her grin. 'Hmph. We'll see,' he replied and returned to his puzzle.

Kara was aware of Martin across the aisle listening in to the conversation. He had been working on his laptop as usual on long journeys, hence her choosing to sit with others in the tour group, but she could sense he was earwigging and had heard her say she had called to the whales in her dreams. Suddenly she had the awful mental image of his tour report, of her featuring heavily in it as some eccentric woman amusing them all with her weird and wacky dreams and visions.

She glanced across and caught his eye. No, he was sincere in his interest, she could tell, whether by intuition, instinct, reading of body language or telepathy. However she was doing it, she was sure Martin was just as interested in the paranormal – yes, that was the word, she reluctantly decided – as she inexplicably now was.

Something Pat was saying infiltrated her thoughts and made her retune her concentration. 'Fairies, you said?'

Pat almost rolled her eyes in exasperation at Kara's lack of attention. 'Fairy terns,' she repeated. 'I was just saying I was wondering whether to try calling to them when we get to Northland. I don't think we'll have much chance of seeing them when there are only about forty-five of them left.'

Kara was on secure ground here. 'If they're nesting, as they should be still, they'll be around. We just won't be able to get close, that's all. I gather the nesting areas are fenced off, but we'll have our binoculars, and our new guide will know where to go.' Robin apparently only accompanied them on the South Island part of their tour. 'They seem very good this tour company so far, don't you think?'

The conversation rolled safely on as the railway headed into the coastal ranges beyond Waipara. They emerged onto the plains again at the Hurunui River, whose braided channel system over gravel deposits epitomised the rivers flowing from the Southern Alps. Unremarkable towns with attractive names such as Mina, Phoebe and Parnassus passed by, as Pat told Kara all about the numerous wildlife holidays she and Owen had been on. After they passed through Parnassus on the Waiau River the scenery became more rugged, and after a brief spell following the Conway River through the ranges they emerged onto the Conway Flat and the sight of the Pacific Ocean again. Here the railway line hugged the coast, closely hemmed in by the ranges on one side and the ocean on the other, to be joined by State Highway One at the settlement of Oaro.

Seeing a gannet swooping low over the waves close by, Kara was reminded of the bird-life on the Isle of Man and managed to interrupt

Pat's flow to encourage her and Owen to visit the Isle of Man. She was relating the abundance of choughs and hen harriers on the island when the terrain flattened out again. Here the road and rail separated, the road continuing to hug the coast, while the railway line snaked inland to approach Kaikoura further north.

As they all gathered up their belongings to leave the train at 'Whale Watch' station, Martin whispered in her ear: 'Did you really call to the whales last night?'

Kara initially glanced down in embarrassment, but then resolutely met his eye. 'I think that's what I was doing in my dream, but I'm not sure. I never saw any whales. I was just waiting for something, but I knew it would come.'

He nodded absently then gave a nod for her to precede him to the end of the carriage. Robin was already outside and directed Kara to the nearby Flukes Café where they were to have an early lunch prior to their Whale Watch excursion.

'Whales, here we come! Yee-ha,' Martin whooped like a cowboy as he stepped onto the platform, and nearly everybody in the tour rolled their eyes as the unspoken word 'Americans' transmitted itself through the non-American members of the group.

*

The whole village of Kaikoura seemed geared around the enterprise, and the professional side of Kara was impressed that it was a locally run venture that had really taken off, thanks in part to the reliability of the whales. She was amused to see that the station was located on Whale Way Road, as the company coach drove them the short distance to South Bay.

Their whale-watching boat was called *Tohora*, a brightly painted vessel with her topsides blue, her twin hulls yellow, and a large grey sperm whale along each side above the waterline. As she left the jetty in South Bay, Kara and her companions made themselves comfortable in the enclosed lounge while their Whale Watch guide, a burly Maori by the name of Tamati, explained safety protocols and what they might expect to see.

'Now we know there's a sperm whale out there today,' Tamati told them. 'Our early morning boat spotted one of our semi-resident males called Rua, which means "two" because he has two nicks on his dorsal fin. We're heading out now towards the Kaikoura Canyon, which is two kilometres deep, and it's where the sea mammals and birds gather to feed on the up-welling sea life. If Rua's moved on from where he was spotted, we can try to locate him or any others around using our hydrophones to listen out for their communication clicks.'

Pat nudged Kara in the ribs. 'I bet our calling to them works. I just know we'll see one today.'

Kara felt confident too, but mostly because the company proudly claimed a ninety-five percent success rate, as long as conditions were favourable enough to go out in.

As they made their way out to sea, Tamati chatted to the dozen or so other tourists on board while Robin concentrated on his tour group. All of them had opted for the boat trip rather than plane or helicopter rides, Loris and Wayne included.

To separate herself from Pat's incessant chatter, Kara turned to the Japanese couple seated next to her, still known to all rather formally as Mr. and Mrs. Tutsumi, as this seemed their preference. Their spoken English was limited, but they seemed to be coping with the demands of the tour quite happily. Kara admired their compact but powerful binoculars, which they let her try. Once the wildlife numbers picked up however, Kara resorted to her own binoculars and, with the aid of her New Zealand sea bird guide and Robin's help, had soon ticked off the Cape Petrel, and the Little and Hutton Shearwaters from her list of possible sightings.

She noticed Martin was without binoculars, so after a while she lent him the use of hers. Murphy's Law saw to it that he was the one who suddenly gave a loud shout and gesticulated off to their port bow as he spotted a spouting whale. The *Tohora* headed rapidly towards it before slowing right down well before reaching the spot. As she idled her engines, her passengers scrambled out onto the observation decks, eager to catch sight of their quarry.

The giant sperm whale – not Rua as it turned out – performed beautifully, resting on the choppy surface and spouting occasionally through his blowhole. They cruised slowly at the required distance beside him for nearly twenty minutes while the passengers took their photos with the blue sea and the sky, and the mountain backdrop of Kaikoura in the distance.

The intense blue and sparkling sunlight made Kara blink. She had taken off her sunglasses just while she filmed the whale on her camcorder, and for a moment she was unable to distinguish anything other than blue light. A blur moved into her vision, and now she saw that the whale was approaching the boat quite close. The *Tohora*'s skipper gently manoeuvred the boat to try to maintain the required distance, but the whale seemed to have other ideas and kept coming closer, seemingly eyeing them up in curiosity for several minutes. Some of the passengers were beginning to mutter in alarm at his proximity, while others were enraptured by his boldness. As one of the latter, Kara leaned over the rail as far as she dared. Just then the whale rolled on his left side slightly, allowing his huge right eye to break the surface and look directly up towards Kara. Then, his curiosity apparently satisfied, he took a breath, closed his blowhole, raised his huge tail flukes alarmingly close to the boat and dived vertically into the depths. Cameras clicked and camcorders whirred around her, but Kara just stood and watched.

She felt sad to see him go. She had felt again that connection between intelligent beings. She had looked into his eye and he into hers.

Their mission accomplished, the *Tohora*'s skipper turned the boat and headed steadily back to South Bay. On the way a small pod of Dusky dolphins bobbed and weaved in the bow wave as the skipper applied the throttle to give them a good ride. After two and a half hours on the water a boat full of happy tourists finally reached the jetty.

Robin congratulated the group on such a full-on and close-up encounter. 'We don't often get it as good as that,' he told them as they assembled by the coach that would take them to their hotel.

'That's because my wife called them in on the train coming up here,' Owen told everybody with a broad grin.

Pat hit him lightly on the arm and looked embarrassed, and there was muffled giggling from some of the Australians in the group, but Kara saw Martin's glance at her.

On the coach he sat down beside her. 'Is there anything you can't do, Madame Merlin?'

'Yes, turn young men into frogs,' she replied. 'Honestly, it was just coincidence that he came so close.' She paused. 'It's you, you know. You're leading me on with all this malarkey, encouraging me to look at all these crazy websites.'

'But you're the one who started all this with your talk of fairies,' he countered. 'I'm just following your lead, and throwing in the odd contribution of my own occasionally.'

'We're both as bad as each other, basically,' she laughed.

'No, you're further along the line than I am. You've seen the light. I haven't yet.'

'Seen the light? Whatever do you mean?'

'The fairy light. You said it touched you and after that all the other coincidences started.'

Kara was silent. She remembered the light coming over the water towards her, it reaching her and touching her, its lingering warmth, the feeling of connection. 'It was like I briefly tuned in to something,' she muttered, 'but it's left enough residual connection to show me how to make the connection stronger. Something's leading me somewhere and I know I'm going to find it.'

'A self-fulfilling prophecy,' Martin said. 'If you believe it will happen, the chances are it will.'

Kara snapped back to reality. 'Yes, like I believe I'll win the lottery!'

'Yes, but who *truly believes* they'll win? It's never more than an ardent wish, is it? Anyway, wishes for personal gain never come true. It's not in the nature of things.'

'Maybe, maybe not. You're probably right though. The universal consciousness wouldn't work for treasure-hunting, unless there was going to be a decent outcome from it.'

'And what about dowsing? Can't you find treasure with that?'

'I'd like to see it done!' Kara retorted. She had a sudden recollection of the whale's intelligent eye looking up at her and she smiled. That was treasure enough.

NEW ZEALAND'S NORTH ISLAND

CHAPTER FIVE

Kerri, their North Island guide, was the female counterpart to Robin. A spirited, twenty-eight year old brunette, she had shepherded and entertained her flock for the past week, and shared her encyclopaedic knowledge of New Zealand's flora and fauna. Now at the Trounson Kauri Park in the Far North of North Island she gave them an important and more sombre message before they disembarked the coach.

'The giant kauri trees once dominated Northland,' she announced. 'Now they're restricted to a few specimens in the Waipoua Forest and elsewhere in reserves such as this. This is because early European settlers came along and felled nearly all the kauri to use as ship- and house-building material. Now they're under a new threat from a fungal disease, which we don't know much about yet. That's why I asked you all to clean the soles of your shoes before we set out this morning from Whangarei.'

The group gathered outside the coach, adjusting hats and sunglasses to suit the bright sunshine they were finally bathed in. Kerri led them first to the information boards then into the shade of the forest park. They had to walk a short distance along the designated boardwalk before they came up close to one of the forest giants.

Looking straight up the sheer elephant skin-like bark, Kara could see the first branches were already high up in the surrounding sub-tropical forest canopy. The upper kauri branches spread out in splendid isolation to embrace the sunlight. The sheer presence of them was truly majestic. They weren't the tallest of New Zealand's trees, but they were the most massive. Kara got as close to one of the trees as the boardwalk allowed, heeding the frequent warning signs not to tread on any of the delicate roots, and pressed her palm against the scaly bark in a conscious effort to connect with it.

A tui was calling noisily but melodically from up in its branches, and she looked up to see the iridescent greenish-black bird with its comical twin white chin bobbles. Its song switched from clicks and chuckles to fantastic warbles and trills, as though it was speaking to her. That morning they had visited the Bird Recovery Centre in Northland's largest urban area, Whangarei, and heard its long-term resident tui, called Woof-Woof, speaking clearly in keeper Robert's voice. This forest tui was now singing its heart out to her, and she heard voices behind her remarking on its beauty.

She turned to find Owen filming it, while Pat stood by, entranced by its song. Suddenly it flew down, weaving through the branches towards them before veering off to the left to find another perch in the neatly labelled lemonwood tree they had recently passed.

'Wow, that was something!' Owen exclaimed. 'I know we've seen a few tuis since we've been here, but that performance took the biscuit!' The tui started up its song again from the lower branches of the lemonwood tree. 'I think I can get a close-up of it,' Owen muttered, creeping back down the boardwalk towards the bird, followed by an unusually silent Pat.

Kara sat down for a moment on a thoughtfully provided bench and took off her sleeved shirt to reveal a thin sun-top. Here in the sheltered forest they were out of the cool southerly wind that had dominated throughout the whole tour, keeping temperatures down. One thing she had learnt about New Zealand was that the weather was just as changeable as at home, but the sun was extremely fierce when it came out from behind the clouds.

Apart from Pat and Owen now some way away, the rest of the tour group had gone on ahead, so she felt like she had the forest to herself for the moment. Other little birds – silvereyes, she recalled, having studied the bird book – were flitting about the undergrowth. Suddenly a whistling whoosh of wings announced the large native pigeon, or Kereru, flying by. With all the comings and goings of the birds and their singing, the forest felt truly peaceful and safe. She had read there were no dangerous creatures here to speak of, apart from the white-tail spider introduced from Australia, which could give an unpleasant bite, and another rare spider, akin to black widows, which inhabited the nearby coastal dunes. There were no snakes, and it was now only the comparatively recently introduced wild pigs that could be aggressive. Unless you tried to dig up or investigate some ancient sacred site, she suddenly thought, remembering some of the websites she and Martin had looked at. Whoever they were and wherever they came from, the ancient peoples who wandered these forests must have truly found paradise, she thought.

A leaf fell down from the heights, spinning in a shaft of sunlight to land at her feet, and she picked it up, a souvenir from the Maori god Tane. The warmth of the sun felt good on her skin and she wished she could have sat there much longer, but that wasn't possible. Kerri had told them they only had an hour to get around the boardwalk trail, which should have been plenty long enough, even for ardent naturalists who stopped every few paces to photograph something.

As she sat there, reluctant to move, a bright golden glow on the trunk of the adjacent kauri caught her eye. A globule of gum had oozed out and set like amber. The sunshine seemed to diffuse out of it, as though it were lit from within. Liquid light, she thought, like my Vitamin D capsules.

The teardrop of gum on the grey bark fascinated her, seeping from the tree like its life-blood. Light is life, and life is spirit energy, her thoughts told her as she gazed at the glowing orb. So spirit energy must be light! A ripple of what felt like static electricity brushed her skin, making the hairs on her arms stand up. The sunshine had fired up the numerous cicadas, their loud chirping sounding like white noise, but in it she heard again Manannan's voice telling her: 'Connect your dream life to your waking life.'

The amber-coloured gum shimmered in the heat, and the bark of the tree took up the shimmer, rippling like skin. Enchanted, Kara followed the rippling wave, like the slow and gentle breathing of some giant being, up into the green mist of the dragon's breath.

Owen and Pat found her still on the bench.

'Come on, Kara! You can't go to sleep here! We're late as it is,' Pat said shaking her by the shoulder.

'Oh, I wasn't asleep. I was just enjoying the sunshine,' Kara protested feebly, wondering if she had indeed nodded off for a moment and dreamt her strange thoughts. Struggling to regain normality, she reached for her shirt, which had fallen off the bench, then stood up. 'Did you manage to film your tui?'

'Yes,' Pat replied. 'It sang for ages and then we saw some silvereyes and a lizard of some kind, so we were much longer than we should have been. The others must be way ahead by now.'

Owen was already striding purposefully along the trail, consulting his watch.

Kara put her hand on the warm kauri bark one last time, bidding farewell to the tree, before following Pat and Owen along the trail. Something had spoken to her. She was sure of it.

She hardly noticed the rest of the trail as she hurried down past a stream and up the hill the other side to catch up with the tour group who were busy putting donations in the collection box at the end of the trail. She put a twenty-dollar note in, feeling especially generous towards the majestic trees and their battle against the attacking fungus.

Back at the car park where their coach stood waiting, Julia and Henrik approached her.

'Did you find something interesting?' Julia asked. 'You took a long time to catch up with us.'

Kara was still affected by her strange experience and was unwilling to share it with people who might not understand. 'Nice trees,' she just said. 'Very friendly.'

Henrik nodded in agreement. 'They had something of Tolkien's Ents in them, don't you think? Shepherds of the Forest.'

'Talking trees, you mean?' Kara smiled. 'Yes. I think they did talk to me.'

*

That evening they were staying at the nearby Top 10 Holiday Park, as it offered a guided night walk of the same reserve they had visited earlier that afternoon. It was the most basic of the accommodation offered on the whole tour, and the group had to divide themselves up appropriately between the available chalet units. Kara decided to take up Fig and Berni's suggestion she should share with them. They were a mother and daughter in their late forties and twenties respectively from England, who had never disclosed why Fig, the mother, was called by that name. Kara wondered if she would have the chance to find out that night.

The holiday park had access to a swimming hole on the adjacent river, and after settling into their unit Kara, Fig and Berni decided to freshen up with a plunge into its cool waters before attending the communal barbecue. As they ambled damply back from the river past the substantial wooden shelter where the barbecue was to take place, they greeted the two eager Australians, Mike and Alan, who were already getting the barbecue heating. Beside them stood a cool box full of venison and vegetarian sausages, and lamb steaks brought with them that morning from Whangarei. Kerri was organising the salads and baked sweet potato, or kumara, onto the serving area.

'We'll be starting cooking soon,' Kerri advised the bedraggled swimmers.

The three women hurried to get dried off and presentable before joining the rest of the party at the wooden shelter. Other campers and holidaymakers were also beginning to light up their stoves and barbecues around the site. Soon the air was filled with the smell of cooking meat and fish and the chatter and laughter of people enjoying themselves on holiday.

Kara couldn't help noticing how much of a cohesive entity the tour group had become. Even Mr. and Mrs. Tutsumi had managed to integrate with everyone by now, if only with polite small-talk, but Kara still found herself clinging to the small group she had so far got to know. Fig and Berni had now notably added themselves to that number, with Fig sweeping Kara up into her dominion as easily as a river in flood catches up a log. A strong personality, Kara chuckled to herself while watching Fig put Alan in his place over some trivial issue. *But she flows in the right direction.*

*

Darkness fell quite swiftly and it was time for the group to assemble for the return trip the five kilometres back up to the Kauri Park. Having seen it in all its glory by day they were now going to experience it in a different guise, as this was the speciality of the holiday park: the guided night walk.

Since their tour group was rather large, the holiday park's guides split the group in two. Kara was with the group that included Martin, Julia and Henrik, and her new room-mates Fig and Berni. They set off quietly following Sue their guide through the dark forest in the reverse route from the other party.

The first item of interest was a rough wooden box that could be opened up to reveal large waving antennae, as several giant grasshopper-like weta stared back at them while everybody took turns to look. The rare kauri snails were less exciting but nevertheless another item to tick off in the 'seen' section of their wildlife lists.

The cicadas serenaded them still from the trees as they progressed along the banks of the little stream, looking out for eels. Tiny pinpricks of light sparkled at them from the vegetation, and Kara was well aware, without having to be told, that these were glow-worms, although fairy lanterns would be a more fanciful explanation. She whispered as much to Martin, who was ahead of her on the path, and she saw his grin by the flash of his white teeth. Martin had been keeping himself glued to his laptop again recently, but Kara felt it was more than just his travel report he was engaged upon. She would have to ask him about it.

Everybody froze in their tracks as a nearby owl began calling its own name: 'more pork'. In the distance to their left another morepork answered almost immediately, followed by a third to their right. The owls' triangular conversation lasted some minutes, but Sue eventually moved them silently on.

They all jumped when a piercing screech shattered the stillness of the forest quite close at hand.

'Kiwi,' Sue whispered, shining her torch at where she thought the bird was, but the kiwi was only going to oblige further as a rustling emanating from the bush.

It could have been quite eerie standing there in the dark with all the screeching and rustling going on, but again Kara felt the peace of the forest, and everybody in the group was too engrossed in tracking down the source of the sounds to let any primeval fear of dark forests trouble them. When the other group passed them on the route, the two guides conferred and compared notes. Kara stood aside from the rest to feel the presence of the forest, her other senses finely tuned to compensate for the lack of visual stimuli. She laid her hand on the nearby kauri tree to steady her.

It started in the soles of her feet. Then the electric tingling rose like gooseflesh up her legs and reached the base of her spine. Transfixed, Kara felt it rising up her vertebrae to her shoulder blades, and she shivered involuntarily. The white noise of the cicadas once more filled her head, and through it she thought she heard voices whispering away in the forest. Straining to identify any words, she closed her eyes. A spot of royal blue light appeared behind her eyelids, gradually brightening and enlarging as the whispering drew nearer.

'Kara!'

It was Martin whispering loudly to her and shaking her by the shoulder. She opened her eyes to find him staring intently at her, a look of real concern on his face.

'Are you OK?'

'Yes, of course. Why do you ask?'

'Pat and Owen noticed you seemed to be... out of it, and alerted me. They said they'd found you just like that earlier here today. You obviously didn't notice we were all setting off, and just seemed to stand there like you were away with the fairies again. They're waiting for us to catch up.'

Kara looked up the track to where the red glow of the guide's torch was stationary. 'Oops,' she said as she strode briskly in that direction. 'I was just listening to the forest,' she whispered to Sue and the rest of the group by way of apology.

'You have to be careful here,' Sue told her in a voice that spoke of mystery and intrigue. 'I'll tell you why back on the coach.'

Martin nudged Kara. 'I think I know what she's going to say,' he whispered. 'I was reading about something strange in these parts.'

'Let's see what she says,' Kara whispered back, 'and you can tell me if you're right.'

As soon as they set off on the short coach ride back to the holiday park, Martin asked Sue to tell them about the mystery she had mentioned earlier.

'Ah yes,' Sue said with relish into the coach's microphone. 'Now we're all safely back on board I can tell you about the tourists who got lost in the forest.'

'They weren't called Hansel and Gretel were they?' quipped Jackie, a dentist from Sydney. She and her market research analyst husband, Mike, were celebrating their silver wedding anniversary that day, and were busy passing round beer bottles from a couple of crates they had brought onto the coach for everyone to celebrate with, as Kerri had warned them that the holiday park didn't allow drinking on the site except in the individual units.

'No, they weren't,' Sue replied with an indulgent smile, accepting a beer bottle, 'but I'll keep them anonymous. I don't actually know a lot of the details, just that some time back some tourists and a guide went off into the forest north of here and disappeared. Three months later they turned up and thought they'd only been gone for a day or so. How weird is that!'

Kara turned to look at Martin on the seat next to her, and he nodded as though he'd already heard about it.

Bill, a retired Canadian accountant and partner to literary agent Nancy, now started up with a ghost story about his old office block in Toronto, which turned out to be quite spooky and convincing. Kara had never been especially interested in ghost stories before, but after hearing Bill's tale of the night watchman checking the building was secure, then hearing a noise and going back in again to find previously secure doors unlocked and chairs moved around, she wondered whether there mightn't be something in it after all. Or perhaps it was just the beer and the darkness of the surrounding countryside that made it all seem more real?

The night had begun to cool as they got off their coach and thanked their guides. It was already getting late, so the group began to disperse to their units. Kara was glad to join Fig and Berni in a cup of tea on the veranda of the unit she was sharing with them.

Fig was a real cuddly 'Earth Mother' sort, sporting wild and curly greying hair, wearing colourful hippie-style clothing and drinking only fruit and herbal teas, whereas her daughter looked like a high-flying city financier, with her elegantly polished nails, chic bobbed hairstyle, and casual clothing of a label Kara couldn't identify. Nevertheless, Berni had been game to muck in with all the activities and wildlife watching, showing a keen interest that belied her urban appearance.

'So, Kara,' Fig said warmly, handing a mug of the holiday park's regular tea to her 'guest'. 'You've taken a while to come out of your shell, but you're getting there, aren't you?'

'Mother!' Berni snorted with an exasperation that sounded habitual. She turned to Kara. 'Please excuse my mother's directness, but she lives alone and has forgotten the common courtesies.'

'I don't live alone,' Fig said genially to Kara. 'I have Fergus, and he doesn't mind my way of talking. He's my cat – or my "familiar" as Berni refers to him. She reckons I'm a witch – which I am of course!' She chuckled to herself as though at some private joke.

Berni hurried to explain. 'My mother is an artist and poor as a church mouse, so she supplements her income by making herbal potions and soothsaying at local fairs and things. Actually she has quite a following and regular clientele now, so she must be getting quite good at it.'

'Really?' Kara commented in amazement at meeting yet another person on her New Zealand tour who might give her more insight into what had been happening recently.

' I could give you a reading, if you like,' Fig offered. 'Your aura looks quite interesting, actually.'

'Mother, you promised me you'd leave all that for the duration of the holiday!' Berni scolded her wayward parent. 'We don't want to be upsetting people we've got to live with day to day.'

'I don't upset people,' Fig said to Kara, pointedly ignoring her daughter. 'I only tell them what they want to know or, if it's useful, what they need to know. I would never dream of telling someone anything hurtful.' She sighed. 'But she's right. I did promise.' She flashed a sudden smile and added: 'But I'd just like to say to you that you're on the right track. You're seeking for yourself, and you don't need any help from me.'

Fig could tell from Kara's dumbstruck expression that she had hit the mark, and she nodded to herself in satisfaction, while Berni shrugged helplessly and tried to bring the conversation back to a more rational topic.

'Julia and Henrik tell me you're the Director of the Manx Wildlife Trust. What does that entail exactly?'

Kara sipped at her tea before embarking on a brief career résumé, not wanting to bore the pair too much with her life. She was keen to ask them more about themselves, but Fig had one more question.

'And do you greet the fairies when you cross the Fairy Bridge?'

Kara looked at her in surprise. 'You know the Isle of Man?'

'Oh, yes. I've been there many times – for this and that,' she replied enigmatically. 'It's famous for its fairies. I was wondering if you'd met them yet.'

Berni sighed pointedly, but Kara had to smile. Fig was astonishingly good at what she did.

'Not yet. But I wouldn't be surprised if I did one of these days,' she laughed while looking meaningfully at Fig.

'You have to be ready to meet them,' Fig advised. 'They won't come to you otherwise.'

'Have you met them then?' Kara asked, realising she was being serious.

'Oh yes,' Fig replied, putting her finger on her lips as if to say that was all she was permitted to divulge.

Berni tapped her head and nodded at her mother. 'Quite mad, but we have to indulge her, I'm afraid.'

Kara decided to rescue her from her embarrassment about her mother. 'So what brings you both here on this tour?'

'The need to get away,' Berni said with feeling. 'This last couple of years has been simply awful for me, and I was in desperate need of a holiday well away from my usual sphere and... former partner,' she admitted. 'I realised my mother hadn't had a holiday in years either, and we hardly see anything of each other, so we decided this sort of holiday was the only one that would suit both of us.'

'And has it?' Kara asked.

'Perfectly,' Berni replied. 'Everybody's really friendly, I don't have to do any organising, just sit back and enjoy it all. It's been well worth it.'

Kara recollected Fig's first comment and picked up on it. 'I suppose I must have seemed rather unfriendly at first. In fact, there's still about half the group I haven't really spoken to yet.'

'Dear oh dear,' Fig rebuked her gently. 'And we're nearly at the end of our travels together.'

Kara looked ashamed. 'Well, I think I know where they're all from by now, but I've not really had much to do with the two sets of Aussies, the Canadians Bill and Nancy, and the German couple, whose names I've forgotten.'

'Silke and Karl,' Berni told her.

Fig shook her head as Kara went on: 'You see, I'm not usually a very sociable sort of person. I get easily tongue-tied and can't make chit-chat.'

'Then you must make it your personal mission to spend time with each of the couples you haven't engaged with yet,' Fig told her.

'What if they don't want me with them?' Kara objected.

'There's no reason whatsoever why they shouldn't want to talk to you,' Fig reassured her. 'Trust me. You're a nice person.'

'Just a bit shy,' Kara admitted.

'You're getting over that, obviously. I've noticed you deep in conversation with that American writer, Martin.'

Kara sighed. The gossip mill was firing up again. 'We discovered a mutual interest, but it's rather taken over for him now. He's spending all his spare time looking up websites now. He'll probably start writing a book about it all next!'

'Well, that's what holidays are all about,' Fig said, gathering the empty tea mugs together and taking them inside to the small kitchen sink. She continued speaking to Kara over her shoulder. 'Encountering new experiences, meeting new people –'

'I just came to escape and have a rest,' Berni interrupted with a yawn. 'Talking of which, I'm off to bed. I've got a good book on the go, and I don't get a chance to read during the day. Night-night.' She disappeared off inside the unit and shut the curtains on the world outside.

Fig finished rinsing the mugs then returned to her chair on the veranda. 'I'm afraid Bernice doesn't understand my interests,' she apologised to Kara. 'Takes after her father, if it's the one I think he was.' She patted Kara on the knee. 'Now you just keep seeking and you'll find what it is you're looking for. Talk to people and listen to what they have to say. You're lucky you live where you do. The energy's still strong there.'

Kara was starting to find Fig just a bit too weird for comfort. 'What energy?'

'You'll find out when you're ready.'

In other words, Kara thought, you don't know what you're talking about and are just trying to impress me by sounding mysterious.

'Keep seeking the dragon's breath,' Fig added, engaging Kara in all seriousness with her golden hazel eyes. 'Speaking of which, I must clean my teeth and get to bed.' With that concluding remark, she disappeared inside.

Kara sat on a while longer enjoying the cool evening air. She looked up at the stars in the sky. The moon was approaching full but was not yet up, so she could clearly see the brightest stars of the Milky Way stretching in a bright arc across the dark sky with the easily recognisable constellation of an upside-down Orion at its northern end. She mulled over what Fig had said about 'dragon's breath', recalling her thoughts on that same subject in the shop in Arrowtown. Was it just another strange coincidence among the many so far, or was some predetermined plan being played out here? If Fig did know more, it was obviously like some Masonic or fairy secret that couldn't be divulged to the uninitiated. Fig had talked about 'seeking' as though it were some official term. And what on earth had she meant by 'dragon's breath'? Kara had the strangest suspicion she already knew, or would soon find out.

With a sigh of frustration she stood up, stepped around the curtain and shut the sliding door. Berni was already reading her book in the top bunk, while Fig was still getting changed into her nightclothes ready to occupy the lower bunk. Five minutes later Kara was in the unit's double bed and bidding them goodnight. She hoped they didn't snore – she suspected Fig might – but as she began to ponder the events of the day, sleep quickly took her.

*

Seven white doves circled overhead then alighted on the edge of the roof, cooing and bobbing their heads. Kara looked up and watched them from her patio chair, and they in turn tilted their heads sideways so they could look down at her. With a clap of its wings, one of them flew off, closely followed by another, and a few moments later two more took flight, following their companions out of sight over the nearby treetops.

The three remaining doves sat there contentedly enough, assessing the surroundings, taking their time in the bright sunshine before one of them dropped down suddenly with a brief flurry of wings to land on the patio beside Kara's chair. It cooed and strutted around in and out of the shadow of her chair, while Kara sat motionless, hardly daring to breathe lest she frightened it away. Eventually the dove moved back into the shade right under her chair and settled down on the warm paving stone, closed its eyes and went to sleep. A second dove then flew down, joined its friend and it too was soon asleep only inches from Kara's feet. The third dove stayed where it was on the roof, as though keeping watch.

Kara felt privileged to be so trusted by the doves that they would fall asleep right beside her. She sat quietly immobile, at peace, enjoying their trust. After a few minutes they woke up, strutted back out into the sunshine and flew up to join the dove perched on the roof. A moment later they all three took flight, soaring up into the blue sky directly towards the sun so she could no longer see them.

*

Kara realised it was the sun streaming in through the gap in the curtains onto her face that had woken her. She felt suddenly bereft, missing the doves of her dream. They had seemed so real, and were certainly a result of the previous morning's visit to the Bird Recovery Centre in Whangarei. There had been a whole flock of white doves there, some flying around, others inside an aviary. But the dream had seemed so personal. The birds had chosen her and come to show she was accepted. Whatever the reason, she felt still that sense of peace and tranquillity the birds had brought with them, just like she had felt in the kauri forest, at one with nature and the earth.

Sounds of movement from the bunk beds prompted her to claim the bathroom first then quickly dressing in shorts and T-shirt she stepped out of the unit into the fresh morning air and the loud song of the forest birds.

She was not the first up. The German couple on the tour were already sitting on the veranda outside the next unit drinking coffee. She had really only passed the time of day with them up till now so, remembering Fig's advice about talking to people and listening, she decided now was the time to get to know them a bit better. Besides, it would have seemed churlish to ignore them when nobody else was around.

The woman was in her mid-sixties, Kara guessed, but her husband was possibly in his late eighties, though extraordinarily spry still, managing to keep up with all the activities except the glacier walk, she recalled. Despite the age difference they seemed to fit together like yin and yang, with a self-containment and ease with their own company that Kara found herself envying as she nodded to them.

She racked her brains to recall their names. Hers was a bit unusual – Silke, she remembered with Berni's help from the previous night – and he was called Karl. They always talked to each other in near perfect English, rather than German, so it was only the initial introductions that had disclosed their nationality.

'Good morning. It looks like it'll be a lovely day again,' Kara began a touch diffidently in case she was interrupting their peace and quiet.

'Morning, Kara,' Silke replied warmly. 'It is a beautiful morning. Would you like to join us for some coffee? Or would you prefer tea? I think we've got rather a wait until breakfast is provided.'

'Thank you. I'd love some tea.' Kara sat down on the white plastic chair Silke pulled forward for her.

'Do you take milk and sugar?'

'Just milk, thank you.'

As Silke disappeared into the unit, Kara turned her attention to her elderly husband, Karl. He reminded her a bit of Prince Philip in his lean build and Germanic looks. She felt her tongue instantly tie itself into knots, as all she could think of now was the famous television series *Fawlty Towers* when Basil Fawlty had German guests in his hotel.

'"Don't mention the war",' Karl quoted with a smile.

'How on earth...?' Kara spluttered, embarrassed in the extreme to be caught red-handed with such thoughts. 'Are you a mind-reader?'

He shrugged. 'That depends on what you would call mind-reading. Technically no, I'm not, but the expression on your face was instantly recognisable as "the Basil Fawlty moment",' he chuckled. 'Don't worry, I'm used to it and it's actually quite funny for me to see that expression coming over people's faces, though fortunately it's happening less often these days. No, it's my wife who's the mind-reader,' he added as Silke came out of the unit and put a mug on the table in front of Kara.

'Are you really?' Kara asked her, intrigued.

Silke sat down again between Kara and Karl and picked up her own mug. 'I seem to have quite a few telepathic moments,' she replied. 'With our family and Karl for the most part, but occasionally with friends or people with whom I feel a close connection.'

Kara thought for a moment. 'I don't have anybody I feel close to any more since my parents died and I seldom see my brothers. Maybe if I did, I'd be into telepathy too. Do you have to be physically close to the person concerned, or does it work over long distances?' Kara noticed Fig emerging from their unit swathed in a towel and heading left towards the swimming hole. Fig gave a wave then a discreet thumbs-up of approval that Kara was taking her advice.

Kara waved back as Silke began to answer her question. 'Not at all. I seem to know when my daughter is about to phone even when she's often in another country from me, or even another time zone. It's that quantum physics thing, isn't it? Once atoms have had some kind of interaction, the connection is maintained even over huge distances, even across the universe, so they reckon.'

'Yes, I've heard that theory,' Kara agreed, 'and it could explain all sorts of bizarre things. Such as ghosts,' she added, remembering Bill's story last night.

'Silke reckons you tap into another dimension when you dream or see a ghost,' Karl chipped in.

Kara thought about that for a moment. 'Do you mean that when you die you go to another dimension?' she asked Silke.

'Your energy must go somewhere. As Einstein famously pointed out, energy can't be created or destroyed. So your spirit energy must go somewhere, so let's call it the fourth or fifth dimension, rather than heaven.' She looked at Kara to test for her reaction at such religious heresy.

'Oh, I'm with you there,' Kara replied. 'My scientific upbringing needs an explanation for things like that. Other dimensions I can just about cope with.'

'It's the only way I can account for some things that have happened,' Karl agreed, 'and I'm not religious either although, at my advanced stage in life, I think I'm entitled to some wishful thinking about life after death.

But I have to admit, I distinctly heard my mother's voice shortly after she died. I was going through a rather difficult patch at the time, admittedly, and didn't care to confess to anyone I was hearing voices. Maybe it was just stress. But Silke is quite aware of her mother communicating from beyond the grave, and I've seen evidence of it myself.'

Kara was fascinated. 'Really? How?'

'My mother's photo falls over when I want a "yes" answer to a question,' Silke explained. 'It only happens in the middle of the night, so I don't see or hear it ever. But in the morning, sure as eggs are eggs, the photo's lying face down if she agrees with what I want to do.'

'And how often has that happened?' Kara asked, somewhat dubious.

'Oh, three or four times. It's only really important questions I bother to ask her about.'

'And has she answered "yes" each time? I mean, how do you know if she's answered "no", if the photo hasn't fallen over?'

'Good question,' Silke laughed. 'I suppose I only ask her questions I want her approval for.'

'Did you have a very close relationship with your mother?' Kara continued. 'I was wondering whether my parents might do the same for me if I tried asking them things.'

'Yes, I did. I never really knew my father. He was killed in the war, so my mother and I just had each other.' Silke touched Kara gently on the hand. 'If you want to speak to your parents then just try it. You might not get an answer straight away, or one you're aware of at first, but wishful thinking is usually positive. I thoroughly believe in self-fulfilling prophecies, whether good or bad. If the whole world is negative then bad things happen. If we all start to think better thoughts, the world will turn around.'

'Yes, I've heard lots of people think that now. But it only seems logical.'

'Exactly. You can only hope so anyway.' Silke swilled down the last of her coffee. 'Well, it looks like everybody else is up, and I just saw Kerri stick her head out of the communal kitchen to see if we're ready for yet another hearty breakfast.'

Kara set her mug down and stood up. 'It's been very interesting talking to you both. We must chat some more. Fig was right. She told me I needed to talk to people more and listen to what they had to say. I'm going to come away from this holiday quite a different person, believe you me! I think I'm even starting to believe in ghosts now.'

CHAPTER SIX

For Kara the highlight of the month-long tour was always going to be the trip out to the nature reserve of Tiritiri Matangi Island in the Hauraki Gulf off Auckland. Kerri had promised them that here they would see the birds they may previously only have heard. The conservationists had cleared it of all introduced predators such as stoats and rats, and had planted thousands of native trees to allow a sanctuary for the most endangered of New Zealand's birds and reptiles. It was a shining example of what could be done with sufficient determination, enthusiasm and vigilance.

On boarding the island's daily ferry, Kara was most impressed by the care taken to ensure nobody accidentally brought any mice over in any hand baggage. Equally impressive was the friendly reception an elderly and very tame takahe gave to them as they landed on the jetty. He strutted around like a blue dodo, making it quite clear to all the visitors that this was his island.

They were quickly divided up into groups, depending on their preferred walking speeds and fitness levels, and allocated a guide. Kara's group's was Val, a retired lady of great enthusiasm for her voluntary job. On the walk up through the bush trail to the summit of the island, Val paused by a thicket. Quietly she pointed to a pair of large blue-grey kokakos, one of the wattlebird species, perching in it. Their mournful call sounded like a squeaky gate, with a 'kokako' periodically thrown in. Kara managed to get a good bit of video and several spectacular photos of them. Further up the hill Val took them through a wooded area hung with sugar-water birdfeeders. Flocking around them were numerous saddlebacks, their bright chestnut saddles in stark contrast to their otherwise black plumage, and the mellifluously singing bellbirds.

As Val guided them higher up through the bush, views over Auckland city and the Hauraki Gulf opened to their right, allowing a sea breeze to cool them briefly before the trees swallowed them again.

The humidity level was high, and Kara was pleased to reach the summit finally, where several more takahes greeted them outside the very welcome café.

Kara browsed in the gift shop then bought herself a bacon, lettuce, avocado and tomato sandwich that she took to eat on a grassy hillock. Sitting by herself, looking out across the sapphire blue Hauraki Gulf towards Auckland's elegant skyline, she felt astonishingly happy. The holiday had lived up to all its promises: not only due to the sheer quantity of wildlife and habitats she had seen, but also because of the strong friendships she had made. Julia and Henrik had already promised a return trip to the Isle of Man to see more of it and visit some of the numerous Manx Wildlife Trust reserves. Martin had spent another interesting evening with her checking out websites, and he had told her he too intended to try out the island from a travel writer's point of view, featuring the mystical antiquity of the place. Owen and Pat had promised to come and see the choughs and hen harriers maybe next year, while Fig had said she would certainly call in on Kara during her next visit, although she failed to specify the purpose of that visit. Knowing Fig's interests, Kara felt it might be for a witches' coven or gathering of druids, but perhaps she just had friends or business interests there. Silke and Karl had even hinted they might add the island to their itinerary next time they were in the British Isles visiting the English side of their seemingly extensive family.

It wasn't just the friends she had made that had left Kara feeling so happy, however. Most of all, she felt a whole new world had opened up to her: a mysterious world of strange happenings and otherworldliness, of promises of more to come and doors yet to be opened. She felt excited at the prospect of discovering more when she returned home and had regular access to the Internet, and more than anything else she was anticipating reading the John Michell book she had ordered.

Before her eyes the sparkling blue waters of the Hauraki Gulf had an almost electric quality to them, and the splendid volcanic presence of uninhabited Rangitoto Island and the other numerous volcanic cones dotted around the narrow isthmus that made up Auckland, provided an almost tangible link with the earth's inner sun. Kara could feel the sun above, the sun below and the sun in her heart, and was transported into the blue light.

*

The people around her wore skirts or kilts made from woven flax leaves attached to a waistband, and some had cloaks of feathers. A grey-haired old fellow holding a tall staff in his hand approached her from the summit, and she felt she recognised him. He exuded what the Maori called mana, *meaning authority or power.* Mana, Manannan; *the two words alternated in her head like a mantra until she couldn't separate them.*

The elder smiled and nodded at her, raised his staff high and spread his arms towards her in a welcoming gesture before extending them and turning to encompass the surrounding landscape in a gesture signifying 'we live here'. Kara followed his gesture and saw to her surprise that Rangitoto Island had a very different look to it. Its flattened cone outline was markedly different and it seemed to have primitive wooden settlements around it, with wooden boats pulled up on the shore. The vegetation looked denser and more mature than might be expected in only the six hundred years since its last eruption.

'You have managed to cross the bridge,' the old man said. 'We felt you coming and have helped you as best we can. Many others have crossed before you and many more will do so. You should try to help them too. Your kind needs to return. You have forgotten too much and been taught too much falsehood, but you, Kara, respect our Mother Earth, and she has welcomed you back.'

'Who are you?' Kara asked.

'We are the keepers of wisdom, and we are here to help. You will find us again in the sacred places and with the dragon's breath. Keep seeking.'

*

'Excuse me. Are you Kara Groves?'

Kara opened her eyes to find a young man shaking her shoulder, his uniform that of a reserve warden. 'Yes?'

'That's a relief. We've been looking all over the place for you, thinking you'd got lost or fallen down a hillside or something.'

Kara looked around and realised the café area behind her was now deserted, apart from one or two back-packing types who were obviously staying overnight at the island's hostel. She scrambled to her feet and saw by the shadows that the day was getting late.

'But I've been here all the time,' she protested. 'Didn't anybody see me?' She put her hand over her mouth in alarm. 'Oh no! Have they gone without me?'

'They waited as long as they could for you, but the ferry had to leave promptly for all the other passengers to get back to Auckland. You were told to be down at the jetty on time.'

'Yes, I know. I must have fallen asleep or something.' She looked at her finder. 'What do I do now?'

The young man smiled to reassure her. 'Any other day you'd be stuck here for the night but, unusually and luckily for you, we have some guests here today who've come over independently, and their boat hasn't left yet. I'll radio in that I've found you then I can run you down to the jetty in the ute. We've got Kerri's cell phone number, so I'll contact her and she can arrange with you what to do once you get to Auckland.'

'What a stupid situation! I'm so sorry for all the trouble,' Kara apologised. 'I've never done anything like this before.'

'Not to worry. My name's Murray, by the way. Let's get back to the office up there, and I'll let them know you're coming.'

While Murray busied himself with the radio and cell phone, Kara made use of the toilet facilities. While washing her hands she looked in the mirror at herself. What on earth would the others think of her? And poor Kerri must be beside herself with worry at losing one of her flock.

As soon as she emerged Murray whisked her over to a Toyota 4WD, and they sped off down a track.

'Kerri asked if you could walk or get a taxi to your hotel,' Murray told her, while grappling with the steering wheel as they negotiated a rather rutted part of the trail. 'It's Rydges, not far from the Sky Tower. You can't miss that!'

At the jetty there was no sign of the elderly takahe, but a large launch sat there, its engines throbbing gently and the crew waiting to receive her on board. Kara felt about six inches tall under their scrutiny, and wondered who the visitors were who had condescended to wait for her. A crewmember showed her to a seat in the rear cockpit, from where she could see a group of about half a dozen people occupying the saloon cabin.

As ever she was wearing her white baseball-style cap emblazoned with the Manx Wildlife Trust's flying tern logo, but which was so ancient that it bore the Trust's former name. One of the party stuck her head out of the cabin and smiled at Kara, as if to reassure her she was welcome on board, then noticed her cap.

'Manx Nature Conservation Trust?' she read. 'You've come a long way! Are you a member?'

'I'm the Director,' Kara told the woman sheepishly, still embarrassed by her predicament. 'And we're called the Manx Wildlife Trust now, like all the rest.'

'Well I'm blowed!' She turned to her colleagues in the cabin. 'You'll never guess who our rescued castaway is – no less a person than the Director of the Manx Wildlife Trust.'

Kara felt even more embarrassed now at the aggrandisement of her position until the woman turned back to her and said reassuringly: 'Come on in and meet the team. We're all part of various UK woodland and conservation trusts on a tour of successful nature reserves, exchanging ideas about what really works.'

'That sounds like a fun job!' Kara commented as she crossed the open cockpit and entered the cabin. When she saw who else was inside her jaw dropped.

'Fancy meeting you here, Paul!' she declared, holding up her hand in greeting to a tall man near the centre of the group. The men and women around him parted to let her through then resumed their conversations. In their close professional circle, people were always meeting up with acquaintances at gatherings and conferences in various parts of the world.

Despite her initial friendliness, Kara now approached Paul with some trepidation. They had been close friends many years ago early in their careers, when they had both worked for the Bucks, Berks and Oxfordshire Nature Trust, as it was called then. If she had stayed there they might have got really close, but a better job had turned up in Norfolk and she had left, with some regrets, but young and eager to develop her career. He had certainly gone on to develop his own, as she knew he was now high up on the board of the Woodland Trust.

'I never knew the Woodland Trust had the funds for this sort of junket,' she stretched up to speak close to his ear, above the noise of the launch's engines and the conversation around them.

'And I never knew the Manx Wildlife Trust had funds to send their directors across the world,' he countered with a broad grin and a twinkle of warmth in his familiar grey eyes.

'They don't. I'm on holiday – I decided to spend my inheritance,' she added quickly, lest he thought they paid her too much.

'And I suppose I'm spending mine,' he admitted. 'Or rather, this is all being paid for by my father and stepmother. It's her money really. My dad married a very wealthy woman, lucky sod!'

'What, they paid for all of this?' she asked, indicating the boatload of people.

'Yes. I did say she was wealthy. I think I may have told you about them once. Actually it's to tie in with their fortieth wedding anniversary later this year. They were coming out here for a holiday, and this trip became possible at the same time, so they organised both. They've been on... I guess the same trip you're on!' he ended with a laugh of glee at the coincidence. 'I met up with them here on the island today, and we're getting together this evening at my hotel for dinner.'

The penny dropped for Kara. 'You don't mean Silke and Karl, do you? Of course, I remember now you saying you're half German.' She looked again at his eyes, and now realised how like Karl's they were. 'If I were better at recognising people, I might have seen some semblance of you in your father.'

'Well, he is looking pretty old now, but he's still sprightly for his age.'

'You're telling me! How old is he?'

'Eighty-eight. I know Silke keeps a careful eye on his health and well-being and must be feeding him some kind of elixir of youth, but he says it's having plenty of grandchildren and great-grandchildren that keeps him young.'

'Plus the money to enjoy life,' Kara said enviously.

'Life hasn't been at all easy for him, especially with my mother dying quite young,' Paul pointed out. 'But everything changed when he met Silke. It was like the awful bad luck disappeared, and everything's been good for us all in the family since then. It was she who encouraged me to develop my interest in ecology and conservation, and she's helped fund some projects I wanted to get involved in.'

'So she's like a fairy godmother to you all then?' Kara joked, grabbing at his arm to steady herself as they crossed over the wash of a freighter heading out of Auckland harbour.

'Yes,' Paul admitted, considering her words carefully. 'My fairy godmother. I hadn't thought of her like that before, but you're right. She is.'

*

'And then Paul invited me back for dinner at the Hilton where they were staying, even though I was still in my sweaty, old day clothes!' Kara told Martin, when she finally made it back to Rydges Hotel later that evening and found him working at his laptop in the bar. She sat down on the seat next to him. 'I managed to have a shower in his room and he called Silke – they're actually staying at the Hilton tonight – who brought round these clothes of hers for me to wear. Fortunately we're a similar- enough size, though her shoes are a bit large for me. They kept slipping off under the table. But we all had a lovely meal, and they were so nice. Silke's very interested in conservation work and wants to help with our reserves in some way. We're actually raising funds to purchase a new section of land, so she's going to chip in a good bit for that.'

'Serendipity strikes again!' Martin commented. 'If you hadn't missed the boat, you'd never have met Paul. By the way, why did you miss it? You're not one for being late normally.'

'Well, that's the strange thing. I don't know how it happened. I was sitting after lunch looking out over the bay at Auckland, and the next thing I knew, this warden was telling me I'd missed the boat. Because we were to make our own way back to the jetty, I wasn't attached to any group, so nobody missed me till the final count.'

'Yes, it turned into a mad panic then, as we all thought you must have fallen and hurt yourself somewhere. It's quite a big island to search. We all wanted to join in the hunt for you, but Kerri insisted we get on the ferry, otherwise we'd all have been stranded there and most people are catching flights tomorrow.'

'There really wasn't any need. I was in full view of the café area all the time. Surely somebody noticed me sitting there?'

'I expect they were concentrating on the lower part of the island at that time. They assumed you'd already left the summit. So why were you still up there? You must have fallen asleep.'

'I don't think so. I'm sure I was sitting up when the warden spoke to me.' She suddenly had a flash recollection of a dream being interrupted, but she had been too anxious and busy since then to have recalled what it was.

'Well the main thing is you got back safely and even had a useful meeting out of it, by all accounts.' Martin tapped the screen of his laptop. 'Meanwhile, I've been discovering all sorts about those Caucasian bones found in the forests up north. Apparently over the years they've found quite a number of skeletons in caves and elsewhere, many in these strange, coffin-like boxes, and all the authorities do with them is hand them over to the local Maori for disposal, thinking they're theirs, but the Maori know they're not and just bury them in a local Anglican cemetery. The Maori elders are fed up with all the fuss and bother and don't want anything more to do with it all and, according to one source I've been communicating with, they're hiding or destroying any new bones they find.'

'Really? So this evidence that the Patu-paiarehe people existed is being ignored?'

'In effect, yes. Apparently there were even reports as recently as earliest colonial times of these people up in that area, but they seem to have died out since then. You can still see spirals and bowls and things cut into rocks all over the place here, which are supposed to be their work, as they're apparently similar to ancient stone carvings found in Ireland.'

'You have been busy, haven't you?' Kara said in admiration for the way he had taken up the hunt for evidence of her supposed fairy folk.

'Yes, well, it's turning into quite a ghost hunt or cover up, depending on how you like to look at it. The latest snippet I've found is that they could be the bones of early Portuguese sailors stranded here.' His face suddenly lost its sparkle. 'There was a rather disturbing discussion section on the website, though, which accused the writers of allegedly making it all up for European racial superiority reasons. It was all getting a bit nasty, and I didn't know what to believe in the end. But whether it's true or not, I'm really fascinated now at all the other stuff I've found and the implications for world history. You've really set me off on a new course here, Kara.'

'It's funny, isn't it? We've both had our minds opened to something strange by coming here to New Zealand. It's like there's something in the air here that allows new ideas to collect and disseminate themselves into unsuspecting travellers.'

'Or maybe it's just us,' Martin theorised. 'Suspending disbelief while we're on vacation. What's the betting once we get home we'll forget all this and get back to normality?'

'No, I don't think so,' she replied thoughtfully. 'Something's happened to me here. Something's definitely happened. I've seen the light, and it's blue.' She shook her head as if clearing fuzziness from it. 'I feel like I have a job to do, but I'm not sure what it is yet.'

'Perhaps you'd better sleep on it,' Martin suggested helpfully. 'Despite your long snooze this afternoon, you look crap.'

Kara laughed at his forthrightness. 'OK, I get the hint. See you in the morning for our last day here.'

*

She stood looking into a dark pool. Around its edges willows dangled their fronds in the water. The full moon reflected brightly on its surface, dazzling her, but as her eyes adjusted she saw her own reflection under it, her face a round white shape, shimmering gently. As she watched another round face appeared near hers, followed rapidly by others: faces of people she recognised, some living, some dead. Her parents were there, as was a good friend who had died a few years back, but she also saw the faces of some of the people on the tour: Fig, whose wild hair now resembled Medusa's head of snakes; and she was sure she recognised Sharon from the shop in Arrowtown. Then there was Silke, whose dark brown eyes disappeared into the depths.

As she stood there a thin stream of green mist rose in a coil from the moon's reflection in the centre of the pool towards the heavenly moon, while from above a second stream of white mist descended in a coil around the first, forming a double spiral.

From the depths of the pool were uttered the words 'dragon's breath'.

*

The coach was waiting for them outside the hotel to take them on the last stage of their tour to Auckland Airport. Only Silke and Karl were missing. They would be staying on longer in Auckland with their son. Everybody else was busy exchanging email addresses, while Kerri double-checked that all those who were headed for the airport were assembled and their luggage was safely stowed.

'Well, that's about it, then,' Kerri announced once they were all in their seats on the coach. 'This is where I say goodbye and wish you all a safe journey. I'd like to thank you all for making this tour such a pleasant event. I hope you'll all come back to New Zealand for another visit in the not too distant future.'

There was a loud murmuring of assent followed by generous applause for Kerri. She waved farewell then stepped off the coach. The doors slid closed and their coach driver pulled out of the forecourt into the Auckland traffic.

Kara felt like she was leaving something behind as they headed out on State Highway 1 towards the airport. As the road opened up, she could see to her left the distinctive flattened cone of Rangitoto Island prominently occupying the harbour, and with a jolt she remembered her dream or vision or whatever it was while on Tiritiri Matangi Island, of the wisdom-keepers welcoming her and telling her she had a job to do, and that they would help her. Then she remembered again her dream of last night: the moonlit pond and the clearly defined faces of Fig, Sharon and Silke watching over her like three fairy godmothers. In Sharon's presence she had first thought of the words 'dragon's breath'. Fig had actually spoken them to her, and it had seemed to be Silke's voice in the pool of her dream saying those same words.

ISLE OF MAN

CHAPTER SEVEN

The flight from London's Gatwick Airport touched down on the damp tarmac of Ronaldsway Airport, Isle of Man. Through the aircraft window Kara had seen the approaching island as they flew down its east coast. She could identify every bay and headland, recognise the farms and white-painted houses, and as they circled over Castletown in preparation for the approach to landing, the solid familiarity of the town, with its impressive castle, seemed to be welcoming her home.

Stepping onto the tarmac and smelling the bracing, salty air again, she smiled. This was indeed home. Early February was proving its usual blustery self, and she hung onto her handbag as it threatened to be whisked away across the airfield by the stiff breeze. Upon entering the terminal building all was peace and calm. Kara walked the short distance through to the baggage reclaim area where, soon afterwards, a klaxon announced the start of the carousel and the arrival of the luggage.

Amongst those waiting she recognised a couple of faces, and gave them a warm smile, while through the dividing windows to the main concourse was a family she knew waiting to greet a passenger from her flight. She waved at them and they waved back.

After her almost two-day journey from New Zealand she had intended to get a taxi back to her home in Douglas, but while struggling with her luggage trolley outside she met another acquaintance, Tony, a Trust member who often came to help on the 'Midweek Muckers' workdays on the reserves.

'Welcome back, Kara!' Tony said, catching hold of the end of the trolley, which was threatening to roll off the kerb into a waiting taxi. 'You're looking well. How was New Zealand?'

'Awesome!' she replied in the Kiwi vernacular. 'But it's good to be home. I don't know, there's something about this place that just grabs you and won't let go!'

'It's the weather!' Tony laughed when another strong gust of wind threatened to send her trolley into a spin. 'Do you need a lift? I'm heading back into Douglas. I've just dropped off my son and his wife here.'

Exhaustion was setting in for Kara. She had already endured a coach connection from Heathrow to Gatwick where she had had a long wait on top of the twenty-six hour journey from Auckland, which included a tedious two hours in transit at Los Angeles airport negotiating US immigration. 'That sounds wonderful, Tony. Thank you.'

'Good. My car's just up there across the road. Here, let me push your trolley.'

Kara gladly yielded control and followed Tony across to the car park, casting a quick nod of recognition at the famous Manx palms planted in the central reservation of the dual carriageway outside the airport. The tree was actually a native of New Zealand, known there as the cabbage tree after Captain Cook discovered the young sprouting leaves were edible. It was introduced into the Isle of Man in the early eighteen hundreds and was now visible island-wide in gardens and parks. Kara had read up all about them as soon as she had encountered the familiar-looking trees on her visit. She had bid them farewell in Auckland, and now here they were welcoming her home again.

Tony sensed her weariness during the twenty minutes' drive back to Douglas, and neither spoke much except to say hello to the fairies, each in their own fashion, when they crossed the tiny Fairy Bridge.

'Old habits die hard, eh?' Tony quipped. 'Though I've heard it's not the original Fairy Bridge.'

'Really?'

'Apparently so. The real one's reputedly less accessible on an ancient track over the stream somewhere nearby. When the tourist buses came on the scene Ballona Bridge was adopted as the new one.'

Kara was silent, struck by the sense of power emanating from the area around the bridge. They were out of it now, but she had encountered a prickling, electrostatic energy that rose up her spine to her heart, and a kind of magnetic force trying to hold on to her. How could that be if, as Tony said, this was not the real bridge? She shook her head in disbelief, attributing the sensation to the disturbance of jetlag, but she was puzzled nevertheless.

*

It took several days for the jetlag to resolve. Sure enough, the John Michell book was waiting for her, but she resisted starting reading it until her correspondence was cleared, her fridge restocked and her laundry ironed. By then her eyelids were dropping, and she couldn't have read had she tried. She had allowed herself only a long weekend to recover before starting work again, and arrived there on Monday morning as ready as she was able to tackle the backlog. Planning progress on the new premises was still slow. The building was in poor shape, needing gutting and re-roofing, so there were numerous reports of proposed developments to catch up on, as well as general wildlife matters to attend to, phone calls to return and meetings to prepare for.

The sheer number of emails awaiting her attention was daunting, and she decided to spend her lunch-break trying to clear as many as she could. To her great delight there were two already from fellow travellers, and she hastened to open them. The first was from Martin, telling her he had just finished reading the John Michell book and was eagerly awaiting her response to it. He was already planning a trip over to the Isle of Man in the summer, and could she recommend a reasonably priced hotel, as this new travelogue would be aimed at those travellers not so well endowed financially? She sent a brief but friendly reply with the information he needed, adding that she'd be in touch further once she'd read the book. She then opened the email from Berni. After the preliminary greetings it read: *Mum doesn't have a PC so she asked me to tell you she'll be over in late June and will contact you then.*

'That's quick,' Kara muttered.

'Sorry?' Jill Bridgewater, the office manager, was passing her open door on her way to make a cup of coffee and thought Kara was talking to her.

'Oh, I was just talking to myself,' Kara explained. 'Two people I met on holiday are both coming here in the summer, quite independently. Isn't that great?'

Jill visibly shuddered at the thought. 'That depends on whether you like them or not. I can't think of anything worse than being descended upon by people I've met on holiday.'

'Well, these two are very nice in different ways. One's an American freelance travel-writer-cum-researcher of weird happenings and tales, while the other's a kind of Gloucestershire white witch, I think.'

Jill blinked in astonishment. 'I thought it was a natural history tour you were on, not a New Age convention.'

'It was. It's just that events conspired to get us all talking about... such things,' she finished tamely, not wanting to embroil Jill in all the entanglements of her holiday.

The office phone began to ring and, since Jill wasn't at her desk to answer it, Kara lifted her handset.

'Manx Wildlife Trust, Kara Groves speaking,' she said automatically.

'Kara! It's Paul Driesler here.'

'Paul! Where on earth are you phoning from? Aren't you still in Auckland or somewhere equally far-flung?'

'No, well, yes, I suppose. I'm in Germany now at my parents' place for a few days. Look, I just wanted to confirm with you the arrangements for their donation to your new reserve purchase. They'd like to come over in the summer to see what they're putting their money into.'

'Really? That's great! I'd be delighted to show them round, and we can organise a publicity photo shoot of them, if they don't mind. Would it be OK if I just emailed the Trust's account details to them in the meantime? Then they can do a bank transfer rather than risk sending a cheque.'

'Yes, of course, but I thought I'd give you a ring anyway and say how much I enjoyed meeting up with you again.' He paused, awaiting her response.

Kara blinked away a blue spot that had formed in front of her eyes. The connection to Paul was as clear as though he were in the next room, and she pictured him standing in an elegantly furnished room, the sun pouring through huge French windows which looked out onto tall winter trees in the distance beyond. 'I really enjoyed it too, Paul,' she heard herself saying from his mobile phone, as though she were in the room right next to him. 'Why don't you come over too?'

She clearly saw him give his reply. 'I was hoping you'd say that. I'll have to fit it in with my schedule somehow. But I'd better let you get on with your work now. Lots to catch up on, I expect.'

'You're telling me!' Her eyes fell on the office wall planner in front of her. 'Paul, if you're coming over, try to make it for when our orchid meadows are in bloom mid-to-late June. That's after the TT races, but if that's not convenient at least come before the Manx Grand

Prix starts in late August, so you'll be able to get around the island easily.'

'I'll check out the dates. Mid-to-late June you say?'

'That's right.'

'Well, I'll get back to you on that. Speak soon. Bye for now.'

'Bye, Paul.'

It wasn't until after she had replaced the handset that she remembered Fig was supposed to be coming to the island at about the same time. And possibly Martin. Perhaps she had done too good a job of selling the island to everybody. Still, it would be nice to have them all at the same time as a kind of holiday reunion, and it would make it easier on her showing people around the reserves as a group rather than having to make repeated visits, which would affect her day to day work. It would certainly make an interesting article for the Trust's magazine, especially if Silke and Karl were willing to be photographed at the site of the new reserve.

As she sat back in her office chair she recalled the incredibly vivid sensation of actually being with Paul in Germany. Through her ground-floor window she could see one of the three mouse-brown Loaghtan sheep that cropped the small area of grass at the back of the building. The ram had four horns, the lower two almost encircling his head, and now he suddenly reminded her of pictures of ancient tales of Pan, Herne the Hunter and horn-headed shamans summoning the spirits of nature to impart their wisdom. The ram looked up at her through the window, his mouth chewing, showing his yellow-stained teeth. Their eyes met, but he did not supply the answer to her question: did she really see where Paul was?

It was as though there had been a definite connection of the kind Silke had spoken of, but much clearer. She was sure there was a proper term for it and, after a short struggle with her memory, it finally came to her – remote viewing. Was that what she had done? The way to check would be to email Paul and ask him to describe the room he was in to see if it matched her mental image.

He would think her crazy. At this stage she didn't feel she wanted to jeopardize anything, as there had been a certain degree of warmth to his enquiry and an eagerness to meet up, which she reciprocated. Seeing him again had been so easy, like long-term friends who only see each other once in a while but click again instantly.

It occurred to her now that she hadn't asked Paul about a wife or partner. Surely if there was one, she would have accompanied him on a trip like that? Unless she was working and couldn't take time off, or had a sick parent she couldn't leave, or had children still at home, or an elderly dog... The list of possibilities was endless. It was more than likely he did have a wife, a lovely man such as that.

With a sigh she turned her attention back to her emails and carried on working.

*

The snow that had beset the whole country that winter returned with a few flurries of flakes on her journey home, but fortunately it didn't settle. Switching on the lights in her Victorian terraced house, she dumped her bag full of work-related reading on the hall floor, and headed back out to the car parked a short way up the street for the couple of carrier bags full of food shopping she had just bought.

Her house was on a tiny back street of Douglas, overlooking the steam railway station and the large Tesco supermarket. It was an ideal location, as it meant she could easily walk around town, to the bus station and ferry terminal and any evening entertainment, without worrying about taking the car. The house was a bit on the dark side, surrounded as it was by houses behind and tall trees in front towards the railway. It was private and sheltered, however, and Kara had made it light and cosy inside. She liked smelling the whiffs of coal smoke when the steam trains were running, and hearing the regular blasts of their whistles, prior to starting off on their trip to Port Erin in the south-west of the island. Less welcome was the blast of the Douglas lighthouse foghorn during one of Manannan's occasional 'cloak' episodes, and the roaring of visitors' motorbikes up and down the nearby main road in the middle of the night during the TT races fortnight, as they headed to and from the ferry terminal.

Kicking off her shoes, she put the shopping away, popped some carrots and potatoes in a pan to boil with broccoli in the steamer on top, placed her piece of hake ready in the microwave then sat down to watch the early evening news with a glass of French white wine she had won at a raffle. She longed for the New Zealand wines she had become used to, and resolved to look out for some here, now she knew what to look for.

As usual the television news was doom and gloom, and she wondered why she bothered watching it. If the end of the world ever came she supposed she would need to know about it, she thought, and pottered across the lounge to her kitchen to finish off the cooking.

When she sat down again in front of the TV with her dinner, she noticed the John Michell book on the sideboard against the wall. As she finished her last mouthful of fish, the news turned to sport, so without hesitation she turned off the TV, found her reading glasses and opened up *The Sacred Center*.

At eleven-thirty she wrote a lengthy email to Martin.

Hi there

So he reckons the Old Tynwald Hill was the centre of British and Irish Druidry! I confess, I've never been up there and wasn't even really aware of its existence. It's tucked up an isolated valley, as you could see from the map, but I'll have to go and check it out now, though it doesn't look like there's too much to see. How incredibly important that site must once have been! I expect you can't wait to see it now.

All that other stuff about the alignment of churches, roads and towns in Britain and Europe is mind-blowing. And he even says the people of Man were known even in the ninth century as great navigators. They were also brilliant surveyors, but that's exactly what the pre-Maori people were called – The Surveyors – and they seemed to get around the most inhospitable terrain. They certainly knew a lot more in those days than they've been given credit for.

I blame it on the Romans deliberately destroying the Druidic culture and subsequently slandering it, as they feared its power. I'm all fired up to read more about the Druids now. By the way, it's true about the reservoir being built over Druidale. It's hard to imagine that it was possibly a sacred grove once.

Something that struck me while reading it was how my name fits in with the landscape there: Groves obviously fits with the sacred groves of Druidale, but also the pyramidal hill immediately north of Old Tynwald Hill is called Carraghan, which means nothing more exciting than 'Rocky Place' in Manx, according to my book of walks. I know I'm trying to find connections and look too deeply into the significance of all this, but I just feel such an incredible draw to the place, like I'm meant to go there.

Well, I'd better stop rambling on. Just wanted to say how excited I was after reading the book, as it lived up to all my expectations. And I love the way he says the Isle of Man 'has always been known as a place of enchantment' and that it was probably the seat of learning for the children of Scottish and Celtic kings. Whoops, still rambling on. Must stop and go to bed.

Cheerio for now, Kara.

*

Manannan stood before her on the cliff-top. Behind him seagulls were hovering in the updrafts of the cliff, their yellow legs dangling in ungainly fashion beneath them. The sun was from her left, due south, and Manannan's staff cast only a short shadow to the north. He was dressed in a white cloak this time, and round his forehead was a circlet of gold.

'The light is within you,' he told Kara. 'And it has changed from blue to white. You are seeing what is there to be seen, and must find what is as yet hidden. Listen to your guides and you will find the way to wisdom, but do not go alone.'

Around his feet in the folds of his cloak were seven white doves. At the wave of his staff, four of them flew off: north, south, east and west. The remaining three strutted towards Kara. One sat on her feet, one perched on her head, though it felt almost weightless, and the third took up position on her left elbow, close to her heart. They began to coo, first one, then the others, their cooing vibrating throughout her body, resonating up and down her spine until, in a blinding flash of white wings, they all took off and flew to the north-east behind her. She turned round, watching them flying towards Snaefell and the central hill range, towards Old Tynwald Hill.

*

By the end of the first week back, Kara was starting to get back into her normal sleep pattern. The weather was still very chilly and not conducive to jaunts up into the hills. She also felt for some strange reason that she wanted somebody with her when she drove up to the Old Tynwald Hill site, and decided to put off going until Martin's visit in the summer.

In the meantime, she had managed to clear some of the backlog at work, and on Friday she and the reserves manager, Vicky Costain, were visiting the proposed new reserve site with representatives of the Department of Tourism and Leisure, the Department of Agriculture,

Fisheries and Forestry, as well as the members of the House of Keys for Patrick and Rushen.

The proposed new reserve was situated on the south-west coast overlooking Niarbyl Bay, and would complement the two existing reserves in that area at Dalby. Adjacent to the new area ran the Raad Ny Foillan, or The Road of the Gull, round-island coastal path. Kara reminded her guests how wildlife tourism was becoming increasingly important for the island's economy, and that walkers and hikers on the path could make use of its information board. The highly successful Basking Shark Project was an important draw, as were sightings of cetaceans and other sea mammals from the cliffs. Choughs, puffins and Manx shearwaters as well as occasional exotic birds blown in on Atlantic storms all did their bit to draw eager 'Twitchers', Kara explained.

Having said her piece, she stood near the cliff top, hanging on to her flapping scarf, while Vicky pointed out the proposed new reserve boundaries. A couple of large herring gulls hovered in the updrafts, giving Kara a strong sense of déjà vu as she suddenly remembered her dream about Manannan. It was a shame there were no white doves to complete the scenario, she thought wistfully, but the sturdy, bearded figure of the DAFF representative almost stood in for Manannan. He even had a walking stick, but that was as far as the likeness went.

Her gaze followed the gulls as they swooped out towards Northern Ireland, their white bodies showing clearly against a large, dark cloud scudding in on the stiff westerly. Alerting the group to the impending shower, she set off back to the road in the company of Margaret Quayle from the DOT&L.

'I'm still astonished at how successful our Wildflowers of Mann Project has been,' Margaret commented to Kara as they strode across the rabbit-cropped turf. 'We get so many letters from tourists who appreciate seeing all the old wildflowers in the verges and hedgerows. It just goes to show what can be done when different departments cooperate.'

'I just wish we could get the bluebells under control,' Kara replied. 'But the Spanish bluebell has well and truly taken over from our own true-blue ones. Now there seem to be as many pink and white ones as blue, especially around Douglas.'

'Ah, you can't beat a proper bluebell wood, can you?' Margaret said wistfully. 'When I think of paradise, I think of the bluebells under the beech trees in Groudle Glen.'

Kara smiled. 'It's funny you should say that. That was one of the first places I visited when I came to the island. I walked down the Glen from the parking area on the Laxey Road, and just as you approach the viaduct, where the banks get steeper, I just had to stop and stare in amazement at the beauty of it all. The sun was streaming down through the fresh green beech leaves onto the patches of bluebells below, with the stream sparkling beside them. I don't know how long I stood there and soaked up the sight. I've never forgotten it. In fact, I think that's where I'd like my ashes strewn when the time comes.'

'I know exactly where you mean,' Margaret nodded in agreement with Kara's sentiments. 'Oops, here it comes,' she cried, as the threatened rain descended on their heads and both women dived for the sanctuary of their cars.

Vicky hurled herself into the driving seat of the MWT utility truck as Kara collapsed into the passenger seat. 'That was a close call,' Vicky said, starting the engine to begin the demisting process. 'They seemed impressed with our plans to make it as public-friendly as possible, without encouraging over-intensive use.'

'I don't suppose we'll ever be crawling with visitors here,' Kara remarked, remembering the restrictions on Tiritiri Matangi Island to one boatload of visitors a day, despite its proximity to the city of Auckland. 'Not unless the weather ever becomes more reliable. But that's the beauty of this place. It's only really busy during TT, and even then there's plenty of room to spare. Not like the Channel Islands.'

The windscreen had cleared enough to see out of by now, so they headed back up the coast road towards the crossroads at Round Table, under the shadow of South Barrule. Kara looked up to the cloud-shrouded summit on her right, picturing the extensive hill fort there and those people of old who had built it. She felt again that strong connection with antiquity that was such a part of her life here.

Vicky had been quiet for a while when suddenly she said: 'We've all noticed a difference in you since your holiday, Kara. You seem a lot happier, if you don't mind me saying. Not that you looked miserable before, don't get me wrong, but you just somehow... I dunno... seem radiant now.'

'It's all right. I know what you mean. You're right though. I do feel happier in myself.'

'What happened then?' Vicky pried, wanting to relate the gossip to the others on the staff.

Kara looked down at her lap. What had happened to her in those four weeks? Her mind had been opened to other influences, not only by the friends she had made, but also by the whole series of coincidences and synchronicities that had started at Doubtful Sound with her contact with a fairy. Or had it begun before that? All the people she had met on her trip had all booked their tickets well in advance, so the wheels of fate were set in motion up to a year ago, about the time she first developed her interest in optimal nutrition and complementary therapies.

'I don't think it was just the holiday or the lovely people I met in the tour group. Since I started taking my vitamins and minerals, I've begun to feel healthier, more alive. I call my Vitamin D capsules 'liquid light' and they've seemed to 'enlighten' me. There was an old guy on the trip who looked very well, and his much younger wife was heavily into nutrition and was feeding him all these things, like the elixir of youth, as his son called it. Oh, and you'll never guess who the son is!'

She sensed Vicky tense as though this was the big revelation. 'Go on, enlighten me. Who is he then?' Vicky asked eagerly.

'Paul Driesler of the Woodland Trust! He and I were colleagues years ago at BBONT, as it was then, and I met him in Auckland quite accidentally,' Kara happily let slip in a bout of wishful thinking that startled her in its intensity.

Vicky took her eyes off the road a moment to look at Kara, and saw the smile on her face. 'Ah! So is he the reason you've gone all sunny?'

Kara's smile slipped. 'Not really,' she admitted. 'I think I would like it to be, but I've no idea whether he's married, single, divorced or whatever.' She couldn't believe how she was confiding in Vicky like this. She had never had a female friend to whom she had told her innermost feelings before. Something had changed in her.

'We could always find out,' Vicky said, taking up the challenge on Kara's behalf. 'I have a few contacts there I can discreetly ask.'

'Perhaps you'd better,' Kara agreed. 'He's coming over this summer with his parents – our mystery benefactors, by the way – and I ought to know whether he's available or not before I start flirting too much with him.'

'You? Flirt! I can't imagine it.'

'Well, I'm not completely a crusty old spinster, you know. And I have rather realised that old age is looming and I don't have a companion to share it with. Seeing Paul's father and stepmother so happy together, even though he must have married her in his late forties, got me thinking.'

'Especially when you met up with Paul.'

'And that,' Kara conceded.

They continued in silence as Vicky negotiated the narrow stone-walled back lanes to St John's in the driving rain. As they passed the lower slopes of Slieu Whallian, Kara thought ruefully of the suspected witches, often an older woman living alone such as herself, who were once rolled down the hill in a spiked barrel. She suddenly had such an incredibly vivid mental image of one such horrific event, of the jeering crowds and the poor woman being forced into the barrel, that she gasped out loud.

'What's up?' Vicky asked.

'I was just thinking of the witches being put to death here. It's truly dreadful how cruel people can be when they believe, rightly or wrongly, that somebody's a bit different from themselves.'

Vicky looked askance at her. 'There you see. That's something that's different about you since your holiday. You seem to be very interested in fairies and witches and things.'

'Do I?' Kara struggled to think when she had mentioned fairies, then recalled a discussion with Jill and Vicky over the teapot earlier in the week. It had all started when Vicky had mentioned the local name for red campion was 'fairy flower'. Kara had gone on to ask if there were many other fairy-related flower names, so they had consulted the *Wild Flowers of Mann* book in their reference library and found that harebells were 'fairy thimbles', and that local herbalists were called 'fairy doctors' until quite recently. Kara had also read out to Jill and Vicky that fairies supposedly avoided yellow flowers, and that verbena was considered a potent charm against bad luck.

'Oh, our talk about the flowers, you mean,' she continued. 'It's as well to keep on the right side of "Themselves", especially being the Comeover that I am, even a Stopover by now, I suppose.'

'I've heard that since the Manx language died nobody sees fairies anymore,' Vicky told her, joining in the spirit of the conversation.

'So why do we all still greet them when we cross the Fairy Bridge?' Kara retorted. 'And what about all the kiddies learning Manx at school now? The language is on the comeback, so perhaps the fairies are too!'

'Perhaps you're right. I'll have to start looking out for strange lights about the place,' Vicky joked.

'Strange lights?'

'Yes. Didn't you know that's how fairies often appear to people – as lights?'

'I thought that was UFOs.'

'Well perhaps UFOs are fairies – we're just interpreting them differently now.' Vicky sounded like she was being serious.

'What, they fly about in saucer-shaped craft, you mean?' Kara asked incredulously.

'Well, possibly not those UFOs. But perhaps the lights people see over crop circles are really fairies.'

'Now there's a thought,' Kara had to admit.

They drew up at the crossroads in St John's by Tynwald Hill – the new, principal one as Kara had to think of it after reading John Michell's book. He had written that it had been designated as the national Tynwald, as opposed to simply the northern regional Tynwald, at the end of the eleventh century, so that Norwegian King Magnus Barelegs didn't have so far to travel from his castle at Peel. Upon reading that she had immediately thought of Julia and Henrik, picturing Henrik in mediaeval clothing whispering important advice in King Magnus's ear. Her imagination seemed to be in overdrive these days.

Once over the crossroads the road to Tynwald Mills passed right beside a megalithic tomb, indicating this site had been important for a very long time. Again a shiver ran up Kara's spine as they crossed the long axis of the site, linking Tynwald Hill to St John's church and the megalithic tomb. She remembered John Michell had drawn a distinction between long geographical axes of alignments, such as located Old Tynwald Hill in the centre of both the Isle of Man and the British Isles, and leylines, which he reckoned were of a more local nature between important features on the landscape. Others said that leylines were supposed to be lines of force or energy, so that might account for her shivers. Maybe she was becoming sensitive to the forces concerned, like a human divining rod.

At home that Friday evening, while listening to the wind battering the trees outside, Kara emailed her thoughts on leylines to Martin. His response the following day was brief but mind-blowing, referring her to a leyline website.

Check out the Dragon Project – sleeping at sacred sites and recording your dreams (e.g. Delphi,) - and Earth Lights as a geophysical or electromagnetic explanation (foo fighters of World War 2). See also 'dragons breath' mentioned as link with feng shui and geomancy. Feng shui supposedly controls the flow of the dragon's breath or chi/qi! I feel it poses more questions than answers, and the website itself doesn't support the idea of energy lines. I'll leave it to you to do the reading. What did you make of Michell's last chapter on cosmological prototypes and sacred numbers? Regards, Martin.

Kara read Martin's email through three times then looked up the website he had referred her to.

Three hours later, at nine-thirty on Saturday evening, she sat back on her sofa, stunned again by the sheer volume of information on geomantic concepts. The more people found out about ancient beliefs and science, the more complex it all became. She hardly knew whether to believe the sceptics or the believers. On first reading Michell's book she had rather skimmed through the chapter Martin referred to, thinking it rather too obscure with its references to sacred numbers, but now she gave it another look, even though her eyes were tired from staring at her computer screen for so long. It was full of the importance of certain numbers for political and societal organisation throughout the world's civilisations, especially the number twelve. Mathematics and cosmology explained the world's principles and functioning without the need for priestly interlopers, or so her reading seemed to be taking her. The more she read, the further along the trail of wacky ideas she travelled, and the more plausible the ideas sounded. She felt seriously confused by it all.

It was all a far cry from fairies – more 'faery' she decided. She was noticing a subtle difference in her reading between the two spellings. 'Fairy' was the little people, 'Themselves', whereas 'faery' seemed to have connotations of ancient wisdom and practices long lost to modern peoples, and was taken quite seriously by many writers. The word 'subtle' seemed significant in some way too, she had noticed. It crept up everywhere, usually but not exclusively connected to the word 'energy'. She felt herself being sucked into some deeper, mystical way of thinking that connected her back in time to ancient peoples. Her eyes were being opened to matters unconventional and strange, but she felt it had significance for her now, whereas she would have laughed at it before.

A 'subtle' pathway had opened within her when the fairy light reached her at Doubtful Sound. Whatever it was, it opened her ears and eyes, and made synchronicities and connections happen that she actually noticed and responded to. The past was speaking to her and leading her to a different future.

CHAPTER EIGHT

Another light fall of snow had fallen overnight, but Sunday morning dawned with a bright blue sky and Manx Radio reporting that the roads were clear. It was the kind of day that necessitated being outdoors, so Kara phoned her friends, Tina and Matt, and asked if they fancied a walk in Glen Helen. Tina and Matt were both in their thirties and both still working in the now precarious finance sector. Keen supporters of the MWT, they had helped to organise and cajole corporate sponsorship for many of the social fund-raising activities. Of prime importance in their lives, however, was their Labrador-Collie cross, or Labradollie, appropriately called Dolly. Tina and Matt paid for a dog-walker to take Dolly out during the week, but that meant that they were eager to go out walking at the weekends.

'That sounds good,' Matt readily replied. 'We'll pick you up at ten-thirty as usual then perhaps we can go for Sunday lunch at The Hawthorn afterwards. I'll book us a table, if you fancy it.'

'Sure do!' Kara agreed. 'See you soon.'

She and Dolly were best friends, as Kara would look after Dolly when Tina and Matt went away on holiday or on weekend breaks off the island. During Dolly's longer stays, Kara would take her into the office, where she was happy to sit or potter about, even going through to the front of house shop and entertaining the customers. Best of all, Dolly would come out on reserve visits and, being the docile and obedient dog that she was, Kara was quite happy for her to enter places where dogs were not normally allowed. In gratitude for this care of their 'baby', Tina and Matt often involved Kara in their activities, especially the occasional Sunday roast.

She was standing on the main Peel Road in her walking boots and warm clothing, clutching a carrier bag with a change of shoes, when Tina and Matt's estate car pulled into the entrance to Kara's road. Dolly was safely in the rear of the car, and Kara made herself comfortable on the back seat as Dolly put her head over the seat to say hello with a whine of pleasure and a quick lick of Kara's hand.

It was a twenty-minute drive up the TT course to Glen Helen, passing The Hawthorn pub on the way. The car park serving Glen Helen and the two restaurants there already had a couple of cars in it when they arrived, with another car turning in soon after them. After adjusting hats, scarves and boots, the three humans set off at a brisk pace up the left hand side of the wooded valley along the broad path. Dolly forged ahead, tail held high, before stopping to sniff at various scent markers amongst the snow and dry beech leaves while her companions caught up with her. At the small waterfall at the confluence of the Rhenass and Blaber Rivers they stopped while Dolly had a long drink. They then had to cross the little wooden bridge over the tumbling Blaber River that drained the peaty slopes of the hills to the east.

Kara stopped in the centre of the narrow bridge and stared upstream into the swirling rust-coloured river. Her head was still full of John Michell's book, and she found herself trying to place where she was in relation to the West Baldwin Valley and the Old Tynwald Hill, as Michell called it, although she had since noticed that the Ordnance Survey map simply marked it 'Tynwald Hill (Site of)'. She turned to Matt behind her who, although a relative newcomer to the island, knew a lot about it, as he was an avid studier of maps and all things geographical.

'Which hill do you reckon those waters are coming from?' The glen was still closely wooded so they couldn't see the surrounding hills to identify their shapes.

'Why, is there a problem with the water or something?'

Kara had to laugh at his natural enough assumption of her professional interest. 'No. I was just trying to work out where the West Baldwin Valley is from here.' She realised she wasn't making any real sense and, on impulse, decided to come clean. It was all very well communicating with Martin by email, but she felt the need for people close at hand to discuss her new fixation with, and somehow she felt that Tina and Matt fitted the bill. They had really only talked about conservation or doggy matters before, but her instinct told her to confide in them.

Matt didn't give her the chance to explain, however. 'That's probably Slieu Ruy, if I picture the map rightly. Red Mountain. That's just about right for the colour of this water. But we've got a map in the car. We can check it up.'

'And Slieu Ruy is on the western flanks of the West Baldwin River?'

Matt nodded slowly. 'Er, that's right. We did a walk up there from Greeba a short time back, which took us up over Slieu Ruy and Lhargee Ruy. I remember now the view from the top of Slieu Ruy was pretty amazing in all directions, but it definitely overlooked West Baldwin. Why do you want to know?'

'I'll tell you over lunch,' Kara replied enigmatically, seeing Dolly sitting waiting on the other side of the bridge.

'Sounds intriguing!'

They returned down the much narrower, rockier path that led to the wishing chair. The shaded valley was still icy, and they trod carefully on the washed away sections to avoid falling into the torrent flowing a short drop below.

When they arrived at the wishing chair they usually all took it in turns to sit on the cold stone throne and make a wish. Dolly, who knew the ritual well, trotted off up the steep bank behind it to investigate a scent trail. While Kara waited her turn she leant against the large beech tree on the riverbank in front of the throne. She became aware of a tingling sensation in her legs and arms that grew stronger as her fingertips touched the smooth bark of the tree. Just like with the kauri tree in New Zealand, she felt a strong connection with the beech tree, and looking up she saw the same rippling pattern up its trunk, like it was breathing or shimmering in some strange light.

If earth energies are potent here, she thought, perhaps that's why the wishing chair was put here. But this tree is close to the spot and its roots are reaching down into the earth. If I make my wish here it might stand more chance of coming true.

She closed her eyes and let her thoughts take her where she wanted to go – to meet the fairies.

*

Behind her eyelids the light became steadily brighter while the smell of sunshine on a grassy bank almost overwhelmed her. Another kind of lightness overcame her; she felt as though she was floating on gossamer wings. Warm and glowing with energy, happy in the extreme, she danced barefoot and weightless on the grass. As she danced she heard a humming noise, a chorus of invisible voices from the ether. She found a note and joined the harmony, the humming vibrations guiding her upwards, so she tried singing a higher note. She resonated better now, felt even lighter, as though she was outside her body and mingling with eternity.

*

Dolly's paw tapped her leg. Cold air bathed her face and the ground felt firm under her feet. Kara opened her eyes and looked down into the dog's intelligent brown eyes. It was as though Dolly was calling to her, rounding her up like a lost sheep and bringing her back from wherever she had gone.

Stepping round from behind the beech tree, she noticed Tina and Matt were no longer by the wishing chair but standing in the middle of the large, stoutly constructed wooden bridge, anxiously calling her name.

'I'm here!' Kara called back to them. She got back on the path, with Dolly almost glued to her side, and walked the short distance to the lower bridge where Tina and Matt met her, relief written large on their faces.

'We couldn't see you!' a shocked and teary Tina told her. 'We thought you'd fallen in the river and been washed downstream or something. We were calling for ages.'

'We sent Dolly off to look for you in the end,' Matt rebuked her, but also clearly relieved she was safe. 'Where did she find you?'

'Behind the tree right next to the wishing chair,' Kara told them slowly, feeling a rerun of events in New Zealand, first by the kauri tree then on Tiritiri Matangi Island. 'I never left the spot.'

Both Tina and Matt looked puzzled. 'But you can't have been!' Tina protested. 'You'd have heard us calling you.'

'How long was I missing?' Kara asked, beginning to feel anxious herself now.

Tina and Matt exchanged glances. 'A good ten minutes, I should think,' Matt answered.

'Oh,' Kara said rather quietly. She noticed Dolly was still glued to her leg, and she began to fondle the dog's head, feeling reassurance from the animal. 'Thank goodness you knew where I was, Dolly.' She gave a final couple of pats on Dolly's shoulder, signalling Dolly could stand down from protection duty, then looked back up to Matt and Tina. 'I'm sorry for worrying you so much, but I really can't explain it. It might have something to do with what I was going to tell you about over lunch, but you're going to find it all very weird, so be warned.'

'It certainly was weird,' Tina admitted as they crossed over the bridge following Dolly, who knew it was time to head back to the car. 'I suppose that will prepare us for what you're going to tell us, will it?'

Kara shrugged. She had no idea what was happening.

*

It was just as well they had reserved a table, as the long, narrow room of The Hawthorn was beginning to fill up with Sunday diners. Dolly was comfortably asleep in the car, but the nerves of her owners were still rattled. It was Matt's turn to drive, so Kara and Tina ordered a gin and tonic each to steady their nerves, while Matt made do with a half of beer.

Sitting at their table by the window Kara raised her glass. 'To Dolly! For finding me, wherever I was.'

The other two repeated the toast to Dolly, but Tina immediately asked: 'Don't you know where you were?'

Kara shook her head then smiled. 'I suppose in days gone by, they would have said I was away with the fairies. People have disappeared, never to be seen again. Nowadays they put it down to alien abductions.' She heard Tina's sudden intake of breath, and hurried on. 'Not that that's what I think happened but, while I was in New Zealand, some very strange things happened to me that seem to be getting more... inexplicable.'

It took the whole of the meal for Kara to tell about her experiences and new acquaintances as a result of it all. In fact they needed to order coffee too, as Kara still hadn't completed her tale by the end of their bread-and-butter-pudding.

To her relief, Tina and Matt seemed to accept her story without ridicule, probably because of what they had all just experienced.

'So what's the significance of West Baldwin?' Matt asked, as Kara finally finished her tale of fairies, dragon's breath and mystical trees.

'Ah, that's the John Michell book I was telling you about. It's apparently a sacred centre, though he doesn't attribute mystical powers to it or anything remotely like that. It's just a very significant ancient site at the geographical centre of the British Isles, and so he reckons it was of prime importance to the druids.'

'Well, some writers reckon the Isle of Man is actually Avalon – the island in the mist,' Tina told her. 'And I'm sure I've read somewhere that Arthur was supposed to have been killed in the battle of Camelyn in Scotland, and that his Camelot was actually at Carlisle. So the Isle of Man could have been the mystical island to the west. Mystical because of the druids, perhaps.'

Matt was sceptical. 'I didn't know you read such stuff! And I've certainly not heard that one before. It strikes me that anywhere and everywhere claims Avalon or Camelot as its own.'

'Well, I don't know about Avalon either,' Kara intervened, 'but John Michell certainly describes the Isle of Man as a place of enchantment.'

'Wow!' Tina sat back in her chair, hands clasping her full belly. 'What an amazing story, Kara. People have been saying you've changed since your holiday, but they were putting it down to a holiday romance, not being bewitched by fairies!'

'It's not just the fairy thing,' Kara continued, 'but all the coincidences that kept happening, and which are still happening. Would you believe it, but seven of the people I made friends with all want to visit here this summer?'

'Really? The Isle of Man Tourist Board will have to start employing you,' Matt told her, fishing for his wallet to pay the bill. 'Well, we'd better go and wake up Dolly. Perhaps she can tell us where you were.'

*

The snow of earlier had turned to rain. Kara spent the rest of the afternoon catching up on household chores then reading through a conservation magazine, where she came across an article written by Dr Paul Driesler about the potential resurrection of elm tree stocks. She had to smile at yet another amazing coincidence, having so recently met up with him again. There was a photograph of him standing in a tree nursery, talking with the arboriculture scientists who were trying to establish Dutch elm disease-resistant trees. The photograph did him justice, she thought.

Her train of thought led her to fetch her laptop and connect to the Internet to check her emails. She felt little surprise at finding one from Paul.

Hello Kara,

Just to confirm that the funds for the reserve have been transferred. I'm now arranging with my parents to come across on the ferry and visit from June 19th to 26th. We've decided the island warrants a whole week to do it justice, so we're booking into a hotel for that period. I'll let you know more details in due course.

My father's getting over a chesty cough he developed since their flight back from New Zealand, but Silke's been feeding him plenty of Vitamins C and D and he seems to be on the mend. They both send their greetings to you.

Silke the fairy godmother, Paul had called her. Kara had a flash of recollection of seeing Silke, Fig and Sharon's faces reflected in a moonlit pond, a column of mist linking the moon to its reflection. Connections, she mused. It's all to do with connecting with something.

As she looked at her inbox another email came through, this one from Martin. She opened it immediately.

Hi,

I've just booked to come on my fact-finding tour of the Isle of Man. I fly in on Saturday June 19 for a week, so will be there for the summer solstice, if that's at all significant. Let's say we stake out the old hill on that day! Tell old Manannan not to put his cloak out over the island during my visit.

By the way, you really need to check out another book I've discovered all about NZ energy lines and 'The Surveyors'. It's called In Search of the Southern Serpent *by Hamish Miller and Barry Brailsford. The review reckons NZ's the most amazing place in the whole world for the strength of its earth energy. No wonder you connected up there! I've ordered a copy myself.*

He had added the website she needed to look at, so she clicked on the link and twenty minutes later was ordering the book and a couple of others for herself. She then went off to make herself a cup of tea and some sandwiches to last her the evening. Sitting back down in front of her laptop, she said out loud: 'I just need Fig to tell me she's coming over the same period and we'll be complete. I wonder if any more will announce they're coming over.'

Her thoughts crossed the world to Sharon, the third fairy godmother of her vision, but she very much doubted that a shop assistant from Arrowtown would turn up on the Isle of Man. She had done her job in New Zealand, stocking the fairy book and giving Kara the magazine, setting Kara firmly on a new path.

CHAPTER NINE

Daffodils bloomed in the grassy courtyard in front of the Manx Wildlife Trust's premises at Tynwald Mills as spring slowly edged its way in. With the improving weather the Midweek Muckers had started cracking on with maintenance on the nature reserves. The purchase of the land for the new reserve was progressing smoothly, but the delays and planning issues of the new MWT premises in Peel were causing frustration for everybody concerned. On top of that, news from around the world seemed to feature earthquakes, fires and floods so much recently, the doomsayers were having a field day. Now the volcanic ash cloud from Iceland was causing travel chaos around the world for millions of people.

For Kara, however, life was worth living. On a sunny day in April she looked out of her office window and felt that first promise of warmer days to come. Lunch alfresco, she decided on impulse, picking up her sandwich box. She stepped out into the sunshine and headed for the Wildflower Garden by the old mill.

Created in 2003 as a showcase for wildflowers, the Wildlife Garden made use of the old tenter field behind the woollen mill, where cloth was hung up on tenter frames and hooks to dry. The field was cleared of bracken and gorse, allowing the existing bluebells and wildflowers to grow, while the old mill-race fed a small pond. Kara walked down the paved path, noticing that the butterfly border was just starting to send up the first early shoots of summer perennials. Beneath the sheltering trees at the end of the plot stood an upright stone with a bench attached, where she sat down to eat her lunch of mixed nuts and hummus and beetroot sandwiches.

As she ate she listened to the thrushes, blackbirds and sparrows singing at their nest-building. It helped clear her brain of work matters so she could take some time out to plan her own busy schedule. Her office year planner was filling up with events and socials leading up to the Trust's AGM in May and beyond. She would have to make sure that she had free time for showing her visitors around in June. A trip to the Curraghs Meadows to see the hundred thousand orchids in bloom was definitely a must-see for them all. Vicky, the Reserves Officer, gave guided tours each afternoon of the third week in June, and Kara was sure Vicky wouldn't mind adding an additional tour at the end for her visitors.

As well as keeping track of all the other projects on the go under her team, Kara was assisting Stephen Coote, the recently appointed Volunteer Co-ordinator, to organise volunteers for the bumblebee and mammal surveys. The Trust was thriving socially, with a strong corps of volunteers, but the financial crisis was biting with a noticeable decline in corporate funding. Paul's parents' donation couldn't have come at a better time, and Kara wanted to make sure they felt appreciated during their visit. She was also quite proud of her little empire, and was keen to show it off to Paul. With thoughts of him in mind she finished her sandwiches, had a little wander around the rest of the garden, noticing the bluebell spikes beginning to poke through the soil, and headed back to her office.

There was a customer in the shop as she passed through. The woman, who was in her thirties, already had an armful of goodies to buy and was now browsing through the packets of wildflower seeds grown locally by the Wildflowers of Mann Project. Kara smiled at her and succumbed to her second impulsive decision of the day: to stop and talk.

'Do you have a large garden?' she asked the woman, who seemed to have come straight from it or else from walking her dog, judging by the mud around the bottom of her jeans.

'No, not huge,' the woman, who sounded Manx, answered Kara cheerily. 'But it's a bit wild and I want to enhance that. I've just signed our family up for your bumblebee survey, by the way. You're Kara Groves, aren't you? I recognise you from the newsletter.'

'Yes, that's right. And you are…?'

'Rowena Kissack. I gather from a friend of mine, you've recently enjoyed a holiday in New Zealand.' Rowena put down the flowered apron, jigsaw puzzle and children's book on sharks onto a display table, as a sign that the conversation might take a while.

'Oh, yes. It was the holiday of a lifetime,' Kara informed her, feeling quite relaxed about chatting to her, whereas before her holiday she had always found it a bit of an ordeal talking to customers. 'And I got so much out of it. It's a fascinating place. Very… powerful.'

Kara felt her mind disappearing into the mists of Doubtful Sound and pulled herself back. 'Who is your friend?'

'Fig Green. She was in your tour group, I understand.'

'Fig! Well I'm blowed. She said she visited here sometimes.' Kara felt the need to probe more about her enigmatic acquaintance, who she suspected of being a white witch. It was possible that Rowena might have similar interests. 'How is she?'

'She's very well and busy planning her next visit here in June. She's actually staying a few days with me and then with another friend.' Rowena thought for a second. 'Perhaps you'd like to come round some time for a meal and a glass or two of elderberry wine while she's over?'

'That sounds lovely. It'd be great to meet up with her again. She's quite a character, isn't she?'

'She certainly is – and very respected in her field.'

'Which is?' Kara wanted to hear it said out loud, but was disappointed.

'She's a herbalist, among other things. She's helping me with my herb garden and preparing lotions and balms and things.'

Kara noted the phrase 'among other things', but Rowena didn't seem ready to elaborate. 'Don't tell me, she'll be here for the twenty-first of June.'

Rowena gave a knowing smile. 'Yes, she will. She was quite emphatic on that point.'

Kara nodded at the reference to the summer solstice. 'Perhaps you can tell her that there'll be half a dozen others from our holiday here at the same time.'

Rowena's eyes lit up. 'We could have a party! A Midsummer's Eve party.'

Rather than turning her cold at the prospect of a party, Kara felt a sense of excitement. She felt that Rowena's parties would be rather different from your average drinks-and-loud- music party that bored Kara to tears and she generally shied away from. 'I'm looking forward to it already,' she declared.

'Me too!' Rowena seemed equally excited at the prospect as she gathered together her items for purchase. 'Well, I'd better not keep you from your work. I'll be seeing you again at your bumblebee-surveyors' training session, so we can catch up on details then.'

'Oh, right. Give my love to Fig when you next speak to her.'

'Will do. Be seeing you, Kara.'

Kara wandered back through to the rear of the building towards her office. If she hadn't gone out for a walk in the garden, she might not have met up with Rowena, she mused. And why had she bothered to stop and speak to her? Was synchronicity active again? As she passed the reference-book library she spotted a book about garden herbs and other medicinal plants. With Rowena's recent conversation in her mind, she picked it out and took it back to her office. Still under Rowena's rather mystical influence, she opened the book at random. She hardly felt surprised when a picture of mistletoe appeared, a particularly noteworthy plant for the druids. She began reading.

*

Dolly sniffed deeply at the wild garlic. The glen at Port Grenaugh was full of it as Kara, Tina and Matt began one of their Sunday walks together. The weather forecast was good, and they had decided to bring a picnic lunch. They began their walk by heading southwards across the shingle of the small sheltered bay then up onto the coastal path. It was not a route Kara had taken before, having only walked north of Port Grenaugh previously. The plan was to negotiate the narrow path atop the cliffs, past the little bay of Port Soldrick, over Cass-ny-Hawin Head and then on as far as the next inlet where the Santon Burn, which flowed under the Fairy Bridge, met the sea. Here they would turn back on themselves up a minor road that led past the ancient stone circle of Arragon Moar, until a lane off to the right took them past a farm and thence onto a footpath across a meadow to the main coastal path near Port Grenaugh again.

To their left the waters of the Irish Sea were like a millpond, reflecting the clear blue sky. A warm zephyr blew across their noses bringing the sharp odour of seaweed from the bay, replaced by the more pleasant scent of coconut as they marched in single file through the gorse and bracken to the cliff top. While watching out for choughs or early butterflies brought out by the sunshine they could also see the occasional plane flying low down the coast on its approach to the airport at nearby Ronaldsway. A few sailing boats were out on the water making the most of the fine weather.

Kara had a swing in her stride and joy in her heart as the sun fell on her face. There was truly nowhere else on earth she would rather be. Rolling up the sleeves of her shirt, she basked in the sudden warmth of spring.

By the time they reached the Santon Burn inlet it was lunchtime. A thick sward of tussocky grass, marked on the map as an old earthwork, provided a comfortable place to sit as they delved into their rucksacks. Tina poured out water into a plastic tub for Dolly, who lapped it up eagerly before lying down on a patch of bracken, snapping at passing flies.

Matt finished his first sandwich then reached for another. 'Just for you, Kara,' he said, carefully redistributing the salad contents of the sandwich that were about to fall out, 'I've been studying the map of this area. There's an abundance of old chapels, round houses and tumuli. I even looked up information on Arragon Moar to see if there was anything interesting or any references to fairies, and it was quite intriguing. Apparently this whole area around Santon, Castletown and Rushen is said to be the traditional home of the fairy people. There's a Fairy Hill just the other side of the main road from the Fairy Bridge and another one near Port Erin. And as far as antiquity goes, Arragon Moar itself is reckoned to be four thousand years old.'

'I've not heard of it. It must be one of the less spectacular stone circles on the island,' Kara commented. 'Still, I'll be interested to take a look.' She took a sip of water from her flask. 'Why is this area supposed to be special for fairies, I wonder?'

Matt shrugged. 'The only thing I can think of that might be relevant is that the rocks at Arragon Moar are supposed to be rich in quartz.'

'So?'

'Well, quartz crystal is used for radio receivers, crystal balls, healing charms and the like. Perhaps it conducts certain energies or stores and transmits information from other dimensions. I'm just letting my thoughts run wild here, you understand, just for the sake of coming up with fantastical ideas. But what do you think?'

Kara was intrigued. 'I remember while I was in New Zealand with Martin we read about some ESP experiments. It said that much better results were obtained when a quartz screen was used between the participants than when there was a glass screen. Perhaps you're on the right track, and crystal does somehow carry energy or even information.'

'So we must all tune in carefully as we're passing the stones,' Tina laughed, feeding a small piece of ham from her sandwich to an appreciative Dolly.

After their lunch they continued on the coastal path until they arrived at the end of the lane passing the farm at Arragon Veg. From there it was a short walk uphill towards the Arragon Moar stone circle, which stood proudly on an earth mound on a ridge about fifty metres from the road in some sheep pasture. To the south it watched over the shelter of Castletown Bay, on the near side of which now lay the runways of Ronaldsway airport. The ancient overlooking the modern, Kara thought.

There was no public access to the small, tight circle of upright stones, and the Manx 'hedge', a turf and stone bank topped by gorse surrounding the field, was quite high. To get a better view, Kara climbed the hedge bank on the opposite side of the road by a gatepost so she could study the stones, several of which she could now see were large pieces of white quartz crystal. As she watched, a flock of rooks flew up from the south and settled around the stones, with one perching on one of the white rocks. It made quite a dramatic picture against the skyline, and she took out her camera.

'Are you feeling anything yet, Kara?' Matt joked. 'Any messages coming through from the ancestors or fairies?'

'Not that I'm aware of,' she grinned self-consciously. 'But they usually come in my dreams.'

'But you did go off into fairyland in Glen Helen, didn't you?'

'Yes, but that time I didn't meet anybody specifically. I just seemed to be weightless and singing with some hidden chorus. It's only in my dreams I do things or meet people I can really remember – apart from on Tiritiri Matangi,' she recalled. 'That was daytime, but I don't know if I was asleep or not.'

'It sounds to me like what people today would call an alien abduction,' Tina observed. 'Having memory blackouts or recollections of strange visitations.'

'No way,' Kara laughed. 'I don't meet up with 'greys' or what-have-you. My people seem real, but ancient. It's like they're guiding me in lots of ways, sending messages and helping me meet people, who in turn help me understand it all better. Take you for example, Matt.'

Matt's eyebrows shot upwards in surprise. 'Me? What have I done for you?'

'All your talk about crystals. Your geological training may help explain things and focus ideas. Who knows? And it was your idea to come this way today, specifically because it's rich fairy country, according to your sources.'

'Yes, but I'm only doing it to tease you, Kara. It's not like I'm taking this seriously.'

Tina snorted. 'Are you sure about that, Matt? You seemed awfully engrossed in that book about the supernatural Isle of Man the other night.'

'Well, it was far more analytical and factual than I'd anticipated. It was actually quite a good read, the way the author tried to explain old stories using modern concepts. I learnt a lot about the island too.'

'Well there you are,' Kara said. 'You're starting to do research for me now, as well as Martin in America. I met a woman in the shop the other day, who got me interested in herbs and things such that I got a book and started reading all about mistletoe and how it was considered a 'cure-all' by the ancients. I then remembered that another of the websites I'd looked at with Martin in New Zealand had mentioned mistletoe in an extraordinary article about light and cellular health. The writer was a scientist called Popp, who seems to be researching photobiology, bio-electrodynamics and bio-communication, among other things. Anyway, he reckoned that mistletoe was the only plant he had found so far that could retune your body's cells back to their healthy light wavelength and cure all sorts of diseases.'

'Well I won't be trying it out,' Matt protested firmly. 'Anybody can write anything on the Internet. Besides, I always thought mistletoe was poisonous.'

'So did I!' Tina agreed fervently. 'But I do know it was important somehow for the druids.'

Kara felt a sudden tingle run up her legs into her spine, like energy flowing in. Then the hairs on her arms stood up. She held her arm up to show Tina and Matt.

'Message coming through?' Matt asked. 'Or have you got cold standing still? Shall we move on?'

Kara didn't know what it was. She shivered but the hairs on her arm were lying flat again, and the tingle had gone. 'We might as well. Perhaps it'll come to me in a dream tonight. Perhaps I need to be in a different brain-wave state to actually receive messages.'

'Hey-ho, this is fun!' Matt laughed, skipping a jig on the spot like a leprechaun.

Kara laughed with him. 'Isn't it just?' She nodded up the lane. 'Onwards and upwards!'

*

Kara stood in front of a mighty oak tree within a grove of smaller oaks. Adorning its branches grew clumps of mistletoe, the white waxy berries like glowing full moons in the woodland gloom. A mistle thrush flew onto the lower bough and pecked at a berry. The sticky seeds adhered to its beak, and the thrush wiped them off onto the branch, beginning the birth cycle of a new plant. Pecking at another berry the thrush managed to dislodge its neighbour, which fell to the ground into a patch of bright sunshine-yellow flowers. The moon and the sun merged together into a ball of brilliant white light that floated up towards Kara, settling over her head before engulfing her in light and the fragrant, sage-scented vapour of the dragon's breath.

*

First thing the next morning Kara was on the phone to Tina and Matt.

'I did have a dream,' she announced as soon as Tina answered the phone. 'About mistletoe.'

'Well that's hardly surprising, considering we were talking about it,' Tina remarked.

'Yes. But there was a flower in my dream that worked with the mistletoe to create a ball of brilliant light. I think it was a celandine, but I'd have to check it up.' Kara realised from Tina's lack of response that she was not as enthralled by the dream as Kara had expected. 'Well, I suppose you're busy getting ready for work, but I just thought I'd let you know.'

'That's OK. See you soon.'

When she got into work Kara headed straight for the reference books to try to identify the buttercup-like flower of her dream. She decided it was most likely greater celandine then trawled the Internet to see what was said about it, finding both references to its use as a herbal medicine and possible anti-cancer agent but also toxicity warnings. The same was true of mistletoe. It too had long been used as a traditional medicine but also came with warnings about the berries being poisonous. There did seem to be some research being done on synthetic compounds based on greater celandine as a tumour-busting compound, but other reports seemed sceptical. She felt none the wiser and only wondered whether future research would yield more conclusive benefits to health. She was not sure why she was convinced it was the health benefits of the plants she was so convinced about, but that was what her intuition was telling her.

She had a strong inclination to discuss the topic with somebody, and her thoughts immediately alighted on Paul at the Woodland Trust. She had not been in touch with him for a few weeks now, and spring was already well under way with the June visit not too far off. Her next decision was whether to try phoning him or email. Her hand reached for the phone.

'Paul, it's Kara here,' she announced as soon as she heard him say his name. 'How are you?'

'I'm fine, thank you, Kara. You're lucky to catch me. I'm about to go off for a meeting, but I've got five minutes.'

Kara felt momentarily flustered. Why was she really ringing him? Was it just to hear his voice? Calming herself she got her thoughts into gear to make the most of the short time available. 'Sorry it's so early on a Monday morning, Paul, but I'm doing some research on mistletoe and greater celandine and just wondered if there was anything at all new on the subject of either you were aware of. I've had a quick look on the Internet but I thought of you as a shortcut. I hope you don't mind.'

'Not at all.' She saw him start to doodle an oak tree on his notepad. 'I'm not really aware of anything off the top of my head – no ground-breaking news of any kind. What's your research for?'

Now Kara saw him doodle the moon in the sky. 'Paul, can I ask you a crazy question?'

'What's that?'

'Are you drawing a picture of the moon and an oak tree?' She heard his sharp intake of breath down the line.

'How did you know?'

'I don't know. You could argue, I suppose, that since we're talking about mistletoe and that your job is to do with trees, that you might well doodle that sort of thing while on the phone. But I just had a really strong image in my head of you sitting there in your office and the pad on your desk.' She remembered now the clear picture of him she had when they had spoken before, but she had been too uncertain to ask him about it then. 'Here's another crazy question. When we spoke after the holiday and you were at your parents' house in Germany, were you in a room with French windows looking out to big trees?'

There was a long pause before he spoke. 'What's this about, Kara: all this talk about mistletoe and seeing things? It all sounds a bit... weird. Or should I say 'wyrd' as Terry Pratchett would have it?'

Was he mocking or interested, Kara wondered. She tried to 'see' his face. Interested, she decided. 'You didn't answer my question, Paul. Did I just describe the room you were in?'

'Yes,' he admitted matter-of-factly. 'And now I'm intrigued. You'll have to tell me what's been going on and why you're researching mistletoe of all things.' There was a pause as he looked at his watch. 'But I really must go to my meeting now. I'll be on tenterhooks till I speak to you again. I'll give you a call back soon, OK? Possibly later today, if I can manage it.'

'That's fine. You get off to your meeting. Thanks for your time.'

'My pleasure. Speak soon. Cheerio.'

Kara put down the phone and found she was shaking. What was happening to her? And why was her apparent remote viewing centred round Paul Driesler? Unable to concentrate on any work, she headed out to make herself a mug of coffee.

While the kettle was boiling she wandered behind the partition screen into the shop. It was not open yet, so she was able to stand unmolested in the still gloomy area on the shop side of the partition and study the map of the island currently pinned to it. Her eyes were inexorably drawn to the centre of the island, the location of the Tynwald Hill that John Michell claimed was the original main site. She had deliberately refrained from going there until Martin was with her, heeding the warning not to go alone. Her 'absence' in Glen Helen with Tina and Matt, and having to be rescued by Dolly, had brought home to her that things were happening over which she had no control. She was definitely connecting with something, some energy or intelligence, that was gradually introducing her to new concepts and giving her access to new communication pathways, but as yet she had no idea what it was all leading to.

She felt no fear, however, despite her trembling earlier. That must have been simply from the buzz she had felt from talking to Paul.

The kettle clicked as it switched itself off, and Kara moved back around the partition to the little kitchen area. Coffee made, she headed for her office determined to get some proper work done.

CHAPTER TEN

The email from Lambert Dodman gave her food for thought: not just his name, which she found rather charming, but the fact that she had no idea who he was, and yet he wrote as though they had met somewhere.

Kara, I shall be calling into your office soon and look forward to seeing you. These surveyors are all snails. Regards, Lambert Dodman.

Most odd, Kara thought, sipping her coffee. Why didn't he fix a time? He must have something to do with the new premises in Peel, but I can't think who he is. Oh well. She clicked on the next email and gave Lambert Dodman no more thought until she found herself pondering the idea of writing an article on snails for the summer edition of the Trust's newsletter, prompted, she was sure, by his reference to them in his email.

She busied herself happily for the rest of the morning researching interesting facts about Manx molluscs, both terrestrial and marine. As usual time flew once she became engrossed, and she hadn't noticed it was past her normal lunchtime when her phone rang.

'Paul here again, Kara. Sorry I had to dash off, but it was an important meeting.'

'I hope you weren't late.'

'No, I wasn't. But you'll never believe this.'

'What?'

'The topic of mistletoe came up.'

'What! Really? How was that?'

Paul cleared his throat briefly as though embarrassed. 'It was basically a funding meeting, but one of our committee members started talking about harvesting mistletoe from our woodlands for the Christmas market. Somebody else then mentioned homeopathic remedies and herbal suppliers who might be interested. The idea was rejected for several reasons, but I just sat there flabbergasted at the coincidence. Over coffee afterwards I got chatting to the committee member who had mentioned the herbal remedies. He's a retired doctor interested in 'integrative medicine' as he called it, and he seemed to be well versed in the uses of mistletoe. I didn't ask him about greater celandine though.'

'Well I never!' was all Kara could say.

'I asked Bill, the doctor, if he'd mind if you contacted him, and he said he'd be delighted to help you with any research. In fact he asked for your email address, so he might get in touch first. He's Bill Paget.'

'I'll look out for him,' Kara said distractedly, as she became aware yet again of something strange happening to her. 'In the meantime, I need to find out why I get such a strong connection to you, Paul, that I can see you from here.'

'What on earth do you mean, you can see me?'

Kara struggled to sound matter-of-fact. 'You're wearing a royal-blue tie with green tree frogs on it.'

Silence reigned for a moment before Paul's voice came back somewhat shakily: 'This is getting creepy, Kara. How do you do it?'

'I've no idea, but it's like I'm in the room with you.'

'Whereabouts?'

'Possibly where your laptop is.'

'That would work. But it doesn't account for my parents' house. Where were you then?'

'Well, I could see towards the French windows and garden.'

Paul thought for a moment. 'There's a large mirror on the back wall and I think possibly a display cabinet full of porcelain and Bohemian crystal.'

'Crystal!' Kara gasped.

'What about it?' Paul asked.

'I'm not sure, but that's another thing to do research on. It seems I'm being led in too many directions at once.'

'I'll be intrigued to see where all this is going when we come over in June, as will Silke. She was a bit of a hippie first time around, I gather, and now she's into all the complementary therapies and organic food stuff like you are. As I said, she's certainly keeping my father young on her witch's brews.'

Kara was reminded of one of her dreams, where Silke's voice had emanated from the moonlit pool. 'I think I must have got that impression when I met her. In my mind she's one of the Three Fairy Godmothers.'

Paul chuckled. 'Now, which of the fairy stories are we talking about here?'

Kara had to think hard, until recollections of seeing a Disney film clip helped her. 'Sleeping Beauty, I think.'

'I'll remind her to pack her wand. I must say I'm looking forward to our visit to Fairyland, as you make it out to be.'

'Well don't forget you must all greet them when you drive over the Fairy Bridge,' Kara said. 'We're quite insistent on that here. Even the Queen had to do it.'

'I'll try to remember. Well, I'd better let you get on with whatever you're doing. I sent you all the details of our trip, didn't I?'

'You did. Give my regards to your parents and I'm looking forward to seeing you all in June.'

'I'll be in touch before then,' Paul promised. 'Bye for now. Oh and before I go, what am I doing now?'

'Blowing me a kiss,' Kara blurted out before she had time to think.

'Shit! Excuse my French.'

'I take it I was right?'

'Possibly,' Paul conceded. 'Well, I'd better watch what I say and do from now on. I'll never know if you're watching.'

'It doesn't work like that, Paul. It's only when I'm on the phone to you that I seem to connect.'

'Thank goodness for that. I don't quite know what to make of your psychic abilities. I just know you're quite something!'

Kara grinned. 'And so are you, Paul.'

*

Watching the increasingly gloomy early-evening news later that day Kara could see where the doom- and-gloom-mongers were coming from. European economies had collapsed, and the Icelandic volcano continued to cause travel chaos. Every other documentary or film seemed to be about the supposedly imminent apocalypse as 2012 loomed ever closer. Even worse were the post-apocalyptic films and horror stories of trying to survive the flood/earthquake/riots/meteor impact or whatever it was that year was supposed to bring. Now they were talking about massive solar flares disrupting satellite communications and anything electrical just in time for the 2012 London Olympics. You couldn't get away from it these days. No wonder so many people were turning to more spiritual matters and hopes of salvation by unknown beings. Was she one of them?

Determined not to feel despondent by it all, especially after her mysteriously psychic phone call with Paul, she decided to check her emails. Martin had responded to her queries about crystal.

Until I started reading about it I thought all this crystal stuff was just a load of New Age hogwash, but now I'm not so sure, especially when I read some of my own nation's stuff. Native Americans have been using crystals for centuries. Then there's this current obsession with crystal skulls. There's more on the subject than I can get through, so you might like to read up on those yourself. As far as Bohemian crystal goes, I don't think it's the real thing, just leaded glass.

I checked on Isle of Man geology and there is a lot of quartz there. I feel like I know the place already with the amount of reading I've done, and most references I come across refer to it as a magical place and that you all live in a kind of time-warp there with your continued belief in the supernatural. It's no wonder you've been bewitched.

At the end of his email he had attached a gap-toothed crone flying on her broomstick, winking broadly, but it only made Kara think of those poor unfortunate women hurled down Slieu Whallian in spiked barrels in less enlightened times. Are we becoming more enlightened now, she wondered? Is this what they really mean by the dawning of the Age of Aquarius? We're moving from the sign of the fish to the sign of the water bearer. Perhaps I ought to take up dowsing. Oh Kara Groves, what are you doing?

*

In the darkness the white quartz rocks lining the path up the hill guided her footsteps. Each rock, as she passed it, hummed and buzzed as though a swarm of bees surrounded it. The rocks were not regularly placed, seemingly haphazard along her route, but each was like a navigation beacon leading her onwards to the distant summit. The humming grew louder, more constant, taking on the tones of human voices, resonating with the rocks' own frequency until her head was filled with the constant sound as it reverberated throughout her body. As she continued up the hill her legs became lighter, her walking easier, until she felt she was floating above the ground, held aloft by the cushion of sound. Now she could no longer locate the source of the sound. It filled the earth, the sky and the very stars themselves. She looked up and saw only light.

*

'It was like an out-of-body experience,' she told Paul on the phone first thing at work the next morning. 'Like I was astral flying or something. I felt connected to the entire universe, like I only had to think and I could be anywhere in an instant. Or any time for that matter,' she added.

'So you reckon your fly-on-the-wall episodes with me are you astral flying then?' he asked in some disbelief.

'I don't reckon anything, Paul. All I know is I've been having some very strange and lucid dreams since going to New Zealand. I feel I was directed to meet you there for some reason, and I met a lot of other interesting people besides.'

'Well I can't argue with that. Fairy godmothers or guardian angels, call them what you will, but I can't help feeling we were meant to get back together again, Kara.'

'I'm glad you feel like that too.' Kara looked out of her office window but saw only a busy street reminiscent of Oxford with its golden stone buildings and numerous students walking by.

'Where are you at this moment, Paul?' she asked him. 'My call must have diverted to your mobile phone.'

'I'm walking down a street in Oxford. You can probably hear it down the phone.'

'Yes, I can, but I can also see you again. You've stopped walking and are standing in front of a bookshop window. I'm beginning to wish I could turn off this second sight or whatever it is. I feel like I'm spying on you and I don't want to.' As she said this a Loaghtan sheep looked at her from the grassy enclosure outside her office window. 'Hey! I can do it! I switched it off.'

'I think I feel relieved. Look, I don't think I can wait till June to see you again. It's all very well you seeing me, but I need the real thing. There's a gathering of us woodland folk here in Oxford in a fortnight's time to discuss the implications of this new Acute Oak Decline. It seems it could be as bad as Dutch elm disease. Perhaps you'd like to come over and join us?'

'I'm hugely tempted, Paul. When exactly is it?' She glanced up at her year planner, ready to check dates in May.

'It's Friday the fourteenth at two o'clock. You could stay the weekend and we could visit some of our old haunts.'

It was a blatant invitation, and Kara realised she had an unanswered question still. 'Paul, I hope you don't mind me asking this, but under the circumstances, I need to know. You're not married, are you?'

He didn't sound in the least put off by her sudden change of topic. 'No. I was, but we became incompatible after a while. Nothing dramatic. We just decided we had different paths to tread. Barbara went off to Nepal to help run a school and I took up my post with the Woodland Trust, which takes me all over the place.'

'So you're divorced?'

'Yes. All legal and proper.'

'Good. That's a relief.' She turned back to practicalities. 'I'll get the Seacat and drive down, that way I won't be worrying about volcanic ash clouds. In fact I'll probably have to travel down on the Thursday evening to be there in time.'

'I'll book you a room in a hotel. I won't be getting to Oxford until the Friday, but we'll have the weekend at least.'

'I'll have to be gone reasonably early on Sunday to get back in time for work on Monday.'

'Ah yes, the joys of living on an island. Well, I'll be in touch about the details and I'll look forward to seeing you soon. Must dash now. Bye.'

Kara duly filled in the dates on her year planner, only glad they hadn't clashed with the AGM the following weekend. Tonight she was scheduled for the bee-surveyors' training session when she would meet Rowena Kissack again. It was all go.

Her morning was spent checking with Stephen that all the kits were ready for the surveyors, as well as dealing with phone calls. It was shortly after one of these from *The Manx Independent* that Joyce, the Monday morning shop volunteer, came through to her office to tell her that her visitor had arrived.

'Shall I show him through?' Joyce asked.

'I wasn't expecting anybody,' Kara told her, puzzled. 'Did he give his name?'

'Er, no. I assumed you'd know who it was. Sorry.'

'Not to worry. I'll come out and see what he wants.'

Kara followed Joyce out to the front area of the shop, and saw an elderly gentleman with a walking stick studying the new display of metal garden ornaments in the shape of hares and hedgehogs. As he turned to greet her she gasped. It was the Manannan of her dreams, but this time dressed in tweed jacket and brown corduroy trousers. Otherwise the silver hair and beard and ruddy face were the same.

'Manannan' transferred his walking stick into his left hand and held out his right to greet her. 'Lambert Dodman,' he introduced himself. His voice was warm and mellifluous, and Kara had no hesitation in stepping forward to put her hand in his as he said: 'I'm sorry I wasn't specific on timing in my email, but I could only come when you were ready.'

Kara was conscious of Joyce hovering nearby, apparently tidying books on the shelves. 'Shall we go and find somewhere to sit and talk, Mr. Dodman? It's a bit cramped in my office.'

'Lambert, please. How about in your Wildflower Garden? That would be nice.'

'Of course. I'll just let the office know where I'll be. One moment.' Kara hurried back into the office and called up the stairs to Jill in her mezzanine office. 'I'll be outside for a while. Not sure how long for, if you can take any calls.'

'OK,' Jill's voice called down from above.

Kara returned to the shop, strangely calm considering the circumstances. Lambert was already standing in the open doorway, apparently sniffing the air. 'Well, let's go to the garden, shall we?' he said briskly, stepping out of the door.

Kara followed him to the right, past the fine arts establishment, hairdresser's and furnishings shop, then right again on the road towards the mill buildings and the Wildflower Garden. He certainly had no obvious need of his walking stick, she thought, managing to finally walk alongside him once they were on the road.

'I hope you don't mind not meeting in my office, but –'

'Not at all. I hardly expected it. A bit of privacy is needed, I think.'

They had entered the garden and sat down on the wooden seat by the pond at the entrance. There was nobody else around, fortunately, and Lambert got straight to the point.

'You've come to our attention recently, Kara. Unexpectedly swiftly, I might add, and now the light has become white for you and you smelt the dragon's breath, didn't you?'

Kara gasped in astonishment at his apparent reference to her recent dreams. 'Who are you?'

He smiled at her. 'I understand your bafflement, but it is for you to comprehend. You're making very rapid progress, as I just said, but you're probably wondering where all this is leading.'

'Absolutely!' Kara agreed fervently. 'Until you just said that, I wasn't sure whether I was imagining everything that had happened to me.'

Lambert gave her another reassuring smile. 'All I can tell you is that you're being helped and guided on your path to enlightenment. What you choose to do with your knowledge is totally up to you, but it is our hope that your life will blossom as a result of sharing our ideals.'

Now it was her turn to smile. 'It already has. I've really come out of my shell since my holiday, and met some lovely people as a result.'

'Your reference to snails just then shows you are tuning in. You have been a snail on the earth, but you are becoming a surveyor.'

'What do you mean? That's like what you said in your email, something about surveyors being snails.'

'Exactly. The surveyors follow the lines of energy like snail trails on the land, trails which sometimes spiral into a vortex like a snail's shell. We learn to use the energy lines and connect with them. You now know enough to accept guidance more directly and willingly to try to help this planet survive what is being done to it.'

'Is that what this is all about? Saving the Earth? I don't see how I can do much.'

'It's not just you, Kara. There are many more like you, healing their bodies first with food and light so they can become receptive to the subtle energy. Junk food and electromagnetic interference has meant that much of Mankind has lost the ability to connect with the universe.'

'But since eating better and taking my Vitamin D I've reconnected, you mean?'

Lambert nodded. 'Then you went to a place that was high in energy. It jump-started you, so to speak. Now you're making up for lost time with all your recent research. The network is growing rapidly as others join you on this snail trail, but there are still too many who abuse both their bodies and this planet.'

'So where is all this leading us?'

'You must open your mind and your senses. You are nearly there. Several times you have almost made the connection but have fallen short. Over the last two nights you arrived.'

'But I don't remember arriving or anything,' Kara protested. 'Only this bright light surrounding me and the... dragon's breath as you call it.'

'That was the final connection at this stage. You are now ready to participate and you already know what to do.'

'Do I?'

'Yes. Your friends and helpers are gathering and I will be there too. The rest is up to you.' Lambert stood up suddenly, holding his walking stick like a staff rather than a cane. 'I've taken up enough of your time, Kara. I know you feel very confused, but the path is before you. You just need to follow it now.'

Kara stood up too and looked into Lambert's wise face. She would have called him a wizard in a bygone age, but now he seemed a kind of Professor David Bellamy or Sir David Attenborough – an eco-warrior in gentle disguise.

Lambert held out his hand. 'Until we meet again, Kara. Keep up the good work tonight. The bees are important.'

They shook hands and she realised he was waiting for her to leave, so she set off back down the lane towards the shopping complex, glancing over her shoulder once to see where he was going, but there was no sight of him.

On her return to her office she sat down and ran back over the conversation. It was all too extraordinary for words, as though Lambert represented some kind of mystical group who were out to save the planet. He knew of her dreams, and there was no doubt she was somehow connecting telepathically with Paul.

On the other hand, her scientific and critical mind told her, she only had Paul's word that what she had described about his surroundings was correct, and she had told Paul, Tina and Matt the content of her recent dreams. Perhaps it was all a joke or a hoax at her expense. Perhaps one of her acquaintances had told Lambert to come and wind her up even more to see just how far along her crazy path she would travel. But why would anyone go to so much trouble? It didn't seem credible, somehow.

She felt more disconcerted than encouraged by Lambert Dodman's visit and talk of snail trails, energy lines and vortices. She remembered her earlier thoughts on dowsing and knew that some people dowsed for earth's energy lines using a rod a bit like Lambert's supposed walking stick. She hadn't spoken of dowsing to anybody else, so was she really travelling on a prescribed path and discovering knowledge for herself? And was it a spiral path as Lambert intimated?

She thought of a snail shell, how it wound up to a pinnacle, and of her journey so far of discovery. At the top of a spiral shell was an interior connecting shaft. Was this also true of life, such that through all the layers and levels of existence everything was connected? And were there connecting shafts at certain points on the earth's surface, found by following leylines to earth energy centres?

The more she thought about it all, the more convinced she became. Fairies, dragons, snails and spirals were symbols in geomancy, an ancient lore which modern man had forgotten, but was rediscovering. Lambert Dodman had not been joking with her, she decided. She had trusted him as she would trust David Attenborough. But who was he really? She fired off an email to Martin then forced herself to concentrate on work.

*

There was a good turnout that evening at the St John's school hall for the bee survey instruction. Recent scare stories about declining bee populations around the world seemed to have caught the public's attention. There seemed to be as many theories about what was causing it as there were studies being done: from disease in the hive to cell-phone masts and electro-magnetic influences disrupting bees' navigation systems. It wasn't Kara's place to speculate which was the most likely cause, but several of the surveyors had their own definite opinions, which they readily voiced.

At the end of the session, as young families and business people alike packed away their newly acquired survey kits, Rowena Kissack approached Kara.

'Lambert told me he'd been to see you.'

Why was she not surprised at Rowena's words, Kara wondered? Had she already sensed the connection between the pair? She smiled at her new comrade in the weird fraternity. 'Yes. He seemed to be formally admitting me to some kind of exclusive club or witches' coven. I'm not sure which. You must be a member too, is that right?'

Rowena smiled at the concept. 'You could call us either of those, if you wanted, but we have our own name for ourselves. But membership is by right not invitation. You have earned the right through your actions and now your thoughts to be guided to higher levels of learning.'

'So is Lambert the kind of Grand Wizard?' Kara instantly realised her jesting was inappropriate. 'Sorry, but I'm having awful trouble getting my head around all of this. I really don't know what to think.' She had a sudden flash of inspiration. 'Did Fig have something to do with you hearing about me?'

'She alerted us to you, yes. She felt the connection with you was strong already, so we've been waiting for you to arrive.'

'Is that why she's always visiting the Isle of Man? Because she's part of you lot, whoever you are?'

Rowena nodded. 'Don't forget you and all your friends are invited to our Midsummer's Eve party. Lambert's invited too.' Two boys approached her, obviously her sons. 'I'll see you around, Kara, and on the twentieth of June,' Rowena reminded her.

'I'm looking forward to it,' Kara said with a wave as Rowena left with her young family's barrage of bee-related questions.

*

Martin's reply to her email took several days to appear. When it did, she knew why. He had obviously been reading up all about dowsing and the Dodman connection.

It was one of the earliest writers about leylines, Alfred Watkins, who put forward the suggestion that the original ley surveyor was the Dodman or dowser, and that a snail's two horns are like a surveyor's sighting staves or a dowser's rods. See the chalk figure of the Long Man of Wilmington in East Sussex, with a staff in each hand. I also found out that the Isle of Man has a children's rhyme about snails, to do with good luck. My only thoughts are that 'dod' is like 'dad' a word for an older man – a wise man?

The spiral shape you mentioned is also likened by some to the coils of a snake or serpent/dragon and is one of man's earliest drawn symbols. As regards centres of earth energy, there are numerous suggestions of sacred sites such as Stonehenge, Delphi, Angkor Watt, Thebes, Jerusalem and Mexico City/Tenochtitlan among others. Basically most ancient sacred sites could be reckoned to be an omphalos or 'navel of the earth'. In other words, a connecting point, as you suggested.

Are you thinking what I'm thinking? That perhaps the Old Tynwald Hill is one of these, but the old druids were wiped out and so their secret was lost?

Gee, Kara, I can't wait now till June to come visit the place. No wonder you're anxious about going there on your own. You never know what corner of fairyland you might end up in!

While you're near Oxford you might like to visit the Rollright Stones. They're mentioned in an article I read about psychic archaeology. As part of the Dragon Project back in the early '80s, they were using bat detectors and infrared cameras near megaliths at dawn with surprising results. I haven't found more recent references, so maybe their hopes came to nothing or they've kept quiet about what they found except to the initiated. Your guess is as good as mine!

Keep sending me these delicious titbits. I'm having great fun exploring the fairy world online. By the way, I Google Earthed the walk you did past those stone circles, as I want to try it out when I'm over as part of my travel write-up. Could you see the other circle further back from the road? I finally managed to find Old Tynwald Hill and it shows up really clearly. You get a great panoramic view all around the surrounding hills. The island sure looks beautiful and great walking country. I'll be sure to bring my walking boots. Regards, Martin.

Now why didn't I think of Google Earth, Kara thought? Five minutes later she was lost in cyberspace.

CHAPTER ELEVEN

The golden spires of Oxford welcomed Kara back. During the 1980s she had lived in the area, and she felt wonderfully at home back in the soft landscape of southern England. Her journey down was uneventful, although the traffic on the M6 and M40 was as bad as ever, and she was glad to turn off the motorway, although the lesser roads were really no better.

She had programmed her satnav to find the Bath Place Hotel, and she arrived excited at the prospect of meeting Paul in the flesh again tomorrow. The hotel turned out to be quite different from what Kara was expecting, comprising several early- seventeenth century weavers' cottages clustered around a quiet courtyard and having only fifteen guest rooms. Kara felt instantly at home.

After unpacking her belongings, which included a bat detector she had borrowed from the Manx Bat Group, she called Paul on her mobile phone shortly after six to let him know she had arrived safely.

'It's some hotel this, Paul! I wasn't expecting quite such antiquity.'

'Cosy, isn't it? It's where I usually try to stay when I'm in Oxford, so I know it's comfortable and friendly.' He paused a moment. 'Er, look Kara, I hope you don't mind, but Bill Paget got onto me today and insisted he wanted to meet you this evening. I tried to dissuade him, saying you'd probably be tired after your drive, but he said he needed to chat to you about mistletoe and stuff. I think he sees a convert to homeopathy or herbalism in you, so be warned. Anyway, he's going to be at the hotel reception at seven-thirty. If you want to have dinner with him somewhere nearby and chat about plants, it's up to you. He said if you're too tired or don't want to bother, leave a message for him at reception and he'll understand. He's a nice old boy, so he won't be upset if you decline. It's totally up to you. I got the impression he thought you'd be more interested if I told you that Fig sends her regards. Does that make a difference?'

Once again Kara felt little surprise, as though she already knew this information but it just hadn't registered with her yet. 'Oh, er, yes it does. I'd be glad to meet him. Really. Seven-thirty you say? How will I know him?' Despite her question, she knew she would have no doubts as to who he was, but Paul enlightened her.

'He looks like an archetypal country gentleman – tweed jacket, walking stick, the lot.'

'Does he have a beard?' she asked.

'Yes, well-trimmed. I should have mentioned that. How did you guess?'

'I know someone else just like him. He sort of fits the pattern, though I don't think all country gents have beards. Just certain ones I seem to meet.'

'Right, well I'll let you get on with your evening and I'll meet you for lunch as we arranged. Have a fun evening with Bill. I'm sure you will.'

'Yes, I'm sure too. Thanks, Paul. See you tomorrow.'

As she put down her phone she realised she hadn't seen Paul this time while speaking to him. She was still 'switched off' from visuals, much to her relief, though she wondered how easy it would be to switch on again.

After a revitalising cup of tea and a shower she changed into her smarter set of clothes, more suitable for a possible dinner with a retired doctor than her driving jeans and sweatshirt. Marks and Spencer's casual trousers in a pleasing shade of sage green were matched with a rust-coloured blouse and a dark-green-verging-on-black jacket. Remembering just in time to check her appearance in the mirror, she picked up her handbag and headed down to the residents' bar where she ordered a tonic and bitters, deciding she wanted a reasonably clear head for her meeting with Dr. Bill Paget.

He arrived at seven twenty-five looking just as Paul had described him. He was probably in his early seventies, with a thick thatch of wavy white and dark-brown hair and neatly trimmed beard to match, and, like Lambert, his walking stick seemed more of an accessory than a necessity as he lithely walked over to where she was seated on a large sofa and held out his hand.

'Miss Groves! Delighted to meet you.'

Kara stood up and shook his hand, instantly taking a liking to the man, just as she had with Lambert. His old-fashioned courtesy was charming in this day and age of automatic first names, although at her age she always felt the title 'Miss' branded her rather unfairly as a shrivelled spinster. 'Kara, please, Dr. Paget,' she begged.

'And you must call me Bill. Paul has told me a lot about you.'

'Has he now?' Kara grinned, wondering what exactly Paul might have said. 'Can I get you a drink?' She indicated her own half-finished glass of tonic water.

'Oh, a half of bitter will do for me, thank you. Whatever sort they've got.'

Kara approached the bar and gave the order then returned to the sofa where Bill had now made himself comfortable. She handed him his beer and he took a swift gulp.

'Ah, that's better. What a day I've had!' He took another sip before explaining: 'I don't like cities much and every time I come into Oxford I find the whole traffic situation such a pain. Mind you, it was probably not much better in the days of horses and carts. At least there are bus lanes and Park-and-Ride now.'

'Where do you live?' Kara asked.

'Near Chipping Norton, about twenty miles north-west of here.' He looked at her intently with his dark-brown eyes. 'Near the Rollright Stones, which I believe you've heard about?'

Kara nearly choked on her tonic water. 'How did you know? Are you monitoring my emails or something?' she joked. She thought she had better explain. 'A friend in America told me about them, as we'd been talking about ancient sites, earth energy and leylines. I actually brought a bat detector with me, as I'd hoped to visit the place and see if I could detect any ultrasonic anomalies.'

'Ah yes, the Dragon Project,' Bill nodded sagely. 'Sadly they didn't find as much as they'd hoped in the form of earth energies, but they did detect some odd magnetic fields around the stones and unusual radiation readings in one or two places. It's certainly worth a visit.'

'Look, I hope you don't mind me asking, but what's your connection with Fig Green and how do you know I'm interested in the Rollright Stones?'

Bill swigged back the last of his beer. 'Let's go and find a nice restaurant. I'm famished. Then you can ask me all you want about Fig and mistletoe.'

Kara finished her own drink and followed Bill outside onto Holywell Street. A short walk brought them to a cosy bistro serving Mediterranean food, which at Bill's suggestion they entered. It was reasonably full already with a buzz of noise that would drown out their strange conversation.

'Fig's the expert on the subject of mistletoe. That's how I know her,' Bill explained once their meal had arrived. He shovelled a quantity of hummus and pita bread into his mouth, leaving a smear on his moustache which he sensed and carefully wiped off with his napkin.

The connection was logical, not mystical, Kara thought with relief. It was all getting too much really, this magical world she seemed to be entering – or imagining. Hungry after her long drive, she began tucking into her grilled sardines when she suddenly recalled his comment earlier about the Rollright Stones.

'Before we get caught up in mistletoe, Bill, can you tell me how you knew I was interested in the Rollright Stones?' she asked again delicately.

Bill put down his knife and fork and took a sip of water before embarking on his explanation. 'You may or may not be aware that many different societies believe that all information is out there. You just have to know how to access it. You've already experienced something similar with Paul, I think. You are like an amoeba sending out a pseudopodium towards him and you're now in the process of connecting with him. I on the other hand could be looked on as an amoeba that has fused with all the others, with ready access to all that they know.' He took another sip of water. 'Does that make any sense?'

Kara was taken with the comparison with amoebae. As a scientist it was a concept she could understand. She nodded.

'I've certainly read about the Vedic belief in the Akashic Record,' she replied, 'and that shamans when they're in a trance are supposed to be able to access all kinds of knowledge from somewhere. I admit I've developed an interest in such things recently, but it doesn't explain how I'm "remote-sensing" when I speak to Paul.'

'Is it your intention to get to know him better, if you don't mind me asking?'

'I wouldn't be here in Oxford otherwise, would I?' She was surprised he had found it necessary to ask.

Bill smiled. 'I only wanted to be sure that you knew why you were here. But to answer your question,' he went on, leaning closer to her across the table, 'your consciousness level is expanding beyond what has previously been considered "normal". As you focus your thoughts on one person who is important to you, you become tuned to his thoughts too. He just hasn't been made aware of the bigger picture yet. Take this conference tomorrow. What's it about?'

Kara thought he knew already. 'It's about Acute Oak Decline.'

'And what did you come across in New Zealand that was similar?'

'Kauri tree dieback,' Kara recalled, making the connection Bill was hoping for.

'And what is the bigger picture here?' Bill prompted.

'The earth is in distress?'

'Exactly. And much of mankind is ignoring the fact. More and more people want more and more products to give their empty lives a feeling of worth. If people only connected more with each other, found social cohesion and meaning within their community, they wouldn't need all these products that are costing the earth.'

'People need to look inward not outward for sustenance, you mean?'

'Yes, and it might take some major intervention or disasters for it to happen. There's nothing like adversity to bring people together.'

'Not everyone,' Kara said bleakly. 'There are always those who take by force when the disaster strikes, who go looting and believe it's every man for himself. You can't really expect otherwise.' She didn't like where the conversation was heading. It was like all the doom and gloom on the television these days, but suddenly she latched onto something Bill had just said. 'What do you mean by "intervention"?' She noticed Bill had just taken a mouthful of food so she carried on. 'By governments, do you mean, or revolutionary Greens, or...' she let her recent reading take over her thought processes, '... or fairies, extra-terrestrials, people from another dimension, the Second Coming?'

'You're hoping that mankind can sit back and be saved from all this mess, are you?'

'I think a lot of people are. Personally, I think it's up to us to get a grip on ourselves. That's why I chose a career in nature conservation, but the message just doesn't seem to be getting out to enough people. Education is lacking, or children just aren't interested at school. They're switching off or developing attention deficit disorder or just being... dumbed down.'

'And what is your solution to that?' Bill asked.

Kara gazed at her plate of rainbow-coloured, wholesome food. 'Nutrition for a start,' she replied. 'They're probably malnourished from eating processed and junk foods.'

'And those that are concerned about their health are being poisoned by cocktails of pharmaceuticals,' Bill chimed in. 'Don't get me wrong. As a retired doctor I know the value of a good and powerful medicine, but often they're being used at the expense of alternatives that can be as potent but have no patent, so money can't be made from them. This is where people like Fig come in, but governments are having pressure put on them to curb the activities of the likes of her.'

'Yes, I've heard that. And yet you never hear of anyone dying from herbal remedies, but people die from pharmaceutical complications all the time. It's now the fourth most common cause of death in the USA, I believe.'

'Sad, isn't it?' Bill remarked. 'If they would only fund more research on natural botanical remedies, then many endangered habitats might be saved. The wealth of potential cures in the Amazon rainforest alone is phenomenal, let alone our small woodlands here in Europe. And now they're dying or being wiped out.'

'Is that why I dreamt about mistletoe and greater celandine? Why one of my dreams told me that life is ka qi – spirit energy? Does mistletoe really have some secret property to retune your cells to their healthy state?'

'I can't answer that for you. If there is an answer it must come from official sources. A little knowledge can be dangerous, especially with plants that have toxins.'

'Yes, I know mistletoe berries are poisonous, even though mistle thrushes seem to like them. You can't just boldly go round saying mistletoe is the key to life otherwise people stand the risk of poisoning themselves. But the leaves are OK, aren't they? I bought some mistletoe tea recently in an organic food shop. That can't be poisonous, surely? I've been drinking it!'

'As I said, Fig is the expert here. But I'm keen to access supplies of mistletoe from woodlands and orchards for herbalists, but I was overruled in our recent meeting. Paul supported me, thanks to you, but it wasn't enough.'

Kara nodded slowly as she scraped the last of the fish off her plate. 'So I'm being influenced by your "friends" to influence Paul, among others, to get their acts together and protect the woodlands here?' She thought through her logic for a second. 'So why aren't you influencing Paul directly? You work with him, after all.'

'Some people are less easy to influence than others. Before you met him, I don't think Paul would have supported me in the mistletoe issue.'

A connection suddenly sparked in Kara's brain. 'Of course, mistletoe and oak! The druids' most sacred plants!' She looked at Bill intently and lowered her voice. 'Is that why you're so interested? Are you druids?'

'That's a fairly recent term for the likes of us. We've been around far longer than that.'

'Far longer? How long is that?'

Bill gave an enigmatic smile. 'Just "far longer" is all I'm prepared to say. You'll learn more in due course when you're ready. We have to be careful still, as we've been terribly persecuted in the past.'

'So who among the people I know are in your... group, I suppose I'd better call it?'

'You've met some of them in your dreams, and I think you already have an idea who we are when you meet us now.'

'I'll be watching out for you. Are there many of you?'

Bill tilted his head in a slight nod. 'We're rapidly growing more influential and recruiting support from people like you. It's a race against time to change the way humanity is heading. We have to make our intentions felt.'

'And my mission, along with Paul, is to save the dying oak trees and associated woodland ecosystems.'

'Initially that will be your intention.'

'How much of this can I tell Paul?'

'As much as you feel he'll be comfortable with.'

The waiter came to clear their plates, leaving Kara a moment to reflect on what she had learnt. She felt strangely comforted, and honoured, realising she was now part of a large group of people in possession of ancient wisdom. But surely, all that could be done was being done for a tree as noble and iconic as the English oak?

Nevertheless, as Kara left the restaurant later that evening and walked back to her hotel, she felt Bill's wisdom and guidance had left its mark. Trees were becoming more important in her life, had provided her with some of her moments of connection to whatever it was that had taken over her life. She felt she owed them something.

CHAPTER TWELVE

'I hadn't realised quite how bad the situation was,' Kara told Paul as they left Oxford's Institute of Virology and Environmental Microbiology. 'You won't know until next year whether there's to be any more government funding for research?'

They were heading the short distance down Mansfield Road past Mansfield and Manchester Colleges towards their hotel.

'No. Still you can hardly blame them with all the other troubles they have at the moment. Oak trees must come way down on their agenda. As we discussed, it's largely up to us to do what we can, closely monitoring the situation and trying to control the spread of the disease for now.'

'Yes, that is our intention,' Kara said, not quite sure why she stressed the last word quite so firmly, until she remembered Bill Paget's words from the night before. 'It's funny, but Bill seemed to think you and I could play a big part in that.'

'Did he? How are we to do that, apart from all the normal things we usually do with tree diseases?'

'Intention,' Kara said slowly and thoughtfully.

'I beg your pardon?'

Kara cast a quick sideways glance at Paul. No, he wasn't ready for this kind of thing yet, despite her apparent demonstration of remote viewing – although she hadn't actually proved the veracity of that yet. She would need to see his parent's house to persuade her that what she had seen was real. 'Intention,' she repeated with a shrug of her shoulders. 'Just that. It is our intention to control or get rid of Acute Oak Decline. That is what we must focus our thoughts on.'

Paul looked at her, somewhat bemused by her words. 'You're into your strange world again, aren't you, Kara? Are you saying we can wish away the disease, just by thinking about it?'

They had reached the college sports ground, which their hotel had access to for parking. Paul's mud-spattered Hyundai Tucson Elite looked out of place in the urban environment. As he opened the hatchback and reached in for a well-travelled suitcase, she told him: 'That was the impression I got from Bill. He put the idea in my head. He said together you and I could make a difference.'

Paul closed the hatchback, locked the car and turned round to face Kara. 'Did he now? No wonder he insisted on seeing you.'

Kara could see Paul didn't know what to make of the whole thing, so decided to drop the subject. 'Well, let's go and get changed then shall we go for a walk around the city? I could do with some fresh air.'

It was a short walk back to Holywell Street and the Bath Place Hotel. As a regular customer of the hotel Paul had already checked in earlier to get the car-parking permit, although he hadn't had access to his room then. When he picked up his room key at the hotel reception she realised they were in adjacent rooms, and she wondered whether that had been intentional on his part or just a coincidence of booking. Despite their former association she felt she needed time to get to know him again before she could commit to a full-on relationship, and she hoped he understood.

An hour and a half later, after a pleasant walk around the streets of Oxford, they ended up at one of the riverside pubs. It was just warm enough to sit outside still, and they watched the swans and the college rowers exercising up and down Isis as they consulted the dinner menu.

'So what's the agenda for tomorrow?' Kara asked expectantly after they had given their order. 'Do you have anything planned, or can I make a suggestion?'

'Go ahead.'

She found herself nearly backing off the topic, but plucked up her courage. 'This is weird and wacky Kara speaking now, Paul. I crave your indulgence on this.'

Paul chuckled. 'OK. Fire away. I'm listening.'

Kara relaxed. He wouldn't mind her craziness. 'I want to visit the Rollright Stones, ideally at dawn, but failing that at dusk. I want to check out some things I've read about the place and see if there is something strange there.' She looked down at her lap for a moment, screwed up her courage then gabbled: 'I want to see if there are any magnetic anomalies or ultra-sonic readings that might register on a bat-detector.'

Paul was silent a moment as he took this in. 'I presume you have one with you?'

'Yes,' she admitted, 'courtesy of my friends at the Manx Bat Group. But what we could do with are some dowsing rods. They used to supply them at the Stones, apparently, until their shed got vandalised.'

'Do you want me to supply some?'

Kara looked at him aghast. 'Have you got some with you?'

'No, but I could make some. I've a metal coat hanger I brought with me. We can make a pair from it. I've seen some like that being used in one of our woodlands, and I've always wanted a go.'

'Really? What were they looking for?'

'An old well we knew about, but it had been covered over and nobody was sure where it was or how safe the covering was. We didn't want it to suddenly give way when there was somebody on top of it.'

'What about the dowser? He might have stood on it!'

'She was prepared to take that risk. She found it all right: pretty quickly too, despite it being covered in a thick layer of humus. It was most impressive watching the dowsing rods crossing over. I imagine they must do the same with leylines and things.'

'Apparently so,' Kara said, amazed at Paul's revelation. 'So while I'm using the bat-detector, you can try finding things with your coat hangers.'

'See, I can be crazy too, sometimes. It's not difficult.' He peered into the crowded bar. 'I could do with a couple of straws, I think, to make handles for the rods so they'll move freely. I'll just go and grab some.'

Kara watched in disbelief as he headed off to the bar to make his request. Moments later he was back clutching several orange straws. 'I got some spares, in case.' He stuck them in his shirt top pocket like a strange buttonhole posy that had lost its petals. 'Now all we need are some wire cutters for the coat hangers.'

'Perhaps the hotel can help with those.'

'No, it's all right. I have a toolbox in my car. My father taught me to always be prepared.' As if making a mental checklist he asked her: 'Now then, what about the magnetic anomalies? Short of hiring a gauss meter from somewhere, do you have a compass?'

'I do! I keep one in my handbag.'

'Why?'

'Why not? It's more useful than some things kept in handbags.'

'I'm sure.' Paul chuckled. 'We're made for each other, Kara, you with your compass and me with my coat hanger and straws. Together we'll get things done.' He picked up his wine glass and held it out to her. 'To us!'

Kara smiled and raised her glass, chinking it against his. 'To us!' She had another thought. 'And the survival of the oak trees!'

'May they live for ever,' Paul murmured sincerely.

They sat quietly reflecting on the issue for a moment, watching a pair of swans with two cygnets in tow approach the terrace hoping for food.

'I wouldn't mind coming back as a swan,' Paul said. 'Royal protection, food for free.' He paused. 'Paired for life.'

The male swan honked loudly in agreement, and they both laughed.

*

Next morning, after a leisurely full English breakfast, they packed a rucksack with the bat detector and dowsing rods Paul had made upon their return the previous evening, and set off in Paul's car. The drive up through the gently rolling countryside of north-west Oxfordshire took them along the A44 past stately Blenheim Palace to Chipping Norton, where they made a stop for morning coffee in a delightfully quaint coffee shop on the high street. They had the whole day at their disposal and were in no particular hurry to do anything except enjoy each other's company. After that it was a short hop up the A3400 with a left turn to Little Rollright. Parking at the roadside, they approached the gate that led to the stones.

They were not the only visitors there. Several groups were already dispersed about the stone circle and the nearby Whispering Knights configuration. The Rollright Stones had become a popular destination for seekers after New Age mysteries, as well as for countryside ramblers and those simply interested in ancient megalithic sites.

Kara and Paul stood quietly at the edge of the circle for a while just absorbing the feel of the site. Tall trees flanked the circle by the roadside, shutting it off from modern Britain.

'How many stones are there?' Paul eventually asked, breaking the long silence.

Kara was silent, so Paul turned to her and saw she was gazing into the circle with an unfocused look in her eyes as though her thoughts were elsewhere.

'Kara?' Paul shook her arm gently when she made no response. 'Kara!'

Her eyes suddenly focused and she looked down at his hand on her arm. 'Was I away with the fairies again?'

'It certainly looked like that. What were you seeing?'

'A greenish mist appeared in the centre of the circle and gradually figures appeared in the mist, like ghosts or fairies or even aliens. Perhaps all three, for all I know.'

'And what were they doing?'

'Looking at me, as though asking me to join them. I think I would have walked over there if you hadn't...' she struggled to find the right expression, '... if you hadn't woken me.'

'And then what would have happened? Would you have disappeared into the mist with them, never to be seen again? Or would you have reappeared three months later with tales of alien abductions or perpetual partying with the fairies?'

Kara thought he was joking with her. 'Paul, I really saw it.'

'And I didn't, so what does that mean?'

'You haven't seen the light yet, like I did in Doubtful Sound?' she postulated. 'You're not tuned into their dimension like I am? Who knows? But things like this keep appearing to me now, ever since I went to New Zealand. The place changed me somehow.'

He seemed to accept that. It was all he could do under the circumstances, short of declaring her barking mad. 'I have to admit that your remote viewing on the phone shows something strange is going on with you, and I'm really keen to get to the bottom of it now.' He smiled to show he didn't doubt her sanity then put his original question to her again. 'So, how many stones are there?'

Kara was glad to be back on more certain territory. She tried to recall the information on one of the Rollright websites she had read. 'Apparently nobody ever counts the same number twice, probably because quite a few of the stones are broken. They reckon there used to be about one hundred and five, but a lot have been removed for buildings or whatever. There's about seventy-seven now, or so I read.'

'Shall we start by walking around the outside of the circle with your compass?' Paul suggested. 'We can save the inside for later, in case you suddenly disappear into the green mist, like in the Bermuda Triangle!'

Ignoring him, Kara reached into her rucksack and brought out her trusty compass.

She held it in the palm of her hand and let it settle. North pointed to the nearest stone. 'That's convenient,' she commented, 'but I'm not sure that's right. I reckon north's over there,' she said pointing towards the road behind them.

'Well, let's move on and see what happens,' Paul told her.

They walked on past several more of the irregularly shaped stones and tried again. 'It still points towards the nearest stone,' Kara said in amazement.

'Or the centre of the circle,' Paul suggested.

They continued walking round the circle with the same result. Kara concentrated on watching the flickering compass needle, until she suddenly felt a tingling sensation in her feet that quickly spread up her spine and down her arms to her hands.

'There's definitely something strange here, Paul. I can feel it. Look.' She rolled back her sleeve and showed him her goose bumps. 'Let's see what happens when we go inside the circle.' So saying she stepped through the gap in the nearest stones and walked towards the centre. The compass needle began to rotate and couldn't settle, as though each of the stones was attracting it.

Peering over her shoulder Paul was astonished. 'Wow. That's weird. There's certainly something odd here. Let me have a go with those dowsing rods.'

Kara gave him the rucksack as she continued to watch the spinning compass needle in almost hypnotic fascination. 'Have you used them yourself before?'

'No. I've no idea whether it'll work or not.'

He slotted the coat-hangar short ends into the straws and held them loosely in each hand, his elbows at his sides. The metal rods swayed and rotated with the effects of his movement then settled, pointing ahead of him. He began slowly walking to the centre of the circle, the rods gently swaying with his walking movement and crossing over occasionally, but with no obvious pattern.

'What are you actually trying to find?' Kara asked him, after he returned to her, none the wiser.

'I don't really know.'

'I have a feeling you have to actually have something quite clearly in your mind, so you know what to focus on. Otherwise you could be looking for water, oil or buried treasure.'

'That's a point. So what am I looking for?'

'Energy lines, I should think.'

'Right. Now how exactly do I picture those?'

'Like the feeling you get when you walk under power lines. That sort of static charge, perhaps? Try that.'

Paul shrugged, looking a little sheepish amongst the other visitors to the stones, but cleared his mind and thought hard. He then set off slowly towards the centre of the circle again. Every so often the rods would cross over, but he wasn't sure if it was anything other than his own movement causing it. At the centre the rods stayed crossed.

'You have to find the start of the spiral,' a young woman watching him nearby told him.

'Sorry?'

'The spiral of energy from the centre. There are seven rings to it before you reach the stones.'

'Are there?'

The young woman smiled. With her hand-knitted, golden-brown sweater, rainbow scarf, orange paisley skirt and Wellington boots, she certainly looked the epitome of a dowser. 'Shall I show you?'

Paul looked at Kara, who shrugged that it was up to him. Deciding he wasn't going to get anywhere as a complete novice, he handed the woman his dowsing rods.

She smiled then stood at the centre of the circle, concentrating on what she was doing. She began by walking a circle of about one metre radius. The rods responded by uncrossing then crossing at one point on the circle. She repeated the circle to be sure, and the rods responded in the same way as before. She looked over at Paul and Kara.

'The spiral starts here, where they cross. Now I just have to try to follow the spiral outwards.' So saying, she began walking forwards. The rods quickly uncrossed, and she retraced her steps until they crossed again. She moved sideways and stepped forwards with no result. Stepping back to the crossing point, she repeated the procedure in the other direction and found where the rods crossed again. 'This is the path of the spiral,' she declared. 'You just keep moving forwards and sideways in the same direction, finding where the rods cross and that is your spiral. It's easier to see if you can put markers on the ground to show where your crossing points are, otherwise you rather lose track of the pattern.'

She handed the rods back to Paul. 'Have a go. See how you get on. I'll help you get started.'

As Paul stood in the centre and readied himself, the young woman laid her hand on his shoulder. 'My thoughts may help focus yours,' she told him.

'OK,' Paul said rather dubiously, but willing to give it a go. He made the same manoeuvres as the woman had and found the rods crossing. Kara stepped forward and put a pebble on the ground to mark the spot while Paul move forward and tried to find where the spiral led. At the next crossing of the rods Kara marked the spot again.

After four spots the young woman let go of Paul's shoulder and said: 'Try on your own now.'

By the time he reached the outer stones Kara had laid seven pebbles on the ground, and a small crowd of onlookers had gathered. The young woman found herself answering their barrage of questions. Kara and Paul stepped quietly out of the circle and wandered off along the path towards the other main part of the Rollright Stones, the Whispering Knights, which stood about four hundred metres away further into the field. They were both silent as they crossed the more open space, digesting what had occurred.

Near the Whispering Knights was an information board that told them the group of four tall uprights and one fallen capstone were the remains of a dolmen dating from about 3500 to 4000BC, and were considerably older than the Kings Men, or stone circle, which was probably from the same period as Stonehenge and Avebury at about 2000 to 2500BC.

Paul looked towards the Whispering Knights. 'How do we know she didn't put the idea of a spiral in my head? Of course I found one, as she told me I would. It doesn't prove there was actually one there.'

Kara frowned and looked back wistfully towards the stone circle. 'I'd like to go back there at dusk, when there aren't so many people around. It was distracting having a crowd watching. I sort of felt I should have been feeling more than I was.' She looked up at Paul. 'I feel I missed the message there in the Stones.'

Paul sighed. 'If I hadn't seen the compass going crazy, I'd have said forget it. But I must admit to being curious.' He checked the time on his watch. It was one o'clock already. 'Let's say we head off to Stow-on-the-Wold and find a café or something for a bite to eat, while away the afternoon and come back this evening.'

'Good idea. But I just want to see if the stones here affect the compass.'

The Whispering Knights, however, were all quiet on the magnetic front, so the pair headed back to the car. The young woman they had met earlier was waiting for them on the roadside.

'I hope you didn't mind me butting in like that,' she said apologetically. 'But it seemed important that you found what you were looking for.'

'Thank you,' Kara replied. 'We're not sure if we did find it.'

'The energy was a bit quiet today. I checked the NASA space weather website.' She looked at Kara intently. 'You managed to see it though, didn't you?'

'Hang on a moment. You've lost me there,' Paul interrupted, baffled by her comment about energy levels 'What NASA website is this?'

'It tells you about daily geo-magnetic energy flows and forecasts. It can depend on the sun's energy, cosmic radiation...' She saw their nods of comprehension and realised more detail was not necessary. 'So some days may be better for locating or using earth energies than others.'

Kara now picked up on the young woman's earlier comment. 'You asked me if I saw it. What did you mean?'

Her eyes flashed in excitement. 'The dragon's breath! Like me, you saw the green dragon's breath in the centre of the circle, didn't you?'

'Yes,' Kara admitted. 'But is that all you saw?'

She looked startled now. 'Why do you ask? Did you see more than that?'

Kara felt reticent about revealing what she had seen to a perfect stranger, but Paul proved less defensive. 'She saw either ghosts or fairies, or even aliens, she's not sure which,' he told their new acquaintance.

'Lucky you! Some people are able to connect to the next level, and I'd love to know how.'

'Well, I wish I could tell you, but I've no idea why I see things that others don't.' Kara suddenly realised her last remark was incorrect. 'But you saw it. You're the first person I've met who's also seen something.' A moment's fleeting intuition made her touch the young woman lightly on the arm and ask: 'You don't know Fig Green, do you? Or Dr. Bill Paget?'

She saw Paul suppressing a smile that quickly turned to a gasp of surprise when he heard the woman's reply.

'Yes. I know Bill, and I've read Fig's book and some of her articles.' She giggled as she saw both Kara and Paul's expressions.

It was looking like the start of a lengthy conversation and Paul was getting hungry. 'We were just off to find some lunch somewhere.

Why don't you join us and then we can chat all we like…' His pause invited her to tell them her name.

'Melissa. Melissa Brown. Like my jumper!' she grinned, evidently pleased by the invitation. 'The only trouble is, I came here on my bike and I've got a huge pot of carrot and coriander soup at home nearby waiting to be eaten. It would make more sense if you joined me for lunch if you don't mind slumming it a bit. Oh and…' she looked directly at Paul to make her confession, 'I already know who you are. You're Dr. Paul Driesler, aren't you, of the Woodland Trust?'

'I am indeed. And this is Kara Groves, Director of the Manx Wildlife Trust.'

'Delighted to meet you, Paul and Kara,' Melissa said warmly. 'So, how about my offer?'

Kara and Paul looked at each other in obvious agreement. 'Carrot and coriander soup sounds delicious,' Kara spoke for them both. 'Where do you live?'

'Not far. Back to the main road, up through Long Compton then head towards Wychford Woods.' She gave more detailed instructions, concluding: 'Drive past Holmcott Farm and, immediately on the right, you'll see a track leading between two beech trees. Up the track two hundred metres and the dilapidated hovel is where I live. Just mind the potholes as you go up. If you want to head off and get parked you can have a look in the garden while I make my way on my trusty bike.'

'Can't we give you a lift?' Paul asked.

'Thanks, but I'd rather ride. See you there!'

CHAPTER THIRTEEN

'Serendipity, coincidence or the interconnectedness of things: which is it?' Kara posed the question as they got into Paul's car. Melissa was still removing the padlock from her bicycle and waved as they passed her.

'Well of course people with similar interests read each other's journals and get to know of each other. It happens all the time,' Paul replied, ever the rational scientist.

'True, but it's still weird that she happened to be at the Rollright Stones exactly when we were. I'm just wondering whether I told Bill I was hoping to come here today. I think I may have done. Perhaps he told her to come.'

'Now you're starting to sound like a conspiracy theorist. Melissa implied she's often at the stones,' Paul objected.

Kara felt rather put down by his comment, and sat in silence while they drove through the village of Long Compton. They soon spotted the road leading to Wychford Woods, just as Melissa had described, and Kara's mood began to lift as they began scanning the road ahead for their final waypoints.

'There's Holmcott Farm,' Kara observed, pointing to a large and well-maintained farm complex, 'and that looks like where we turn off at the two beech trees.'

The track was indeed full of potholes, and Paul took it gently. The beech trees increased in number as they proceeded, and it was only when they rounded a bend that they spotted Melissa's 'hovel' through a beech copse underlain with a mass of bluebells.

'Oh my goodness!' Kara muttered as they parked on the track outside it. 'I didn't know there were still any cottages like this left in these parts. I thought they'd all been bought up and developed as holiday lets by now.'

The mud and puddles showed why Melissa wore Wellington boots as her footwear of choice. Her 'hovel' appeared to have once been a tied estate cottage and could have come straight from a Victorian painting. The slates on the misshapen roof were covered in moss and lichen, while the golden stone walls were nearly covered by an ancient wisteria in full bloom. The front door, with its peeling green paint, opened directly onto the dirt track, although off to the side of the cottage was an immaculate hedged garden.

'No wonder she invited us to look around,' Kara said in wonder, peering over the low hedge. 'It's a picture-perfect cottage garden. Just look at her vegetable patch. It must have been there for over a hundred years, with those beautiful old brick paths and borders. And look at that soil! Have you ever seen anything so dark and rich? It's nothing like the rest of the soil round here.'

'Have you seen the size of her compost heap?' Paul pointed out the large mound under the trees at the rear of the garden. 'Mind you, with all these trees around, she's no shortage of leaves to compost.'

Entering the garden by a small wooden gate, they had a good look around, noting Melissa's fondness for using coppiced hazel twigs as fencing and plant supports. Most of the garden seemed devoted to food production of some kind, with ancient apple and plum trees amongst the small area of lawn, and raspberry canes protected by a bird-proof enclosure. Kara identified newly emergent leaves in a flowerbed as belonging to Jerusalem artichokes.

'She'll have to keep those under control,' Kara told Paul. 'They spread like wildfire. Once they're in you can never get rid of them.'

Adjacent to the kitchen was a bountiful herb bed. Varieties of mint were contained in an assortment of coloured pots, with various thymes, sage and marjoram proliferating amongst bunches of chives.

They had finished inspecting the garden and were admiring the magnificent views across the rolling arable countryside to the south, when a tinkling bicycle bell and a rattling of mudguards announced Melissa's arrival. She wheeled her bicycle off to a garden shed, which she locked, then headed back to open the front door for them.

'I hope you like my garden,' she remarked, unlocking the front door and shedding her boots ready to step inside, which she did promptly to turn off the sophisticated alarm system that neither Kara nor Paul had noticed amongst the wisteria. 'Come on in,' she invited them. 'I hate having this alarm, but that's modern society for you. The state of the front of the house is intended to put burglars off. That's partly why I don't paint the front door.'

They both took off their muddy footwear and stepped inside. The front door opened directly onto the main living area, whose flagstone floor was covered in predominantly red Turkish rugs. Inside the cottage was certainly no hovel. Every wall surface seemed to be hidden by impressive bookcases, while the gate-leg oak table by the seedling-bedecked window recess sported piles of paperwork. The appetising smell of freshly baked bread permeated the cottage.

'Come through to the kitchen,' Melissa invited them. 'There's much more room there.'

The kitchen proved to be a modern extension out of proportion to the rest of the cottage. It boasted an oil-fired Aga, a large farmhouse-style table with six chairs, and built-in cupboards with a sizeable area of work-surface for food preparation.

'As you can see, the kitchen is the one area I've done some work on,' Melissa said proudly. 'I always wanted an Aga. It heats the water and the whole cottage, as well as drying my laundry, and my cats wouldn't be without it. Another thing I wouldn't be without is my bread-making machine. I've burnt too many loaves in the Aga, going out in the garden and forgetting about them, so now I just put the ingredients in the bread-maker and forget about it.' She was busy taking the bread out of the machine as she spoke, tipping it from its container onto a wire rack to cool. 'The bathroom is next door if you want to wash your hands while I put the soup on.'

Kara followed Melissa's directions into the small but clean and reasonably modern bathroom. She was rapidly re-evaluating her impression of Melissa from being a caravan-dwelling New Ager to a salaried academic.

As she returned to the warm and sunny kitchen she saw Melissa pointing out to Paul the copy of the Woodland Trust's magazine in which she had seen his picture.

'Dr. Melissa Brown is a lecturer in Biological Sciences at Oxford Brookes University,' he told Kara as he headed for the bathroom.

'Isn't that rather a long drive every day from here?' Kara asked Melissa.

'A bit, but I usually only drive to Chipping Norton then get the bus. It takes a while, but I get a lot of reading done. Houses here are slightly cheaper than closer in,' she went on to explain, 'and I just had to have a decent garden of my own.'

Kara nodded. 'Houses are expensive on the Isle of Man too. I don't have a proper garden myself, but perhaps I consider the whole island my garden. I seem to have wandered over most of it and know most of the plants.' She remembered why they had come to lunch. 'So what's dowsing got to do with Biological Sciences, and how do you know Bill?'

Melissa was busy ladling out soup from a large earthenware pot into a saucepan, which she set on top of the Aga to heat. 'I met Bill a couple of years ago at a local natural history event. We got talking and found we'd both read Fig's book. We also discovered we had other interests in common, and Bill sort of took me under his wing. He's a mine of information on local matters, is Bill. It was he who introduced me to the local dowsing group after I'd said I was interested.'

Her story sounded strangely familiar in that Bill had sought her out. 'Does he know you can "see" things?' she asked just as Paul came back into the kitchen.

Melissa began to set the kitchen table with cutlery and bowls. 'Oh, he sees more than I do. That's who I was referring to when I spoke about some people seeing to the next level.'

'Are we talking about the same Bill Paget here?' Paul asked in disbelief. 'You mean he's some kind of psychic wizard?'

Melissa frowned. 'I really don't know how to describe him. He's just... very knowledgeable about certain topics, especially...' She had to stop to think. 'Well, ancient history for one. Some of the things he says I just wonder where he got the information, if not from the next level.'

'Which is?' Paul asked sceptically.

'The Fourth, possibly Fifth, Dimension.' Melissa stirred the soup then tasted it, adding a couple of turns of the peppermill. 'The Akashic record might be there, where shamans and meditation experts possibly go to when in a trance. All knowledge of the past, present and all possible futures is supposed to be there.'

'So that's how I could know what tie Paul was wearing when I phoned him,' Kara postulated, 'if I was somehow accessing the Fifth Dimension.'

'Don't ask me how it works. I'd just like to be able to do it myself,' Melissa said, ladling the hot soup into bowls.

As they sat down at the table to eat their soup and the fresh bread, Kara decided to mention their evening plans to Melissa. 'I was wanting to go back to the stones at dusk this evening with my bat-detector to see if I could get any ultra-sonic anomalies. Would you be interested in coming with us?'

'I'd love to. But it might be even more interesting if Bill came too,' Melissa replied eagerly. 'Things seem to happen more when Bill's around. It's like he's a lightning conductor for earth energies. He seems to tune them in, or something.'

At that moment the phone rang in the living room. Melissa put down her spoon and hurried to answer it. Kara and Paul couldn't help but listen in.

'Oh, hello, Bill!' they heard her say. 'We were just talking about you.' There was a brief pause while Melissa listened then she replied: 'Kara and Paul are here having lunch with me.' There was a longer pause this time and Melissa looked back at them and pulled an overly dramatic face of amazement. 'Yes, I did meet them there. Paul had a go at dowsing and Kara was finding magnetic anomalies. She said she wants to go back at dusk, and I suggested you ought to be there to help things along.' Without waiting for a reply she continued: 'Kara and I both saw the dragon's breath, but Kara said she saw people in it.'

After she and Bill had made arrangements to meet up later, Melissa returned to the table. 'So, that's all settled. He's going to pick me up just before eight, so we have time to get set up and take preliminary readings before dusk.'

Kara sensed Paul was finding the weekend's events running away with any plans he might have had. 'So we've got the whole afternoon and early evening to fill, Paul,' she interjected. 'What do you fancy doing till eight?'

She saw his look of relief. 'Um, I had been thinking we might visit Snowshill Manor. Apparently they have quite a collection of interesting artefacts there and an organic garden, though we've seen a magnificent specimen today already,' he complimented Melissa.

Kara knew of the National Trust property from her time working in the area previously. She had driven by the signs to it and, from what she had seen of it down the path from the road, it had looked very pretty. It would also give them time alone together away from Melissa, who seemed to have taken over the day. Friendly and interesting as she was, this weekend was supposed to be about getting to know Paul again, and now Kara had committed them to spending the evening with Bill and Melissa rather than having a cosy tête à tête together.

'Oh, Snowshill is lovely,' Melissa agreed. 'You should have just about enough time to get around it, if you leave now.'

It was the excuse they needed to bid a hasty temporary goodbye and thanks for lunch before they got into the car and headed back to

Long Compton. Their conversation during the drive focused on Bill's all-pervasiveness and the strange timing of his phone call.

'It was extraordinary,' Paul commented as they settled into the Saturday afternoon traffic on the A44 to Moreton-in-Marsh. 'He was right on cue, almost as though he had a listening bug in the house.'

'Or his ears were burning, as people say. It's like you know when someone's staring at you. Maybe he's very good at knowing when people are talking about him. You called him a psychic wizard earlier. Perhaps that's a good description of him.'

'He's a psychic lightning conductor as well, according to Melissa, so it'll be interesting to see what, if anything, happens this evening.'

Kara had to smile. 'I think you're quite looking forward to it really, Paul,' she teased.

He nodded. 'Those dowsing rods were certainly doing something. It was only once Melissa put her hand on my shoulder that I really felt a strong response from them. Before that it could have just been random movement generated by my hands, but she seemed to focus the response for me somehow, and Bill sounds like he might be useful with your bat-detector.'

Snowshill Manor was busy with visitors when they arrived. They wandered happily around the gardens, house and displays of clocks, tools, bicycles and Japanese samurai armour, enjoying each other's company. A visit to the café and gift shop completed the pleasant afternoon.

'Shall we try Stow-on-the-Wold or Chipping Norton for dinner?' Paul asked her as they were departing.

'Chipping Norton,' Kara replied. 'Only because it made me think of chips. I never have them at home, so they're a treat when I eat out. I think I saw a chippie when we were there earlier, but I'm not going to order chips, cheese and gravy!'

'Why on earth would you want to do that?' Paul asked in disbelief.

'It's a favourite dish on the Isle of Man.'

'Oh,' he said without further comment.

*

Paul and Kara arrived first at the Rollright Stones, although Melissa and Bill were not far behind. For a brief moment Kara expected Bill to be wearing full wizard or druid's robes, but she quickly dispelled that fantasy. He was dressed just the same as before in tweeds, but this time his outfit included a tweed hat.

Paul shook Bill's hand somewhat awkwardly, as though they had both met unexpectedly at a brothel. 'You're a dark horse, Bill! I never knew you had interests in such things.'

'Most people don't understand what it's all about,' Bill replied. 'They only laugh and mock, so it's only people I trust who get to know the real me.'

'But isn't that true of everyone – or most people?' Kara said, after giving him a quick handshake in greeting. 'There's the public front and the private front. Recently I seem to have found more people I'm letting into my private life.'

'Since your visit to New Zealand, you mean?' Bill asked, heading towards the gate, which he apparently had a key for to unlock.

'Yes,' Kara said, realising suddenly how much her circle of friends had recently expanded. 'Yes, that's true. I think I was always terribly shy and reserved before, and now I've learnt to open up and talk to people.'

Paul was carrying the rucksack containing the bat detector, and as soon as they reached the stones he got it out and plugged in the headphones. He and Bill started a discussion about the best place to position themselves to take ultrasonic readings, but Kara found herself just standing between two of the oddly shaped stones on the edge of the circle, watching the sun dipping down behind the nearby trees. If this was a solar observatory, she thought, those trees wouldn't have been there when this place was built. Perhaps it has more to do with moon or star alignments. Or it's simply a circle.

She realised Melissa was standing quietly at her side watching the shadows lengthening and fading as dusk approached. 'There's a connection here, isn't there?' she said quietly to Melissa. 'I think I'm starting to recognise the feeling now. Certain places, or even just certain trees I've found, call to me, and if I'm not careful I seem to go off into another place and lose all track of time.'

'I know what you mean, although I don't think I feel it as strongly as you seem to. Bill has warned me not to come here on my own, though I did today for some reason.'

'I know what you mean. There's a place on the Isle of Man I want to visit, but I have a really strong feeling I need to go with other people, so I've not visited it yet. I'm planning on going there at the summer solstice along with some friends who are coming over to the island then. I even have a local version of Bill.'

'Really? Gosh I'd love to be there too, but I can't get away then.' Melissa reached for Kara's hand. 'Can I just connect with you a moment? It might help me to feel the energy more.'

Kara felt a little uncomfortable at first, but allowed her mind to forget her inhibitions and concentrate on the atmosphere of the place. She quickly felt a tingling in her feet, which began to travel up her spine. 'Feel that?' she muttered to Melissa.

'What?'

'That tingling sensation.'

Melissa concentrated. 'Ooh!' she suddenly gasped. 'I've got goose bumps and I'm getting a headache.' She snatched her hand from Kara's and stepped aside. Kara had not moved and was looking into the centre of the circle. Melissa followed her gaze and now saw a spiral of greenish mist rising up to the twilit sky. A bat weaved around the mist, as though attracted by it in some way, but never entered the spiral. 'That bat's not going to help with the ultrasound readings,' she commented, turning to Kara, who was still staring at the spiral of mist. 'Kara? Are you all right?' she asked anxiously.

Melissa looked around for Bill and Paul, and saw them on the other side of the circle. Paul had the headphones on and seemed to be engrossed in listening to the sounds they were emitting, watching the bat flying overhead. Bill was standing quietly opposite them looking into the centre too, seemingly in a trance like Kara.

Melissa wasn't sure what to do, whether to let them be, experiencing whatever they were experiencing, or whether to try to snap them out of their trance. She tried waving at Paul to catch his attention, but he was still watching the bat and wouldn't hear her call with the headset on. She walked briskly around the outer edge of the stones towards him, fearful of crossing the middle.

When she finally reached him she tapped him on the shoulder. Paul whipped off the headphones.

'Look at Bill and Kara!' she said urgently.

Paul did as he was told. They were both like statues. 'What do we do?' he asked. 'Are they supposed to be like that?'

'I've no idea,' Melissa replied anxiously.

'Kara told me she'd been stuck like that before and needed to be rescued,' Paul said, now equally concerned.

Bill's voice made them both jump. 'It's all right,' he told them, apparently out of his trance now. 'I wasn't expecting her to make the connection so soon, so I had to join her. She's safe. She's just... "downloading" is the best way I can describe it.'

Bill realised Paul couldn't see the spiral of mist as Melissa could, so put his hand on Paul's elbow. Immediately Paul stiffened as the tingle hit him, and he let out a gasp of surprise as he became aware of the green mist. 'The dragon's breath,' he whispered. 'So it *is* real!'

'You can probably only see the upward, green spiral,' Bill explained. 'But in fact there is a complementary, downward, white spiral, like a double helix. That is what she is downloading from. The contact goes both ways.'

'Contact with what?' Paul asked, almost fearful of being told the answer.

Bill spared him. 'It's not for me to say. Only you can experience it.' He turned his attention back to the spiral of mist. 'The white is fading now.'

'So is the green,' Melissa breathed, spellbound by what she was witnessing.

Paul was already hurrying around the edge of the circle to reach Kara and, by the time he arrived at her side, she had turned to greet him.

'My goodness,' was all she could utter.

'What did you see?' Paul demanded impatiently, holding her by the shoulders and checking her face to make sure she had come properly to her senses.

Kara could only shake her head. 'I'm just trying to remember. It's fading fast, like a dream. Let me think.'

Paul stood back, giving her space. At that moment Melissa joined them, while Bill was making his way across the centre of the circle. Kara spotted him and waited for his arrival. She smiled at him warmly.

'Thank you, Bill, for facilitating. I knew you were there with me.'

'There?' Paul asked. 'Where on earth is "there"?'

Kara frowned, still finding recollection of what had happened as hazy as the green mist of the dragon's breath. 'Another time, or no time. A time between time.' She shrugged helplessly. 'There were people there, welcoming me and...' She looked at Bill and a silent communication passed between them. Kara grinned broadly. 'It's like my antenna has been switched on. I'm receiving, and my brain is fully functioning at last.'

'You've switched on your ESP, you mean?' Melissa asked enviously.

'I suppose so. But it was sort of switched on before, wasn't it, Paul?'

'Yes,' he agreed. 'So can you totally read my mind now?'

Kara laughed. She felt wholly uplifted by the experience, empowered and at one with the world. 'Do you know, Paul, it wasn't that difficult even before this happened. You see, I met the other parts of you and me there, and we've always been together. We work as a team in whatever life we live.'

Bill interrupted by turning to look at the sky and declaring: 'It's pretty much dark now. The bats are taking their rightful place here, and we should be on our way. You and Paul have a lot to talk about Kara, so I'll get Melissa back home and we'll leave you in peace. You know how to contact me in future.'

Kara couldn't hide her grin. 'Yes, I do. Thank you, Bill.'

They all made their way carefully back to the cars in the gathering gloom, promising to keep in touch before Kara and Paul headed off back to Oxford.

Kara was lost in her thoughts initially as they drove on the dark road, but after a while she realised Paul had not asked any more questions and was strangely silent. She glanced sideways at him as he drove, and he sensed her look.

'Explain what's happening,' he told her. 'My whole belief system has just turned upside down, and I want to know what's going on.'

Kara could tell he was unsettled, the scientist in him unwilling to accept what he had seen. She knew she would have felt exactly the same in his position.

She gathered her thoughts. 'I think we were supposed to get together the first time around, but we stuffed up and went our separate ways. When we were both in New Zealand we were directed together. I was delayed long enough by meeting the ancestors on Tiritiri Matangi so that you and I would meet again. And here we are.'

'Do we have any choice in the matter?' Paul asked ambivalently. 'Is life totally pre-ordained by some greater consciousness, or can I refuse to become part of the cosmic plan?'

'Of course we have choice. That's why this planet's in the mess it is. We had the choice to not get together the first time, and we still have that choice, if that's what you want,' she added reluctantly.

Paul slapped the steering wheel with both hands in frustration. 'I don't want to feel pressured or manoeuvred into something. But there again, I enjoy your company, and if all this hadn't happened we could have got somewhere, I'm sure.'

'But...?' Kara asked fearfully.

Paul's tense shoulders relaxed as he exhaled deeply, his eyes on the road. He was silent, and Kara didn't like to push him to say any more. She could tell he was on a knife-edge, and she had to leave him to make up his own mind in his own time.

CHAPTER FOURTEEN

It was obvious from Paul's mood during the drive back to Oxford that he needed distracting with some light entertainment. Kara kept her eyes peeled for likely venues and, on the outskirts of Oxford, saw just what she was looking for: a pub advertising a live band playing Irish music. They pulled in, found a table in the bar and soon their feet were tapping to the lively rhythms as they passed the time in inconsequential chitchat and catching up on each other's lives, as though the events at the Rollright Stones had never occurred. They parted outside each other's rooms at eleven-thirty with a friendly kiss on the cheek and a mutual request to sleep well.

They met next morning for breakfast together before Kara's drive up to Liverpool. Paul was cordial if slightly distant, as though he had been brooding over events and was still having trouble coming to terms with what he had experienced and what Kara had said about their destiny together. But when it was time for her to leave the hotel, he softened, hugging her in farewell.

'It's been quite a weekend, all in all,' he said to the top of her head, his arms around her. 'You've certainly given me a lot to think about, which is why I've been a bit quiet.'

Kara felt that perhaps all was not lost as he stepped back from her. She looked up and saw his friendly face. 'It's only a month till we'll be seeing each other again. Give my best wishes to Silke and your father and tell them I'm looking forward to their visit.'

'I will. And I'll tell Silke all about our exploits at Rollright. I think she'll be fascinated.'

Paul helped her with her suitcase to her car and waved her off on her drive up to Liverpool. The traffic was reasonably quiet heading out of Oxford towards the M40 and Kara was able to mull over the weekend's events as she drove sedately north. She certainly had plenty to discuss with Martin before his visit to the island, and she wondered just what Silke would have to say to Paul about it all. She would have loved to be listening in on that conversation, as she felt Silke was in tune with such esoteric concepts, with all her talk of communicating with her dead mother.

Until now Paul's feet had been planted firmly on the ground, as her own had been before her New Zealand trip. Suddenly the earth was shaking under him and he needed some support. With Bill's assistance, he had told her, he had seen the dragon's breath, and perhaps Bill would nurture Paul's developing awareness through the coming weeks. Paul had been responsive to dowsing, although he was still questioning the validity of it. No, it was her own comments about what she had seen of their destiny together that had most unsettled him, she decided.

Thoughts of what that destiny might be filled her head as she stopped for a late lunch in the picturesque city of Chester, having decided to turn off the busy M6 after the Keele Motorway Services, and head for Liverpool via Birkenhead and the Mersey Tunnel. She always liked visiting Chester, with its black-and-white, half-timbered buildings and sense of ease with itself, and often made it a stopping point if she was too early for the ferry. She still arrived at the Albert Dock in plenty of time for the early evening Seacat to Douglas. As ever, she felt a warm glow about her as she pulled in at the ferry terminal and saw cars with Manx registration plates like her own lined up waiting to embark. After checking in she left her car in the line and walked to the riverside, watching the stalwart little ferries crossing the River Mersey. A stiff breeze blowing in from the sea sent puffs of cumulus cloud scudding over the two golden Liver Birds adorning the Liver Building. The weather conditions looked brisk as ever more cars gathered for the westward journey across the choppy Irish Sea.

It was a crossing she had made many times, yet Kara still enjoyed the thrill of the high speed Seacat as its engines roared once it left the confines of the Mersey estuary and it sped out past the flaring gas rigs. Even more she liked travelling on the slower, roll-on-roll-off ferry, the *Ben-my-Chree*, which docked further north at the port of Heysham. She tended to only use it when venturing to the north of Britain, the timing of the Seacat was inconvenient, or if the weather was likely to be rough, as the Seacat was more prone to being cancelled. The *Ben* was less noisy, having more outside decks on which she could stroll and breathe in the bracing sea air as she watched the land disappear astern and finally appear on the bow. The extra time it took to make the Heysham crossing made the Isle of Man seem even more remote and cut-off from all the trials and tribulations of the mainland. It was a time Kara usually spent in reflection and near meditation, mesmerised by the passing waves. But whichever vessel she was on, it was a time of connection: to the sea, to her home on the Isle of Man and now, she realised, to the universe.

Despite the chattering passengers around her, the Seacat's roaring engines and the thud of the waves against the twin hulls, Kara found her mind drifting as she watched the green foaming water race past the window. She was like a drop of water, but the single drop was part of a sea, and the sea became an ocean, and the oceans together embraced the entire world.

*

As soon as Kara got home and had unpacked, she sat down at her laptop to send an email to Martin. Just as she had sent it, she had the feeling Bill was thinking of her, so sent a thought back of herself safely home. She knew she was still a novice at this collective thinking, but decided while she was at it to send a thought to Paul too. If he received it, he could make of it what he wanted.

Two minutes later she received a text message from Paul enquiring if she was home. Touché, she thought, and sent him an affirmative text with thanks for a fun weekend.

Martin's email reply came back within an hour, just as she was getting ready for bed. She had left her laptop connected online, as she had a feeling he might respond quickly.

Kara, everything that happened at the Rollright Stones is just too incredible, but I do believe you. The fact that even your doubting friend Paul saw the dragon's breath was the clincher. I've been surfing like crazy about these stones, leylines and everything and reckon I'm quite an expert now. I just need to get dowsing, it seems.

I've searched out Fig's book already and hunted for your friend Bill Paget, but only found references to local archaeology and wildlife articles – nothing dramatic. No mention whatever of Lambert Dodman, even though his surname brings up a whole stack of references to leylines and ancient surveyors. I guess he's kept a low profile or that's not his real name. Perhaps he's Merlin in disguise!

Let me know how the telepathy goes. I wish I could receive it, but I guess I'm not tuned in yet. Bye for now, Martin.

After Paul's somewhat low-key reaction to everything, Kara was relieved she still had a staunch ally in Martin. He was as keen as ever to find out background information on any topic she threw at him.

Tired after her long journey she decided to make some mistletoe tea and retire with it to bed. She had some work documents to read through that she had neglected because of the weekend away, as well as thinking about next week's AGM, but her thoughts kept straying to the events of Saturday evening and what she had seen in the dragon's breath.

*

The dove was sitting at her feet, cooing softly, while round about her people of all kinds were gathering. They nodded their heads in greeting, as though the dove announced her as a new member of their gathering. Kara saw an inner circle of twelve people of all races and colours, and knew it was a collection of the wisdom-holders of the world. One of them was Manannan/Lambert. He too nodded in acknowledgement to her as they all sat down and began to join their thoughts.

It was like a whisper of the wind in the trees at first. Kara listened, hearing the voiced intentions as they were uttered. Whatever language was used she understood its meaning, realising that all the cares of the world were being covered by these intentions. She felt her own intention needed to be voiced, so she added her comparatively banal one to the list: 'We must stop the spread of acute oak decline.'

She heard a faint echo and hunted for its source, but it seemed to come from outside the gathering as well as within. She tracked the internal echo back through the crowd, and discovered Fig at the source of it with Silke beside her. Instantly Kara was by their sides, slotting comfortably into their circle. She concentrated on her intention, as one small drop in the ocean.

*

Kara woke with work on her mind. It was the week leading up to the AGM, she had a pile of correspondence and reports to write and she needed to get abreast of things. The weekend had been a very interesting diversion, but she really needed to get her head down to business now. The trouble was she always felt so distracted these days.

She drove along the Peel Road towards St John's, the sun at her back streaming out ahead of her, lighting her path. Her thoughts began to wander with the solar road and she suddenly recalled her dream of the night before. Lambert was part of the inner circle, while Fig was a member of the outer circle, as she now was herself, apparently. She wondered where Bill Paget fitted in to it all, whether he had been a part of that crowd, Melissa too. No, not Melissa, she decided. Melissa hadn't been a full part of the Rollright Stones connection. But there had been somebody else she recognised. She struggled to pin down her thoughts, and it was only as she had to concentrate on her driving more, when a car pulled out from a farm driveway in front of her, that the image of Silke came unbidden to mind.

She remembered Paul telling her a long time back that it was Silke's arrival on the scene, a year or so after his mother's death, that had allowed him to indulge his passion for trees and wood by studying forest management and then move on to research and get his doctorate. Before that he and his elder brother had been running the family sheep and apple farm in Herefordshire, making rustic garden furniture on the side. Silke had been the financial catalyst allowing Paul to break free, actively encouraging his woodland interest which he had inherited from his father, Karl. So Silke was also a catalyst in Kara's meeting up with Paul: initially through their jobs, and the second time because her money had funded Paul's New Zealand trip. Was it all pure chance, or was there really some intention behind it all? Were she and Paul really destined to be partners, as she had learnt from the dragon's breath?

She shook her head in bewilderment as she turned right by Tynwald Hill into the narrow, tree-hung road leading to Tynwald Mills. If you took things to their logical conclusions, she reasoned, then Paul's mother had to die for us to meet. That hardly seemed fair on Paul's mother, but if such was destiny or fate then it had to have been so. Alternatively, everything was random and happened by chance. Kara struggled to find the answer, and was still struggling when she unlocked the MWT shop door, locked it again behind her and walked through to the office at the back.

Jill, always the first to arrive at work and fill the kettle, saw the frown on Kara's face as she walked through.

'How was the weekend, or don't I ask?' Jill asked, fearing the worst.

'What? Oh! It was very interesting and um... thought-provoking.' Kara went to open up her own office door and dump her briefcase before returning to Jill by the kettle. 'This Acute Oak Decline might be as big a problem as Dutch elm disease if we don't get a lid on it fast.' She reached for a mug, inspected it for cleanliness and spooned some instant coffee into it. She didn't normally need a drink until mid-morning, but today she needed to be on the ball and might not have time for a coffee break. 'Still,' she continued on a more optimistic note, 'where there's a will there's a way, as they say, and we must all think positively and get the problem sorted. Either that or it will just die out naturally by itself. But we can't rely on that happening.'

Jill smiled at her unusually chatty boss. Kara's trip to New Zealand had truly been remarkable in the way it had brought her out of her shell.

Taking her mug of coffee through to her office, Kara glanced at the year planner to check on the week's events. Her eye fell on the thirtieth of May, which was a week on Sunday, and she wondered why it rang a bell. All morning as she worked, her subconscious mind was chewing over the problem and suddenly, after a telephone call with Margaret Quayle of the Department of Tourism and Leisure who mentioned an island anniversary coming up, the penny dropped. The thirtieth of May was the actual date of Karl and Silke's fortieth wedding anniversary.

Their recent generous donation for the new reserve, and the fact that they were visiting in June, made Kara decide she should send them a Ruby Wedding card. Now was as suitable a time as any to have a brief lunch break, so she went through to the now open shop and inspected the display of assorted greetings cards. Choosing a nice one with a bouquet of ruby-red roses on it, she took it to the counter where Monday's volunteer shop assistant, Joyce, stood.

While Kara stood at the counter she was aware of the shop door opening and somebody entering. Her transaction complete, she turned around and came face to face with Lambert Dodman. Kara felt suddenly overawed as their eyes met, but Lambert gave his usual warm smile and took control.

'Greetings ladies,' he began, making a point of including Joyce before continuing directly to Kara: 'Just the person I came to see. How fortuitous you're here!'

Kara smiled back at him, sensing nothing happened by chance for Lambert. 'How lovely to see you again! I was just on my way to have some lunch. Would you care to join me, Lambert?'

She had made the suggestion before she realised that she had her usual packed lunch with her, as though the idea had been put into her head.

'How delightful,' he replied, 'although I just need to buy some new mugs here first. I'm expecting a few visitors in the near future and all my old mugs seem to have chips or cracks in them.'

'You go ahead. While you're doing that, I'll go and put this card away and tell the office I'll be out for a while,' Kara told him.

She left him studying the display of porcelain and china mugs. By the time she returned Joyce was packing up a box with half a dozen 'Comical Cats' mugs for him.

'All done and dusted!' he proclaimed to Kara, wielding the white carrier bag Joyce had handed over to him. 'Shall we go?'

They left the shop and headed across the grassy courtyard to the popular café opposite. It was quiet at first, but a coach party of tourists from Lincolnshire entered just after they had sat down. The noise level immediately soared, much to Kara's relief, as their conversation would not now be overheard. She tucked into her Greek salad, waiting for Lambert to taste his broccoli and Stilton soup and settle down to what had brought him to see her.

He supped a few spoonfuls before he began, leaning in across the table to her so she could hear him.

'Welcome, Kara. I saw you last night, which means you've made it up to the next level. We're all incredulous at your progress and, to be honest, I'm not wholly clear myself as to how you've achieved what you have in such a short period of time. Normally it takes years of study and careful guidance by others to arrive at where you are, but more and more people are suddenly shortcutting like you now, which is wonderful to see.'

Kara decided it was time she asked some frank questions of Lambert. 'Can you explain to me who you are, and why you're one of the inner-circle of twelve?'

Lambert nodded and wiped his soupy moustache with a paper serviette, in a gesture extraordinarily reminiscent of Bill. 'Knowledge has been passed down through the ages to those deemed worthy of it. Throughout history and across the world the elders have selected those who can be trusted to share the knowledge. But sometimes people put themselves forward for selection by the twelve. You are one of those.'

'But how could I have done that, if I know nothing about you?' Kara protested.

'What you did crossed our radar. We became aware of you and helped you on your way.'

'And what did I do exactly to cross your radar?' Kara persisted.

'You cleansed your body and fortified it with light. This raised your cellular vibration level such that you could make the spiritual breakthrough when you cleared your thoughts and listened to the silence within.'

It took a moment for Kara to properly digest what he had said. 'So when I saw the light fairy in Doubtful Sound, was that it, my moment of breakthrough?' she asked in clarification.

'Indeed. We all felt the vibration of your tap on the door of our dimension, like a spider feels the insect in its web. But it is worth pointing out that both Fig and Silke were close at hand to help you.'

'But how did they know to be there on that holiday, if I hadn't crossed your radar yet?'

'Time has no place out of your dimension. Retrospectively they knew to be there.'

'I wish I could say "I see" but I don't at all,' Kara complained. 'But can I just ask why I first saw you as Manannan? Is that who you are?'

'You have simply been travelling through the ages. If you saw somebody who resembled me, perhaps he was a remote ancestor.'

'Or not?' Kara couldn't help saying. She felt sure Lambert wasn't giving her all the answers she wanted.

Lambert resumed eating his soup, clearly not going to be drawn further.

Kara tried another tack. 'You keep talking about "our dimension". What do you mean?'

'"There are more things in heaven and earth, Horatio, than are dreamt of in your philosophy",' he quoted to her. 'Dear old Shakespeare seems to hit the mark perfectly, judging by the number of times I see that quotation these days. Now, unless you want me to explain it in terms of quantum physics, Shakespeare will have to suffice for now,' he said and left it at that.

Kara shrugged and picked up the last chunk of feta cheese with her fork. Shakespeare she could handle, quantum physics was out of her realm. But it was interesting that she too had heard that very same quotation fairly recently. It seemed to be in common use in such circles.

There was a crash behind them as one of the coach party dropped an empty tray on the floor. It jolted Kara's thoughts back to the present and her work commitments.

'Well, I mustn't keep you,' Lambert immediately said. 'I'm sure you've lots to do. I just wanted to touch base, as they say nowadays, and remind you that we'll be quite a party at Rowena's. I must say I'm looking forward to physically meeting up with everybody, including your young American friend, Martin.'

'Oh, is he beginning to cross your radar, then?'

'He's come under your sphere of influence sufficiently to prepare him for the solstice events.'

Kara returned to work with Lambert's last remark haunting her. On reflection, it sounded slightly sinister, until she recalled last night's dream. But was it all too much like in the film *Avatar*? Had she been so influenced by that film that it was affecting her dreams of people interacting together on the thought level to achieve a common aim? Her dreams could only be dreams after all, and whomsoever she peopled them with was up to her. Strange, though, that Lambert had appeared today, and that he had mentioned Silke. Kara was certain she had never mentioned Silke to Lambert.

CHAPTER FIFTEEN

To avoid complications Kara had kept her diary free, apart from the most pressing engagements, during the third and fourth weeks of June when she was expecting all her visitors. She didn't anticipate having to constantly be with them, but she wanted to be available if required. Fig would be pretty much self-sufficient, staying with her friends Lambert and Rowena, while Julia and Henrik were not depending on her for anything except the orchid meadow tour. Martin had told her he wanted to fend for himself initially, to maximise his own impressions without being unduly influenced by Kara. The Midsummer's Eve garden party would be the occasion for everybody's grand reunion.

It was Paul, Silke and Karl she was hoping to look after the most, partly as they were honoured guests, but also, bearing in mind Karl's age, she wanted their trip to be as comfortable and enjoyable as possible. Being honest with herself, however, she had to admit the real reason was that she simply wanted to be with Paul.

They had communicated regularly since her visit to Oxford, as much on tree-related matters at first as anything more social. As the visit became more imminent he had started talking about meeting up again, but his tone was restrained. She wasn't sure if that was just his normal, somewhat reserved manner; the one sure thing about Paul was that he was not excitable. Come the day the aliens finally officially landed, Paul would calmly greet them, if that were the appropriate response. That was how he had reacted on seeing the dragon's breath. He had been perplexed, had needed time to think about things, had balanced what he himself had seen with what Kara had told him, and ultimately found a means of accepting it, if not totally embracing it. Certainly she now felt their relationship hadn't suffered as much as she had feared after their Oxford weekend. Whether Silke had managed to influence him at all, Kara had no idea. Her telepathic abilities had not developed that far and she wouldn't want to pry into his private conversations anyway.

She had not dreamt anything unusual recently that she could remember, although she had the strange feeling some mornings on waking that she had had a busy night somewhere or sometime. She had the occasional feeling that she was receiving some kind of telepathic communication from somewhere, whether from Bill, Lambert or the greater cosmos she had no idea. Ideas would pop into her head, seemingly from out of the blue, and when she acted on them another synchronicity became apparent.

The latest of these occurred two weeks before the solstice party, when Rowena phoned Kara to check on how many of her visitors wanted to attend.

'All six of them, if that's still OK with you?' Kara replied.

'Of course. The more the merrier.'

Something niggled in Kara's mind and she spontaneously asked: 'Is it alright if another couple could come – Tina and Matt? They're friends of mine here who I've been sharing some of my experiences with, and they're fascinated by it all. I think they'd really appreciate meeting everybody.' She guessed Rowena's guests would include Lambert and any other 'Manx Elders', as Kara was starting to call them.

'If you think they should attend, then they must be there, of course,' Rowena replied enigmatically. 'It's turning into quite a gathering.'

'If you'd rather they didn't...'

'They'll be more than welcome,' Rowena reassured her. 'Anyway, I think I know them already: Tina and Matt Olsson?'

'Yes. But there can't be any other Tina and Matts on the island, I wouldn't have thought. How do you know them?'

'I've met them at several Trust socials. Last time was the quiz night and we were on the same team.' There was the sound of children shouting in the background. 'Look, I'll have to go. The boys are creating havoc. I'll email you with all the details of how to find our place, if you can forward it to everybody. We'll start at eight and the plan is to see in the dawn. Let's hope we make it!'

*

Thursday the seventeenth of June saw the first scheduled arrivals as Martin and Fig settled themselves in. Saturday morning saw the arrival of Julia and Henrik at Ronaldsway Airport, while Paul, Silke and Karl were on the afternoon sailing from Heysham, arriving early evening. They had all suggested doing their own thing until Sunday evening when they would meet up at Rowena's, which suited Kara as she could get her housekeeping jobs attended to over the weekend and tidy her home in case anybody dropped in.

Despite herself, Kara's eyes were fixed on the eastern horizon late on Saturday afternoon as she took a walk along Douglas promenade. The *Ben-my-Chree* was clearly visible steaming steadily towards Douglas Bay on a relatively calm sea, and she could clearly picture Paul and his parents sitting in one of the lounges, enjoying the trip. Her image was so clear, she thought at first it might be telepathic then decided it was only her imagination, as she couldn't animate the figures or hear their conversation.

The weather that weekend continued fine, so Kara made the most of Sunday afternoon out walking with Tina, Matt and Dolly along Douglas's Marine Drive. As she stepped out briskly along the narrow pavement, with only a rusty railing between her and the swelling sea at the base of the cliffs below, she felt strange knowing that her holiday friends were already on the island and she hadn't yet seen them. They had all phoned, emailed or texted to announce their various arrivals, but Kara's senses were quivering like whiskers, trying to feel their proximity. Like Dolly, she felt she might catch their scent on the summer breeze: a waft of Norwegian salmon perhaps from Julia and Henrik; peanut butter or hamburger from Martin; Fig would no doubt smell wonderfully herbal; Karl and Paul would have the sweet resinous aroma of fresh sawdust about them, while Silke... What would Silke smell of?

Moonlight, came the reply and Kara smiled. Earthy darkness and metallic light with a hint of ozone; the scent came straight to her nostrils. Dolly looked up at her, as though she too had caught Silke's scent on the sea breeze chasing up over the dark cliffs below, until a seagull soared by, catching Dolly's attention.

*

Dolly was invited to the party too. Matt and Tina had not wanted to leave her alone in the house so long, and Rowena had insisted they bring her, saying her two boys would love to play with her. Tina had offered to drive that evening, as well as to bring a substantial amount of food and her favourite non-alcoholic tipple, sparkling elderflower juice, to help see the night through. As Kara sat down in the rear of the car she received her usual welcome from Dolly at the back, even though it had only been a few hours since they parted after their walk together.

The evening was cool but there was almost no wind to rustle the trees or send the paper serviettes flying. Rowena and her husband Tim's house was tucked up a narrow lane on the north side of the TT course near Greeba, on the approach to St John's. With a small shelterbelt of trees to the north, it had an open vista to the other compass points. The setting sun would stream in through the Peel gap, as would any howling westerlies. The house itself was a traditional Manx cottage of white-painted stone with a slate roof, extended piecemeal over the years into a substantial family house. Off to the side was a cobbled yard area, surrounded by outhouses and a stable block, with a gate leading up to one of several large paddocks on the hillside immediately behind the house. A car was parked tidily in one corner of the yard and Tina parked beside it. Kara had hoped to be there already when her visitors showed up and was not disappointed, as the occupant of the parked car turned out to be Lambert. He, along with Fig, was in the garden chatting to Tim, who she recognised now from one of the recent social evenings. Tim was somebody medical at the hospital, Kara remembered, wondering how Tim viewed his wife's interest in herbal remedies.

With Dolly at their heels, they opened the garden gate at Tim's invitation to join the party. There was no sign of Rowena, but Tim and their two young boys had got the barbecue cooking and placed plenty of garden chairs and tables on the stone-flagged patio. Tim came over to greet them with his boys, Juan and Orry, who immediately made friends with Dolly and took her off to play ball. He then led them back to where Fig and Lambert stood waiting, drinks in hand.

Kara and Fig embraced each other warmly as though they had known each other for years.

'Well, you took my advice,' Fig congratulated Kara as they parted from their hug.

'What advice was that?' Kara asked.

'To keep seeking the dragon's breath.'

'Ah, yes. And I found it!' Kara admitted. 'And I think I found it by talking to people I wouldn't normally talk to, also as you advised.'

'You opened up,' Fig said. 'That was all that was needed.'

Kara then turned to Lambert, and they gave each other a more formal hug just as Rowena appeared from inside the house. Matt and

Tina were then introduced all round and led off into the house to deposit their food and drink offerings. By this time another car was pulling up in the yard and, as three car doors banged, Kara knew it must be Paul with his parents.

She waved to them over the garden wall and all three waved back. Dolly bounded forward yet again to meet the newcomers and had to have the first greeting, finding a willing respondent in Karl. Silke and Paul handed over a basket of goodies and some flowers to their hosts. While Paul exchanged a few more words with Tim to allow Karl to catch them up, Silke turned to Kara.

'Paul hasn't stopped talking about you!' Silke murmured in Kara's ear as they hugged.

'Really?' Kara whispered back incredulously, now knowing what moonlight smelt like. Silke was wearing a silver satin top over black trousers, matching her hair. She even looks like moonlight, Kara thought.

Paul was waiting patiently as she stepped aside from Silke. Their eyes met and Kara saw the sparkle of delight in Paul's grey eyes as he laid his hands on her upper arms and stooped to kiss her on the cheek. His hands lingered on her arms as he stood erect again and beamed at her. 'We meet again!'

'So we do!' she grinned back like a schoolgirl. 'Did you have a good journey across?'

'Very comfortable,' he said with a nod of agreement from Silke. 'Manannan was kind to us.'

'Yes, he was,' Kara agreed, adding: 'I was thinking of you,' as she noticed Karl approaching her now. No longer as tall as his son, nevertheless he still had to stoop to kiss her with the warmth a man gives to the woman his son has set his heart on.

'Hello, Kara.' He needed to say no more. In his voice Kara heard the simple greeting given to a family member.

'Hello, Karl,' she replied, squeezing his hand in recognition of his new status for her. 'Welcome to the Isle of Man. What do you think of it so far?'

'Beautiful,' he replied. 'I can see why it has captured your heart.' As you have captured my son's, his words continued inside Kara's head.

Kara could see Paul out of the corner of her eye. It was clear he needed to talk and tell her just what he had been thinking about since their last, rather strained meeting. But the time was not now as Martin, sporting a brilliant orange T-shirt from Malaysia, had arrived at the same time as Julia and Henrik.

Dolly erupted into her welcoming routine and, by the time everyone had settled down, been offered seats, drinks and nibbles and Tim had checked the leg of lamb roasting on the barbecue, the New Zealand Holiday Reunion Party was in full swing. Lambert, Rowena and Tim, Tina and Matt as well as Paul managed to entertain themselves happily enough while the others exchanged news and reminiscences. Julia and Henrik had brought along their photos of the holiday to show everybody, as well as a copy of Martin's article about it from the travel magazine. The Drieslers hadn't yet read the article so as they pored over it, Henrik declared it to be a fair and accurate summary of their experiences. His tone implied it wasn't going to win any literary awards, however.

'You just wait till you see what I'm writing about the Isle of Man!' Martin bragged, sensing Henrik's lack of enthusiasm for his work. 'It's going to really light some fires. What a place!'

It was still broad daylight and coming up to nine o'clock when Tim announced the lamb was ready for carving. It was going to be a long night for most of them, so plates were filled with garlic- and rosemary-scented lamb, as well as from the feast of side dishes laid out inside the house.

Back outside Kara, with brimming plate, cutlery and paper serviette in hand, took a seat beside Paul at one of the round white tables. Martin soon joined them, eager to engage the sceptical Paul in discussion. Fig plonked herself down opposite Kara, with Tina and Matt taking the remaining places at the table, although Dolly sat discreetly at the adjacent table by her new friend Karl, hopefully awaiting offerings.

After a suitable time had passed for people to attack their food, Martin broached the topic he was particularly interested in. 'So, Paul, have you said hello to the fairies yet?'

'At the Fairy Bridge, you mean? Yes, Kara was insistent we should all do so, so we duly obliged when we visited Castletown today. Even my father did, which is quite remarkable. He must have mellowed under Silke's influence over the years.' Paul picked up on Martin's interest. 'Kara tells me you've been helping her research all this stuff about fairies, leylines and dragon's breath. Do you believe it yourself?'

Martin was surprised by Paul's directness. 'Well...' he paused briefly. 'I find it very interesting, but I've no personal experience of anything paranormal as yet. I'm hoping something will happen while

I'm here on the Isle of Man, magical place that everyone says it is. Do you believe it?' he countered.

Paul gave a sideways glance at Kara, who seemed to be holding her breath. 'Not until I visited the Rollright Stones, and even then I found it difficult to accept what I thought I saw. Since then, however, I've been discussing things with Silke and with a colleague of mine, Bill Paget, who was also there. They've explained a few things, and I'm beginning to understand how such things could be possible, but I'm not entirely convinced. Like you, I need more proof.'

'It's funny you should say that,' Matt chimed in. 'We're the same. Tina's been reading all these wacky books recently and has got me interested in them now, especially after what happened to Kara at Glen Helen. I swear we'd never have found her if Dolly hadn't sniffed her out.'

From the next table Dolly whined at the sound of her name and got slipped a piece of lamb by Martin, who was nearest to her.

Kara was busy watching Fig's expression, which stayed quietly neutral during the discussion. Kara decided to bring her into it. 'So, Fig, I've been dying to ask you to enlighten me about greater celandine and mistletoe. Why did I dream about them so vividly?'

It was a direct challenge to Fig to reveal herself for whatever she was: a herbalist, a white witch, or an initiate of the next dimension.

'Your questions about mistletoe led you to Bill and thence to your experience at the Rollright Stones,' Fig stated as though the facts were self-evident. 'You have also started drinking mistletoe tea, so you must believe it has some value.'

'Well, it makes a change from black tea. But is that it? What about the greater celandine?'

'I don't know the answer to that any more than that it's a known medicinal herb.' Fig seemed to relent and let down her guard a fraction. 'Perhaps you've accessed information I'm not yet privy to.'

'Accessed.' Paul immediately picked up on the word. 'You mean from this other dimension that you, Silke and now Kara visit.'

'What other dimension?' Matt demanded. 'And how many of you here are part of this team of "dimension-travellers"?'

Martin was quick to divulge his knowledge gleaned from Kara. 'There's Lambert, Rowena and Silke over there, as well as Fig and Kara here. I also know that Paul's colleague, Bill, is one of them too.'

Kara thought the way he said 'one of them' sounded ominous, as though he considered them as some alien species. She was aware she hadn't seen Rowena as yet in her dreams and wondered whether she was a protégé of Lambert and Fig's who hadn't yet set the spider's web thrumming. She glanced across at the other table and caught Rowena's knowing eye. Rowena then looked at Martin and frowned. Infiltrator. Journalist. The two words came clearly to Kara's mind and she turned back to listen with more attention to what Martin was now saying.

'How do you know it's safe over there?' he was asking Fig. 'How do you know it's not controlled by aliens with some secret agenda, for example?' There was a moment's stunned silence around the table. 'Well,' he repeated. 'How *do* you know?'

'You can't know until you get there,' Fig informed him patiently. 'But when you do get there, there is no hiding of thought or intention.'

Martin looked unimpressed by her explanation. 'I obviously need to go there then.'

'It depends on your own intention, though, doesn't it?' Paul responded, to Kara's surprise. 'It's like heaven or paradise or shambalah, whatever you like to call it. Only the pure in intent can ever get there, surely?'

'I seem to have slipped in by accident, then,' Kara declared. 'I don't consider myself pure in intent.'

'But you were,' Fig contradicted her. 'You had a very strong, pure intent which we all heard. It was the intent Paul and Bill had helped you voice. It was the intent you felt strongly enough about to help carry you across.'

'Me?' Paul queried. 'What did I say?'

'You're saying my intentions aren't pure?' Martin interrupted.

'We don't know what they are,' Fig responded. 'Perhaps you don't even know yet.'

Kara picked up on the guilty twitch of the corner of Martin's mouth. Was his presence here all just a journalistic foray to show the island as a hotbed of weirdoes and nutters? Had he been stringing her along all this time, deceiving her ever more into revealing what she was thinking?

'We can test you out,' Fig suddenly put forward. 'Kara, you suggest how.'

For a second or two Kara was at a loss as to what Fig was driving at, but suddenly a thought implanted itself in her mind. 'We can all go up to the Old Tynwald Hill at dawn and see what happens.'

She saw the smile of approval light Fig's face, and wondered if this had been on the agenda right from the start. The party was scheduled to carry on till dawn, and Kara, Matt and Tina had all taken a day's leave on Monday for that reason. Had the intention all along been for it to end up somewhere significant? She had planned on visiting the hill with Martin that day, for sure, but doubts suddenly started to creep through her mind. She felt herself being manipulated by the elder members, Fig and Lambert, although Rowena was clearly playing a part in it. Did they need to have all these people on the hill at dawn for some strange ritual purpose? Was their intent not as pure as they made out?

It was Martin, of course, who snapped up the bait she had just inadvertently laid. 'What a great idea, Kara! We did plan to visit it anyway at the solstice. It seems more appropriate to do it at dawn.'

'It's only a small hill marking an old meeting site, Martin.' Kara was trying to deflate his over-excitement, but she knew that she and John Michell's book had egged him on, with all that talk of the place being the ancient centre of the druidic world.

Tina and Matt now seemed equally caught up in his fire. 'It'll be a "jolly jape", as they say, if nothing else,' Matt contributed eagerly. 'I haven't stayed up till dawn since I was a student at New Year's Eve. The weather's reasonably kind tonight, so let's get druiding!'

'Exactly,' Fig agreed, adding to the momentum. Kara looked at Paul, who shrugged a 'why not?' to her.

Well, at least I won't be alone there, Kara thought to herself. In fact, we'll be quite a crowd. And with Lambert and Fig with us, who knows what will happen!

CHAPTER SIXTEEN

Sunset on Midsummer's Eve was shortly after ten o'clock. The sky began to change to a turquoise-green, and Tim switched on little white lights in the shape of butterflies festooning a nearby mountain ash tree. While he went on to light oil lanterns around their garden, Rowena shuttled the reluctant boys off to bed. As twilight proper descended, Fig and Rowena appeared bearing a tray full of oak twigs and mistletoe stems.

'What's that for?' Martin asked.

'We're going to make ourselves Midsummer crowns,' Fig told him firmly, brooking no argument. 'It's just for fun, so let me show you how.' She began picking out two flexible oak twigs and binding them together with a strand of mistletoe stem.

'I thought mistletoe was a Christmas thing,' he protested, though following her directions obediently enough as everybody else reached for the necessary materials.

'No, it's important all year round. Traditionally we should be out gathering it tonight to make oil of St John, but I already have enough.' Fig held up the finished circlet and put it on her head to check the fit. 'Custom says that this is the time at twilight when the door to the faery realm is said to open and the two worlds can meet, so who are we to argue?'

Some of the crowns needed a few tweaks and adjustments but presently they were all wearing them, feeling suitably regal or else slightly foolish, like when wearing Christmas-cracker paper hats.

By ten minutes to midnight it was reasonably dark, although the hills behind the house were clearly outlined against the still pale sky. Tim now appeared bearing a silver tray of small glasses filled with what looked like a golden liqueur, each glass decorated with a small sprig of a grey-leaved herb.

'It's not alcoholic, so everyone can feel free to try it' Fig declared. 'It's for the toast at midnight.'

'One of your concoctions, I take it?' Tina asked warily. 'Is this what I think it is?' she asked holding up the grey sprig and sniffing its spicy scent.

'Yes. *Bollan bane*, or mugwort,' she explained to the non-Manx members of the party. 'It's the Manx equivalent of St John's wort, traditionally worn on Tynwald Day, which was of course once Midsummer's Day before it was Christianised. It's supposed to protect you from harm.'

Fig made no mention as to what harm could come to them or as to how safe or otherwise the rest of the ingredients were. Matt and Tina looked at each other cautiously but, with their Midsummer crowns firmly on their heads, they felt reckless enough to sample whatever it was Fig had brewed for them.

As they all heard the grandmother clock in the lounge begin its Westminster chime they raised their glasses, and on the first stroke of midnight Lambert pronounced: 'May the Light be with us!'

They all repeated the toast and chinked their glasses. Kara took a sip of the liquid, which reminded her slightly of syrup of figs. Perhaps that was how Fig got her name, if this was her trademark drink. It was pleasant enough, and she drained her glass then added the mugwort to her oak and mistletoe crown, following Rowena's example. Julia seemed to be struggling with her drink, but politely finished it, declining Henrik's offer to drink it for her.

'So we start watching for fairies now, do we?' Martin asked Kara, his crown slipping slightly towards his left eye.

She couldn't tell whether he was being serious or gently mocking. 'Those butterfly lights look like they might come to life any moment and fly out of that tree,' she joked.

'Hmmm. They do,' he agreed. 'If only they had the New Zealand glow-worms here, we'd think we really were in Fairyland.'

Kara noticed Martin's speech was slurring. He was certainly getting in the spirit of the evening, it seemed, and enthusiastically agreed when Rowena suggested they get out a board game. Not everybody was so keen, however, as Kara noticed Silke heading Karl towards one of the sun-loungers for a nap. Paul came out of the house a moment later clutching a Manx blue, tartan blanket which he spread over his now recumbent father. Dolly had taken a brief interest in the activity before curling up on the ground beside Karl and joining him in the Land of Nod.

The game was based on nature conservation and involved collecting cards of rare and endangered plants and animals while travelling over a world map. There was some skill involved, as participants had to answer wildlife questions in order to win a card. Martin's knowledge proved the least up to the job, but he was magnanimous in defeat, claiming the fairies now flying around the garden were distracting him. Paul was the eventual winner and received a bottle of Fig's 'Syrup of Figs' as a prize.

'Who wants a coffee or tea to see them through till dawn?' Rowena asked as they cleared the game away into its box. A show of hands went up as she specified each choice, and Silke said Karl would have a coffee as she went to wake him. Kara offered to help Rowena in the kitchen with the teas and coffees, and was directed to put slices of rich fruitcake out on a plate.

Dawn was less than a couple of hours off now and already the sky was showing a hint of paleness to the north-east as Kara came back outside, weighed down with a tray of steaming mugs. Karl seemed refreshed after his doze, although Kara was beginning to flag. She was really glad she had decided to take Monday off work, now she realised she would be sleeping for much of the day. Julia and Henrik, used to making the most of summer nights, seemed fit to join the dawn revels, so it was only Tim who would be staying behind to look after Juan and Orry.

Stifling a yawn, Kara stood and sipped her coffee, looking for somewhere to sit. She noticed that Martin was deep in discussion with Lambert, no doubt to wheedle out as much information as he could from the 'dimension-traveller'. Paul, meanwhile, was having an animated conversation with Henrik, Matt and Tina about climate change. Remembering Henrik's comments in New Zealand on the subject she stepped closer to the group, but Silke caught her attention with a wave and directed her to join herself, Karl and Fig.

Kara sat on the end of Fig's sun-lounger and watched Dolly twitching in some rabbit-chasing dream at Karl's feet. It was strange how the dog had attached herself to him so strongly. She commented on this to Karl.

'Certainly, if she were pure Border collie it would be strange,' he agreed. 'They tend to be more one-man dogs. But she looks like she's got plenty of Labrador in her.'

'She has, and perhaps that's the reason she bonds easily with anybody who feeds her,' Kara told him

'Don't we all,' he replied, with a pat of his wife's knee and a soft smile at her.

Kara remembered Paul's remark at the beginning of the evening about how much Silke seemed to have softened Karl's views on mystical things to the extent that he had greeted the fairies at the Fairy Bridge.

'So what do you think about all this talk of fairies and dragon's breath, Karl?' she asked him.

He pursed his lips in thought a moment. 'I've become much more open-minded about many things since meeting Silke. She's had some unusual experiences in life – I put it down to her experiments with LSD in her hippie days – and I've had enough to make me think twice about some things. Sometimes I join in with whatever she's up to, but never with any great expectation that I'll have some psychic experience myself. I don't know what's in all the pills and potions she keeps feeding me, but they seem to keep me fit and well somehow.'

'It's simply good nutrition,' Silke explained matter-of-factly, 'as you've discovered yourself, Kara.'

'And genetics,' Karl added. 'My father lived to ninety-two.'

Fig, who had been quietly enjoying her piece of fruit cake and blackberry tea, suddenly sprang to life and joined in. 'And you, Kara? What of your recent experiences? What have they taught you? Do you think strong intention can alter the future?'

Fig's sudden change of conversation and barrage of questions surprised Kara, but she responded eagerly. 'That supposes that the future is already cast, if you're suggesting you can alter it. But obviously you can change a course of events, so the outcome is different from what it would have been. That goes without saying. But what I think you're really asking is: can just intention change anything? If enough people wish, or pray if you like, hard enough for something to happen, then will it?' Phrased like that she found herself at a stumbling block. Her scientific gut feeling said no, nothing would happen from pure thought, but she hesitated to commit herself to that verdict. 'I don't know. What do you all think? Fig, you first. What's your opinion?'

As the night had cooled and, as though giving herself time to ponder, the Earth Mother pulled her cobwebby shawl around her shoulders and fastened it together with a brooch at her left shoulder. Kara noticed the brooch was fashioned in the form of mistletoe: three small pearls nestling between paired oval green enamel leaves. Fig saw the direction of Kara's gaze, and it helped her to formulate her answer.

'There are serious scientific experiments now that are beginning to show that people can affect outcomes by thought alone. The author of *The Field*, Lynne McTaggart, is working with Fritz-Albert Popp to carefully design experiments to test this out on-line with readers of her book *The Intention Experiment*. It's early days yet, but some interesting results are starting to come through which might confound the sceptics.'

'That's surely the Popp who wrote the article I read, about cellular light emissions and the effect of mistletoe on some cancerous cells?' Kara queried.

'That's the one. He has a whole research establishment set up near Düsseldorf in Germany working on these very issues, and he's by no means the only one doing such research now. So how can the idea of thought's impact on biological systems not be taken seriously?' Fig asked with a dramatic sweep of her hands, which nearly sent her mug of tea flying. 'They're only beginning to scratch the surface of the interface between biological and geographical electromagnetic fields. There's now even a field of study called quantum biology, and I read about a Science and Consciousness Conference in April this year in Tucson, Arizona. Some serious study is taking place now on things scientists once would have just laughed at. It's all so exciting!'

It was not exactly the kind of answer Kara had been anticipating from Fig. She had really expected something more down to earth and 'herbal'. Which just goes to show I shouldn't judge on stereotypes, Kara reprimanded herself. Fig seemed another Melissa: an academic in hippie garb. Talking of hippies, she turned to Silke. 'What about you, Silke? What do you believe about the power of intent?'

'I believe it's possible our thoughts connect to some kind of network that may be independent of time and space. We've all talked about this together, so we are like-minded in trying to make sense of what we ourselves are experiencing. As you are aware, Kara, we are a part of a group linking up around the globe, pooling our thoughts. More and more people are rapidly joining this group. We don't know where it will lead, but we do know that the intention is to lead our world away from self-destruction. Governments aren't setting the right example, so it's up to the people to influence the way things are done.'

'You could be arrested as a terrorist in America for saying that,' Kara said, only half in jest.

'Exactly,' Silke agreed. 'So our intent is to change the world for the better, by numerous ways. Smaller groups of us have our own areas of intent to concentrate on, although there are topics of common interest we try to get everybody focusing on at certain times.'

Karl interjected here. 'They have regularly advertised days when people all over the world are asked to focus their thoughts at a certain universal time on a particular issue.'

'So you believe it too, Karl?'

'I confess I haven't participated myself, although I agree with the principle. It's the same as a World Day of Prayer, but doesn't use that emotive word "prayer" which might put off many people, although the sense is the same. As to whether I believe it or not…?' He shrugged then smiled. 'I'd like to. And I suppose it does give us a sense of belonging to the world community when we know there are people in the Ukraine or New Zealand thinking the same as we are at that moment.'

Fig was raising both her hands in her eagerness to be heard. 'There seems to be a critical mass number of people required to achieve a significant effect, or so some experiments have shown. The more people learn about this, through the Internet or local groups, the more chance we have of the intent taking effect, we hope.'

'So if, when we go up to the Old Tynwald Hill shortly, we all have some strong intent in mind, do you reckon it will radiate out from the druidic centre, or up into the dragon's breath, and spread across the world?' Kara postulated, as it all started to fall into place.

'Is that your intention?' Fig asked.

'Why not? It's worth a try. Surely even you, Karl, can give it a go?' Kara urged him.

Karl had to grin. 'How can I refuse, faced with you lot? There's certainly something about this island and all your talking to the fairies or the ancient folk. It makes you feel magic will work.'

Kara thought of her own experiences with the Glen Helen wishing chair, and smiled to herself. 'So that's settled. We've just got to decide on what our thought intent should be.'

'That's up to you, Kara,' Silke told her. 'It was your suggestion.'

She looked over towards Lambert, catching his eye, and Kara saw the signal between them. This was all pre-ordained. She was being swept along in a tide of events, a willing participant, but apparently being manipulated by the others to achieve the desired outcome: a gathering at dawn at the Old Tynwald Hill to initiate some kind of intention ripple that would spread out from the Irish Sea hub to all parts of the British Isles and maybe beyond. So what should the intention be?

There was a sudden burst of laughter from the adjacent tables. The other nine members of the party had joined their tables together to open out the climate change discussion, which had threatened to become too serious in Tim's opinion. Rowena was beginning to collect up glasses, mugs and plates in preparation for the move up to the ridge between the West and East Baldwin valleys to greet the dawn.

'I reckon we all need to leave the house by four to be sure of being in position and ready for dawn at about a quarter to five,' she told everybody firmly.

As with any large group of people, it took quite a while before they were ready and assembled to pile into three cars to drive up to Old Tynwald Hill. Rowena was driving Julia, Henrik and Lambert; Silke was driving Karl, Paul and Fig; Tina took Matt, Martin, Kara and, of course, Dolly.

The main Peel Road was deserted as they set off east towards Crosby, before turning left by the Crosby Arms up to the back road to Mount Rule. Here they turned left into the narrow, twisting lane up to Baldwin. Just after crossing the stone bridge over the River Glass they made a right turn uphill towards St Luke's church, which stood by itself on open ground surrounded by pasture. The small church apparently serviced the few local farms dotted about the hillsides and the tiny hamlet of Baldwin down in the valley. There was room by the church for all three cars to park on the verge. From there the Millenium Way track led on uphill towards the pyramid-shaped Carraghan, with the aerial-topped summit of Snaefell lurking in the near distance.

Rowena and Lambert had brought enough torches to light the path, although dawn's early glow was already allowing them to make out shapes and silhouettes without too much difficulty. Kara found Martin close by her side, while Paul and Silke kept an eye on Karl, as all twelve of them and the baker's dozen, Dolly, set off in a torchlight procession up the stony track the three hundred metres or so to the site of Old Tynwald Hill.

'So, here we are at last!' Martin's voice was exultant in the fresh mountain air. 'We've waited a long time to get here. I hope it's worth it.' He took a deep breath and surveyed the landscape of open hills and pasture. Apart from their torches, the only lights visible were from occasional car headlamps way above them on the mountain road, from isolated farmhouses and the amber glow of Douglas's streetlights to the south-east.

The track was not too steep until they came to a gap in the Manx hedge off to their left. A path led up through it, but there was no signpost showing a public right of way to a site of interest, and Kara wondered if Rowena had taken the correct path. Very soon, however, the gorse bushes opened out to reveal what they had come looking for: a small circular mound topped by a stone wall. A metal plaque on the edge was all that told them why the site was of any note.

'Not very spectacular so far,' Martin muttered as all twelve of them filed through the gorse gap, gathering around the plaque as Rowena shone her torch on it to read it.

'It says it was last used as a Tynwald Hill in 1428,' she read out, 'but it doesn't say when it was first used. I don't suppose they have any real idea.'

Lambert had already walked around the circle to the opposite side. He now faced south towards Chibbanagh forestry plantation, just visible as a dark smudge on the distant hill.

'According to John Michell, the modern Millenium Way was the legendary *Raad mooar ree Goree*,' Martin told them all, with a stab at pronunciation that made those with some knowledge of Manx wince. 'That translates as the Great Road of King Gorree, or the Royal Road, likened to the Milky Way in your tale of King Orry.'

They all looked up to find the Milky Way, but a band of cloud obscured the sky, which was now too light anyway. Only the brightest stars and planets were still visible to the west.

'Those clouds don't bode well for dawn,' Matt muttered to Kara.

'Perhaps they'll have cleared by then,' she said hopefully.

Following Fig's instructions, the rest of them spaced themselves equally like numbers around a clock face. Dolly stood in the grassy centre of the circle, sniffing it out. Lambert faced south towards the old capital of Castletown, Fig faced north towards Snaefell and Ramsey beyond, Silke faced west towards Peel, and Kara found herself facing east, though more to Laxey than Douglas. It occurred to her that the old hill truly was at the centre of the island and its four major towns, on the sacred Milky Millenium Way running roughly north to south.

Julia and Henrik had positioned themselves between Silke and Fig. Julia had a digital camera and was busy finding camera angles, making sure she would catch the sun on the hill, if it ever managed to break through the clouds.

'That's Slieau Ree or Hill of the King,' Matt informed them, after consulting the old Public Rights of Way map he was never without when out in the countryside. He was pointing to the hill to their north-east, over which the sun would rise. 'We're between six and seven hundred feet up here,' he continued in an effort not to be outdone by Martin, 'and Slieau Ree is over a thousand feet high, so the sun will be late appearing over it. Hardly an actual dawn moment.'

'But it's the time sunlight first falls on this spot that matters, surely?' Tina countered.

'And according to this map,' Matt carried on, ignoring her, 'there's a labelled hill, Cronk y Keeil Abban, just a bit further up the track than this. Was Keeil Abban the original church associated with this site?'

Kara racked her brains for what she had read from John Michell's book. 'I'm sure St Luke's below us was built on top of the old Keeil Abban.'

'Yes, but the map says it's a little way north. Perhaps it just means this whole area of hillside is named after the *keeil*.' Standing immediately to the left of Fig, Matt gazed uphill to see if he could see anything like stone remains higher up, but there was nothing, only pasture with some sleepy-looking sheep.

Lambert had not said a word until now, but he cleared his throat and looked to his right towards Kara.

'Well, it's nearly dawn, Kara. Have you decided on our thought intention yet?'

Kara shook her head. 'I wanted to wait until I got up here, to see what the site suggested to me. Let me think about it for a minute.'

They all stood quietly now, thinking their own thoughts, whatever they might be, while Kara tried to empty her mind. The stillness of pre-dawn on the hillside enveloped her until thoughts of the Milky Way led her to when she had last consciously looked at it in the pristine dark skies of New Zealand.

Oil.

Flying to New Zealand they had crossed America, which was now stricken with a gushing oil well in the Gulf of Mexico, America's worst environmental disaster to date. So many of the evils of mankind were the result of this constant need for oil. Wars were fought over the stuff. Oil companies controlled governments. Earth energy.

The idea poked at her like a whisper passed around the world, and thoughts began tumbling into her head like everyone was speaking to her at once. New Zealand had experienced dawn first, had set the thought rolling westwards with dawn's light crossing Australia and

Asia, Africa and Europe until it had arrived in the middle of the Irish Sea, growing in momentum like a tsunami, until she felt the thought was roaring deafeningly at her with the chorus of voices from across the world.

The sky was lightening rapidly and Kara knew it wasn't long before the sun would appear over Slieau Ree.

'Free earth energy,' she cried out so they could all hear. 'Our intention is that we live harmoniously with each other and with our planet by using clean energy.'

As she said the words she felt a tingle in her feet and the hairs on her forearms rise. She noticed everyone concentrating hard on the thought she had given to them, even Martin, Paul and Karl, before she too put her mind to the task.

For a full two minutes they stood focusing on their thoughts. Dolly was still sniffing around within the walls of the hill, but suddenly she leapt over the low wall as though hit by a bolt of lightning. Her yelp opened the eyes of those who had shut them, so that they all saw the shaft of sunlight find a chink in the band of cloud over Slieau Ree, lighting up the famous TT landmark, Kate's Cottage on the mountain road. The sun's first rays crossed the ridge and raced towards them over the hillside at the speed of light.

Momentarily blinded Kara looked down to the centre of the circle. She could hear a murmuring noise like a distant wind in the trees, which became louder, more like the swarming of bees. Julia had picked up her digital camera from the wall in front of her and was busy snapping photos. Henrik had started to film the events with his video camera, but as Kara looked around to see if the others heard anything she noticed Lambert's, Silke's and Fig's eyes were still closed. North, east, and south they stood. She was west. She closed her eyes to join them.

CHAPTER SEVENTEEN

Kara felt the moment had come to open her eyes. What she saw startled her.

The three other cardinal pointers stood clearly in the shaft of sunlight on the hillside, but around the stone wall their eight friends were mere ghostly shadows, watching but as though from another dimension. Kara tried not to feel alarmed, and looked to Lambert for reassurance. His back was turned to her, however, as he gazed up the slope of Carragheen. She followed his gaze, and could now see what he was watching. From the north down the Royal Road came a procession of about twenty-four shadow people, men and women, walking slowly down the eastern side of the hill. Some held what looked like branches in their hands and, as they drew nearer, she could hear singing like the chanting of monks: harmonic tones sustained but slowly rising and falling. Kara noticed their clothing of homespun Loaghtan-brown wool and leather jerkins was from a former age. Somehow she knew they had walked from Druidale on the other side of Carragheen to this sacred spot for the purpose of meeting the four of them.

When they arrived at the hill they made no acknowledgement of the four already present, continuing with their melodic chanting. Twelve of them planted their oak branches upright in the soil around the edge of the hill and stood by them, while the other twelve positioned themselves on the inside of the circle. Kara found that her space never interfered with that of the shadow woman coming to occupy the western position where Kara stood. It was as though there were two places or times on the same spot. Kara watched intently as the people joined hands and formed inner and outer rings as their chanting slowed right down, increasing in volume. After a minute or two she sensed the air around them beginning to crackle with energy, and their chief, designated by his off-white robe and staff, left the ring to position his staff in a hole at the top of an egg-shaped stone that

Kara could now see at the centre of the circle. As he stepped back to his place to the north of the inner circle, Kara held her breath. A coil of green mist had begun to arise out of the ground and wrap itself around the staff as it snaked up to the sky. When it reached the top it was joined by a misty white coil snaking downwards, just like she had witnessed at the Rollright Stones.

Following Lambert's lead, Kara joined Fig and Silke as they now climbed over the circular wall, somehow avoiding the people standing there already, and moved in to the centre where the staff stood enveloped by its double helix of mist. Lambert stretched out his right hand and grasped the staff, followed by Fig, Silke and finally Kara herself. Instantly the ghostly images of her eight friends disappeared.

Kara experienced no sensation of movement, wind or any mystical happening as the ancient shadow-figures became solid. She and her three companions had simply arrived in another time or dimension.

It was just like in New Zealand, she realised, on Tiritiri Matangi when the ancient people had appeared before her, although this time she was able to connect much better. Lambert was already grasping the hand of the chief like an old friend. The three strangers stationed at the remaining cardinal points stepped forward, hands outstretched in welcome, and Kara found herself greeting the woman from the west.

As their eyes met, Kara gasped. It was herself but clearly not herself, more like looking at her sister. Next to her stood a version of Paul, while one of Martin stood to her south. Casting her eye quickly around the inner circle it was as Kara suspected. Each person had the physical likeness of her friends, and was of similar age, but clearly did not have the same identity. The men had beards and long hair, while both men and women wore circlets of oak and mistletoe identical to those worn by Kara and her companions. She was interested to see that Fig's doppelgänger was somewhat slimmer than the modern version, although Julia's seemed more rotund. To her astonishment, a dog sat at the feet of Karl's counterpart's elderly frame. The dog was larger and shaggier than Dolly and a greyish-brown in colour, nevertheless Kara suspected it was connected with Dolly somehow. Was that why she had taken so readily to the modern Karl?

The chanting came to an end. Kara's twin, seeing she had Kara's attention again, stepped forward and embraced her warmly but silently before passing her on to the tall man at her left-hand side, the one known to Kara as Paul. This man too bent down to embrace her, and the feeling she got was that she had found a long- lost partner. She knew he was actually the partner of her twin, and therefore not hers, but that feeling of possession he had given her was unmistakeable. She smiled at him as they separated, and she knew from his wry smile he was aware of her thoughts. Quickly she moved on, greeting a long-haired Tina then the chief. There was no doubt he was the Manannan-figure of her dreams. Moving on, Kara passed clockwise around the inner circle of people so like her friends, solemnly embracing each one, while her three companions did the same.

Lambert and the chief then moved back to the still-embedded staff at the centre of the circle. After a moment to make sure he had everyone's attention, Lambert began to speak.

'We have come to this ancient meeting place as representatives of our time, a time when mankind has laid waste to his home. We are here to seek your wisdom of the old ways, which we have largely discarded and forgotten. Over our planet this day other groups are connecting with their ancestors, as we all strive to achieve our intent: to live harmoniously with each other and our Mother Earth.'

Although he spoke in modern English, the people around seemed to understand, and Kara found out why once their chief began his reply. He spoke in an ancient tongue, but its meaning was somehow clear to her.

'We welcome you, our brethren. We are here for you in your time of need, but only you can make full use of the skills and intelligence passed down to you. We can remind you of what you once knew, but it is up to the people of your time to put those skills into practice. Our intentions will travel with you when you return, but we know, as you do, that your society has been corrupted by greed and a loss of connection. We must help your people replant their feet in the Earth to source the dragon's breath.'

He reached for his staff and slowly withdrew it from the stone. The image of King Arthur pulling the sword from the stone flicked across Kara's mind, but she had no time to dwell on the thought. She was swept up by the throng inside the circle as everyone began to retrace their steps back north towards Carragheen and Druidale. Fig and Silke were accompanying their counterparts, and Kara's came and put her arm through Kara's while the 'Paul' figure stood on her other side.

'My name is Meriel and you are Kara.' The woman's words translated themselves easily inside Kara's head. 'That means "friend" in our language.'

'And your name means "sea bright",' Kara exclaimed, feeling the sense of the words.

Meriel nodded. 'You and I are connected in time. I am who you are and you are who I am. Bran and I have been told by Selena,' she nodded towards Silke's companion, 'to teach you something of ourselves while we walk up to our village.'

Our village. Kara felt she was included in that term. Had she once lived there as Meriel?

'Yes,' Meriel answered her unspoken question. 'Our group of twelve is one of thousands on this world, who are connected in each life to each other. We are here to help each other through each life cycle, although we don't normally know this. It is normally only in the between times that we are aware of who we are.'

'So how do you know this now?' Kara asked, keeping up with the column of people striding purposefully up the well-trodden track. Meriel's arm was still tightly linked to hers, so they had to keep in step.

Bran spoke for the first time. 'Because we reached a level of knowledge that meant we could access all knowledge,' he replied patiently. 'But soon our culture will be destroyed and nearly everything will be lost to us. We know that here on Mann we will be safe for a while, but then it becomes too dangerous to be found with the knowledge. Only highly trained initiates will be allowed access to it. In your time knowledge has been allowed to leak out once more as the power of Rome has declined. More people are being encouraged to rediscover wisdom, and you are one of those, Kara, helped by your twelve-group here. The world was once closely connected by thought, language and custom, but too many changes have happened and your world has grown apart and fallen into decline. You must work with the many other world twelve-groups to re-establish the connection.'

'The connection with what?'

'With each other, with the Earth and with the other beings in the cosmos.'

'Other beings?'

'Yes. Though not all of them are worthy of connecting with, but if they are not worthy, they cannot connect.'

'Never?'

'No.'

'So who decides if they are worthy?'

'It is not who but what,' Meriel corrected her. 'And if you know the answer to that question, you are beyond the realm of earthly existence already.'

'So how do you know that?' Kara objected.

'There have been a very few who have reached that level and returned to instruct or remind us of our path,' Meriel explained. 'What we do know is that worthy life forms have three bodies: their physical, mental and spiritual bodies.'

'I see.' Kara remembered the dog accompanying Karl's predecessor. 'So is it not just humans here on Earth who have spiritual bodies? Intelligence counts for something, does it?'

'Of course, but not everything. In your time you have machines with intelligence but no spirit. There are creatures like that elsewhere with whom we cannot connect.'

Kara mulled over that for a moment. 'I've seen whales and dolphins that seem to have that spark, but you look in the eyes of a shark and it's lifeless.'

Meriel nodded. 'All matter has energy with which we can connect, but the higher species emit energy of a higher vibration level, strengthening the connection. You know when you're being watched as you feel the energy coming from their eyes. But you wouldn't know when a shark was watching you.'

It felt to Kara as though she already knew all this. Her browsing of the Internet had thrown up many of these arguments already. So Meriel was right in saying that their wisdom was being rediscovered, but too slowly it seemed.

They had reached the shoulder of ground between Carragheen and Beinn-y-Phott. Looking down the valley of Glen Cramman ahead of her, Kara expected to see the expanse of Sulby Reservoir before her, but of course, she realised with a sense of shock, she was seeing Druidale as it once was. Across the far hillside were dotted stone round houses with hearth smoke spiralling from holes in the centres of the thatched roofs. Nearby were pens for pigs and goats, with vegetable plots scattered about amongst the houses.

The procession left the Royal Road and headed down the valley towards a much larger, central round house. If this time is before the Romans came to Britain, Kara was thinking to herself, then this road pre-dates King Orry or Gorree, who was Norse. So how old is this path? What year is this?

Unlike her previous unspoken questions, these received no answers from either Bran or Meriel. They had left the main track to follow the path of the stream, and Kara found she had to watch her footing more on the uneven grass. Meriel too went quiet, concentrating on placing her steps. Ahead of them the dog kept close to his elderly yet robust master, apparently guiding him down the path. Selena was also at his side, and they were both talking with Silke. Kara wondered why it was that only the four of them had travelled here. Why had she come instead of someone like Rowena?

Bran answered her this time. 'The woman you call Rowena cannot pass through the connection yet. Her mind isn't yet as attuned as yours.' He realised Kara didn't understand. 'To make the connection your energy must be on the same frequency as ours. Most people's energies in your time have slipped to a lower frequency, and your brains have stopped functioning to their full capacity.'

'And mine was kick-started back to full-throttle when I went to New Zealand?'

'I understand the meaning of what you say, if not the words,' Bran laughed. 'But yes, your brain is at the right energy level to enable you to connect.'

'So what caused our brains to slip?'

'A long time ago, when the world was as one, there was a natural disaster,' Meriel told her. 'The old civilisation was virtually destroyed. A few survivors made their way to new lands and began again. To begin with all was well, but then it proved that some of the survivors' descendents had lost the connection. Corruption set in, both physical and moral, and where this came from we don't know, as we can't connect to it. What started out as high civilisation descended into bigotry and a desire by some to dominate over all other beings. Balance between male and female was lost, but in your time the female energy is starting to ascend back to its rightful place in some parts of your world.'

In front of her Bran paused as the path narrowed on a steeper section, and the procession had formed a temporary log jam. He turned and looked up at Kara. 'You are thinking now that our chief here is a man, but think on this. Three of your four are female.'

A flood of images poured through Kara's head. Once the world was paradise. The female and the serpent were connected then something came along to spoil it. Wisdom was lost when the female side of humanity was repressed. Wisdom was with the serpent and the serpent is connection. The dragon's breath is the energy that unites the world.

'It's obviously not true that only women connect,' Kara voiced her reasoning. 'But there's a lack of balance. More men need to…' A phrase from the Swinging Sixties sprang to mind. '… tune in and turn on!'

What happened to all that determination of the sixties and seventies to make the world a better place? Flower Power heralded the start of eco-awareness and nature conservation, moving away from the idea that the planet was there to be plundered. Then along came the eighties, the decade of greed and decadence, of the upsurge in fast-food outlets and the death of nutrition, of mass-consumerism and buying everything on credit. Everyone wanted the latest technological gadget to connect to. Now people were almost permanently wired to their favourite technology, becoming machines with no spirit.

'But our technology unites us too,' she continued her thoughts out loud. 'The Internet allows us to connect with each other. But perhaps some people depend on it too much now. We need to stand back from the machines and make the real connection in our communities.'

'Exactly,' Meriel agreed. 'Many people lose track of their community when cities become too big. They become isolated from the connection.' She waved her hand towards the large round house they were now close to. 'This is where our community connects with itself. Our paths connect us with other communities, and the ocean currents and star trails connect us with yet more communities around the world. We are not isolated here, even though we live on this island. Many of our people have journeyed to this place from faraway places, myself included. Thoughts and ideas travel the world, though generally at a much slower speed than in your day. Long-distance connections are only possible through our experienced shamans. That is when we meet in your dreams.'

Kara was beginning to feel overwhelmed by what she was learning. She had the feeling that the time-scale Meriel and Bran had spoken of was far greater than was currently understood. The whisperings of it were only now being unearthed and broadcast by a few outspoken researchers, for the most part derided by the establishment. Now the bookshops were filling with tales of Atlantis, of the Sphinx being far more ancient than supposed, of ancient technology lost over time. How long would it be before heresy became accepted as truth?

'Will it make a difference, knowing all this?' Kara asked Meriel.

'Not until your society fundamentally changes.'

'And how will that come about?'

Meriel looked abruptly away. 'That is not for us to tell you. The future isn't written exactly. I have only been telling you what is already in your head that you haven't yet fully understood. Your future is not in your head.'

The procession had stopped outside the large round house. Kara found herself ushered next to Fig, Silke and Lambert as they were welcomed, still wearing their oak and mistletoe crowns, into the smoky darkness of the round house.

CHAPTER EIGHTEEN

Her eyes grew accustomed to the dim light, and Kara was stunned by what she saw. The interior of the round house looked nothing like the display in the House of Manannan Museum in Peel. That interior had fur rugs on sleeping platforms, a dog lying by an open hearth and a rush-covered earth floor. The only similarity here was the open central hearth. This House of Manannan was more like the British Museum, containing artefacts and treasures seemingly from around the world. Exquisitely carved stone and wooden animals were displayed against walls covered by richly woven hangings. One of the wall hangings had what looked like Central American, geometric designs, while another was distinctly African with giraffe and antelope figures. To her absolute astonishment, she recognised an Australian aboriginal mural comprising many coloured dots in the form of a turtle. Whether the artefacts had actually come from overseas or been copied by means of remote viewing or astral travelling, Kara had no idea.

Occupying the centre of the hut was an enormous stone hearth made of five smooth blocks of granite. Occupying the central granite square was an elaborate wrought-iron grate full of burning logs. This was surrounded by four quadrilateral slabs that fitted together so exactly there was scarcely a gap between them. The whole design looked like a flat-topped pyramid seen from above. On one of the slabs was an earthenware flowerpot containing a healthy-looking specimen of mugwort. On another rested a polished, green malachite bowl containing water. The third slab had what Kara would have called a dream-catcher: a wooden frame woven with cob-web-like threads decorated with feathers. On the fourth slab was the most unexpected sight of all. It was a glowing glass or crystal orb reminiscent of the plasma globes popular back home as scientific *objets d'art*. Kara looked closely to see whether its light came from within or was merely a reflection of the firelight. There was no flickering of flames, she noticed. It held its own light.

Encircling the square of the hearthstones, in the manner of King Arthur's Round Table, stood a large number of ornately carved wooden chairs. These looked Chinese in design, even down to their embroidered silk cushions, as the chair backs were carved with chrysanthemums and the legs were in the form of dragons clutching pearls of wisdom in their claws. Kara counted exactly sixteen chairs, four to each quadrilateral's base, enough for each of the dozen inner ring participants and their four visitors.

Kara, Fig, Silke and Lambert were each directed to a chair next to their counterpart at the relevant cardinal point, so Kara faced Silke across the hearth. All the others were now seated as they had stood around the ring. Bran was to Kara's left and Meriel was on her right.

A hush fell around the circle as Manannan cast his eye around the assembly. 'Welcome to our selves from a time of destiny yet to come.' He gestured with both hands: east, west, north and south. 'I'm sure you have many questions about what you see here, so I will try to enlighten you briefly.' His powerful voice carried easily over the crackling of the logs, so everyone seated around the circle could hear him.

'We are one of several cultural-exchange centres around the world,' he began. 'Each continent has one or more centres like this. After the devastation long ago, certain key elements of knowledge survived with small groups of people scattered around the world. Other knowledge only survived patchily or not at all in some areas. In these centres we aim to gather together the surviving information and pass it on to those that feel the need for it. Not all the surviving cultures have the physical resources or even the will to use the information gleaned by us. That is their right. We do not force this knowledge on others, but their elders know it is here if they want it. Likewise it is here for future generations like yourselves to consult, once you have rediscovered the means of connection. We know that slowly, over the centuries, individuals will begin to find the connection and access knowledge. Then much of what is rediscovered will be lost again under the influence of Jerusalem and Rome. Certain societies become divided as men begin to fear what was formerly honoured in women, so that women and children are denied their rights and the connection weakens. War and conquest take over the planet, and mankind loses personal contact with the cosmic energy. Only in these secret places and in a few more enlightened cultures is contact retained.'

He looked directly at Silke. 'So you are wondering why I, as a man, am speaking for our community. Should not the women have a voice too?'

Silke nodded in assent that those had indeed been her thoughts.

'Society needs a leader to speak for it and coordinate decision-making,' Manannan explained. 'It so happens that this role fell to me at this time, while Selena is my aide. It is our custom to choose an appropriate younger leader from amongst us who is the opposite gender from the current leader. This deputy will inherit the leadership in due course, and acts as a balance to the current leader. In this way our society benefits from the strengths and wisdom of both sexes as well as achieving continuity.'

He now turned to Fig. 'I know your specialty is plants, and that Kara is concerned about ways to combat tree diseases. Selena will enlighten you there.' He moved his gaze to his quarter left. 'Silke, your interests are finding ways to help people combat unhealthy addictions, and also how better to establish connection. Torcull will help you with that.' He nodded at the man who resembled Henrik, who sat next to her, then twisted sideways in his chair. 'Lambert, you wish to improve your already great knowledge of divination and earth energy, and that is Herward's task.' Here he looked over the hearth to where Matt's double sat adjacent to Fig. Herward smiled at Lambert and bowed his head respectfully, which Lambert reciprocated.

'First, however, we need refreshment.' Manannan waved to the doorway and immediately the outer ring members entered the hut bearing trays of simple wooden bowls and goblets. Each bowl contained a selection of cold mutton, nuts, berries, dried fruit and pieces of cheese. There was also a small pile of white, salt-like powder and a chunk of brown bread crusted with mixed seeds. The bowls were passed around the seated occupants of the hut, along with goblets of some dark liquid. Kara sniffed at it, decided it could be some kind of wine, but refrained from taking a swig as she felt some formality was in the offing. She was right.

With no obvious sign from anybody, the twelve seated inner ring members made a toast. 'To wisdom and knowledge!' they cried in unison. The four visitors responded likewise.

As she tucked into the food in her bowl, Kara began to wonder for the first time what their other friends were doing now on the Old Tynwald Hill. How long would they stand there waiting? They would be tired, although surprisingly she no longer felt at all tired. She wished Paul had made it through here too, as she felt it was an experience they should be having together.

Bran interrupted her thoughts. 'You're thinking of your friend, my later self. He clearly hasn't come as far as you have, and that has been a problem, hasn't it?'

She nodded, her mouth full of nuts. Chewing rapidly she emptied her mouth. 'Yes, although I think it will help that his stepmother, Silke, is... knowledgeable is the only word I can think of that's appropriate. It's all about acquiring knowledge and a healthy body to open your mind, isn't it?'

'Yes, a fully functioning brain is essential.'

'And ours aren't fully functioning. We're possibly only using a fraction of our potential. It's like there's been a key chip missing in the circuit somewhere, and mine's been re-installed, but Paul's hasn't yet.' She looked closely at Bran, seeing Paul in him but not enough to stir any feelings, for which she was grateful. She didn't want to give Meriel cause for jealousy. She thought she noticed Bran's family resemblance in the elderly man opposite in Karl's position, and she asked Bran about it. 'Are you related to that man over there?'

'Yes.' He supplied the other answers she wanted. 'Raedwald is my father and Meriel is my partner. Likewise Selena cares for my father in his old age, but she is not my mother. Such relationships do not necessarily follow in each existence but, exceptionally this time, the relationships are all the same in your existence as in ours. That is why we think the strong connections formed, and why we have helped you here now to learn.'

'When I was in New Zealand I seemed to meet or dream about previous inhabitants of that land. Was that part of the connecting process?'

'Most likely. They sensed your presence and made contact, but you were not quite mentally prepared for it yet.'

'No, I certainly wasn't!' Kara laughed. 'I'm not sure I am now.'

She picked a walnut from the bowl on her lap and dipped it in the last of the white powder then sipped her drink. As she did so, she took a look around the circle and caught the eye of Martin's likeness here. He only vaguely resembled the hint of Native American version she knew, with his hawk-nose and dark eyes, but something about the way he held himself and his demeanour were convincing enough. He smiled at her warmly, and she wondered what his role here was. For a brief moment she saw the stars shining in his eyes, but just then

Lambert and Manannan rose from their seats and she had no time to ponder further as Selena rounded up Fig then Kara.

'Let me show you my workplace,' Selena said, leading them outside and across the hillside.

The small round house Selena led them to was more like what Kara would have expected from an apothecary's shop. Numerous earthenware jars were labelled with some kind of runic writing etched onto the surface, while bundles of dried herbs hung from nails in the wall posts. But it was none of these that Selena was interested in. Sitting them on a simple rush mat on the floor, she poured water into a heavy, bronze bowl engraved with mistletoe leaves and studded with berries made of polished moonstones and flowers of clear crystal shards. The water within sparkled with an ethereal inner light.

'Look in there, concentrate on the reflection of your face and ask yourself what you want to know,' Selena instructed them.

Fig shuffled forwards awkwardly on her bottom to get closer to the bronze bowl while Kara held back, allowing Fig first go. Fig seemed to know instinctively what to do and, after a couple of minutes' sitting there, Kara sensed Fig was in a kind of trance. Watching Fig's motionless body, Kara felt herself already in a pre-trance-like state, and wondered if the drink they had been given had some kind of hallucinogen in it.

Selena sat close to Fig, watching her progress carefully to make sure she was all right and not getting lost beyond the point of no return. After about ten minutes Fig stirred slightly. Selena put a hand on her shoulder as though grounding her back to the present, and Fig raised her head from staring into the bowl of water.

A broad grin covered her face as she felt herself coming back into her body, although she swayed slightly as though off balance.

'Well!' she finally managed to say. 'It's almost too much to take in. I hope I remember it all.'

'You will,' Selena reassured her. 'But now you know the path, you can visit again when you choose, as long as you have someone with you on this side to help you back.'

This last remark made Kara feel nervous. Was that why she had been stuck in her absent moments until someone came to wake her? Otherwise would she have stayed permanently 'away with the fairies'?

'Your turn, Kara. Are you ready? Just empty your mind of everything, except the questions you have.'

A picture of Frodo Baggins in Lothlorien looking into Galadriel's scrying dish flitted across Kara's mind, and she chased it out with pictures of dying oak trees. Her face stared back at her, expressionless, and she looked deeply into her own eyes.

She felt herself beginning to sway gently, and after a few moments she noticed the reflections of the wall posts looked more like oak trunks. She felt the wind blowing through the oaks as she swayed with their branches and heard every rustle of each leaf, the buzzing and chirping of each one of myriads of insects living and feeding there, and now she could even hear the healthy hum of the oak sap rising. The tree was talking to her with its vibrations, opening up its secrets. She noticed that ensconced securely on a branch nearby was an outcropping of mistletoe, tapping into the tree's hum and drawing it into itself.

One particular oak leaf drew her attention, and she focused on it. She could see the veins in each lobe and now she could see through the pores on its surface. Her vision magnified again, as she followed the air flowing into the leaf cells. Here the air was divided: oxygen passing to the cells' mitochondria for energy, carbon dioxide to the chloroplasts to combine with sunlight and water to manufacture sustenance. Then down the stem Kara passed, down the twig and branches and finally into the massive trunk itself she flowed, encountering fungal spores and bacteria living within. Down and down she travelled the seemingly never-ending tube ride, the tunnel widening then narrowing again, branching continuously as it became the root system. The tree's vibration had now developed a wobble instead of having a regular pulse, like something was out of phase. Kara sensed all was not well with the tree, but as she emerged from the tip of a root into the damp soil she encountered the tiny rootlets of a plant that hummed strongly to itself. The hum began to resonate with the oak's vibration, until gradually the vibrations synchronised and they hummed in unison. Kara followed the rootlets up to the surface of the soil and out onto the lobed leaves and yellow flowers of the greater celandine.

Kara lifted her face up to the sun and felt her thoughts rising up with the water vapour into the branches above her again. A hand on her shoulder halted her ascent, preventing her from re-entering the cycle through the oak tree.

In the reflection she saw Selena by her shoulder. 'Thank you,' Kara said turning to look at her rescuer. 'I think I was part of a never-ending story there.'

'That's why it's important to have someone with you when you travel across. That is also why your friends were needed with you at the Hill. Their presence will help you back.'

Kara moved her legs out from under her, where they were feeling quite cramped. Awkwardly she stood up, feeling pins and needles as the blood rushed back into her feet.

'Did you find out what you wanted?' Fig asked her.

'I'm not sure,' Kara replied hesitantly. 'I seemed to be experiencing the life of an oak tree. In fact, I felt I became the tree and experienced all the life living on it and within it. It was like being in an orchestra: one that played in tune to start with but then became discordant. I need to find the right conductor to get everybody playing in tune and in time again.'

Fig nodded excitedly. 'With what I learnt we can work together.'

Selena now approached the bowl with what looked like a bronze pestle, and began to drag it round and round the rim of the bowl until a note began to sound, resonating through the bowl and throwing up a pattern of spikes in the water where the reflecting wave peaks combined. Kara had seen a bowl like it in Sharon's shop in Arrowtown, described as a Tibetan singing bowl. The mellow tone seemed to penetrate through their bodies, enveloping the round house with pure sound until Selena stood back from the ringing bowl. The tone gradually subsided, the surface of the water settling again.

'The water also has the knowledge and the intention now,' she said, selecting two small crystal vials from a moss-lined basket. She filled the vials carefully from the bowl before sealing them with moulded wax. 'Water has memory,' she reminded Fig and Kara, handing them the vials. 'Make use of it.'

Kara left Selena's hut feeling like Lucy from *The Lion, the Witch and the Wardrobe* with her curing potion. She saw Lambert and Silke already assembled outside the main round hut, the twenty-four sentinels gathered to accompany them back to the Old Hill. Torcull stood with two small wicker baskets containing white doves suspended from a yoke across his shoulders. Kara wanted to ask what their purpose was, but the procession moved off, everone singing in harmony as they wended their way gently back up the valley towards Carragheen. By the time they reached the shoulder of the hill where they turned south to join the Royal Road, Kara had mastered the ancient words and the tune of two songs. They were travelling songs, seeking safe passage and return home. She hoped there was no doubt about their return.

*

'You came for knowledge and you return with it. May it serve you well,' Manannan told the four of them when they were gathered once more in their ritual places around the hill. It seemed higher and more impressive than Kara remembered it from dawn that morning.

First Bran then Meriel embraced her, passing her anti-clockwise this time around the circle as she bade farewell to the eleven other members of her twelve-group. Returning to her place she noticed dusk was starting to fall. They had somehow spent a whole day in this other time: that of an ancient civilisation on its outpost here in the very centre of the British Isles before the invasions by Romans, Anglo-Saxons, Vikings and Normans. The new scientific thinking of the Renaissance and Industrial Revolution had finally sent the people and their knowledge deep underground into the realms of legend. Only now did they feel able to resurface, as a new way of thinking was growing throughout the world by means of the all-connecting Internet. Minds were being opened, and old paradigms and dogma were being cast aside in the post-industrial world. The old ways were being re-examined and found to have worth. Connection with the cosmos was being re-established, and Kara was a part of it.

With the sun sinking over her left shoulder, Kara felt that mystical anticipation of imminent dusk when the wind drops and all goes quiet. In the gathering twilight Manannan stepped towards the centre of the circle where the omphalos stone sat expectantly. To the sound of the others' singing, he placed his staff in the hole at the top of the stone, just as she had seen him do before to open the connection between the worlds. He then beckoned Lambert, Silke, Fig and Kara in turn to join him around the stone. Closer to it now, Kara could see a carved serpent spiralling its way up the stone to the hole at the top. Just like the hill with the dragon on the cover of *Borrobil,* she thought. The other three had already put their hands on the upright staff held by the stone, so she reached for it too. An orb and sceptre, Kara's connecting mind reasoned.

There was a sudden clapping of wings above the sound of singing. Torcull had opened the lids to the wicker baskets, and four doves flew out and up over their heads. Kara looked up to follow their flight, the air overhead seeming to brighten and shimmer with a heat haze, as the dragon's breath wound its way up to the heavens where the doves had led.

CHAPTER NINETEEN

The shadows fell away to reveal her friends exactly as she had left them: Henrik and Julia were still filming and taking photos; Dolly was patiently sitting by Karl; Martin was talking to Paul. They were all exactly the same. No time had passed.

It was the well-known principle of Fairyland and legend, Kara realised, where time moves independently of the so-called real world. People who went off with the fairies or were abducted by aliens reportedly often experienced time passing at a different rate, whether faster or slower.

She looked around to catch her travelling companions' eyes, and Lambert seemed to raise a finger to his lips in a gesture of silence. She hadn't had a chance to discuss anything of their strange experience with the other three so far, and it was clearly to be kept a secret, at least for the moment.

Unaware of Kara's turmoil, Paul casually turned to her. 'So the sun's up, we're all pooped. Isn't it time to head back to the cars?'

'Yes, you're right. I'm shattered,' she admitted to Paul. The impact of all she had experienced had suddenly hit her, and she felt herself swaying with exhaustion.

Most of the others were already making their way back through the gorse bushes to the Millenium Way, but Martin seemed reluctant to leave the place. He stood staring up towards Carragheen, as though expecting something to appear.

'What are you looking at, Martin?' she asked, straining to see what it was he was fixated upon.

'I thought I saw lights up there for a moment,' he told her, 'but I can't have since it's broad daylight. It must be the sun reflecting off cars on the mountain road, though surely that cloud cover's in the way now?'

Or Martin saw a returning procession with lanterns in twilight, she thought to herself. Did he nearly make it across? If Martin saw lights, might something else show up on Henrik's video that human eyes hadn't noticed?

Paul slipped his arm through hers and began to lead her after the others, while Martin stood wistfully gazing north a few moments longer before following.

When they got back down to the cars, Paul, Karl and Silke were keen to be off to bed. After a hasty farewell to them, Kara grabbed Henrik while she had the chance.

'Before you rush off, Henrik, would you mind if I had a quick look at your video of when the sun came up over the hill? I'd just like to see what it looked like.'

'For sure.' He reached for his camcorder, which he had just put in the back of Rowena's car. After fiddling with it for a moment or two, staring at the screen, he handed it to Kara. 'It should be in the right place now. Press "play" here.'

Kara tilted the camera angle to get rid of glare on the screen then pressed the play button. She was aware of Fig and Martin peering over her shoulders as the screen showed the sun breaking over Slieau Ree and Keppel Gate. Henrik had then swivelled round to focus on the group standing on Kara's side of the Old Tynwald Hill, with his own and others' shadows imprinting darkly on the central area of grass and beyond. At that moment the air seemed to shimmer, and other shadows flitted very briefly across the grass. Kara concentrated hard on the screen, trying to control her excitement, but she saw nothing of herself, Lambert, Fig and Silke moving to the centre of the circle, or even back again, as the tape came to an end.

'Hang on a sec!' Martin grabbed the camcorder off her. 'Let me see that again.' Kara peered over his arm this time, Fig too. 'There!' Martin cried out excitedly. 'Did you see that? That kind of shiver or rippling in the centre.'

'No,' Fig responded quickly. 'I didn't see anything.'

So Fig wasn't going to admit to anything, Kara realised, wondering if she too ought to keep quiet. She desperately wanted to share her experience with someone, and felt cruel keeping it from Martin, who seemed so close to finding his own way. She held her tongue, however, allowing Martin the chance to elaborate.

'It looked like a wriggling worm coming straight up out of the ground and then shooting back in again.' He rewound the tape to play the scene over again. This time Henrik was showing an interest in what Martin thought he'd seen.

'Yes, I think I see what you mean,' Henrik declared. 'There's a sort of hazy line in the air just for a second.'

We're all seeing something slightly different, Kara thought to herself. She called to Rowena to take a look.

'Can you see what Martin and Henrik are seeing?' she asked, suspecting Rowena would probably see the most, if there truly were anything to see.

Martin played the scene yet again for Rowena to watch, and Kara studied her face as she peered at the small screen. Rowena frowned then asked to see it again.

'Well,' she finally said, as Henrik took back his camcorder. 'I agree with Martin. It does look like something comes out of the ground and goes back in again, but perhaps I'm just primed to see that now from what you said. I hardly think we can send it to the BBC as evidence of earth energies, though.'

Martin seemed disappointed at their response. As they began to disperse to their separate cars he asked Kara: 'You saw something, didn't you? Both you and Fig did, and you're not owning up to it.'

'What makes you think that?'

'I don't know. There just seems to be an air of conspiracy between you suddenly.'

Kara was excited by what Martin was picking up on. Had he been mysteriously affected by the place somehow, like she had been in Doubtful Sound? Had he suddenly become more tuned in?

Despite Lambert's caution, she decided to confide in Martin. 'We'll talk about it later. I can scarcely think straight right now, I'm that tired, and Tina looks like she's keen to drive us home.'

Martin gave a broad grin of triumph. 'I thought something happened. Those lights I saw: were they aliens, fairies or what?'

'Later, Martin,' Kara promised.

*

On the hill Kara saw the column of spiralling light glow brighter as the dragon's breath reached up to the stars. She felt the energy of the cosmos pulsing with it in harmonic waves, like the rhythmic tune of some ancient song.

'Music and harmony are the universal language,' the cosmos was saying to her. 'Your civilisation is singing out of tune with your earth. Disconnect from your selfish ways and reconnect to your brothers and

sisters, or you will tread the same path as those who went before in the long-gone aeons. We are trying to help you, but it is your responsibility to open up your minds and listen. We are here amongst you to offer advice and share with you what you need to know. You must just allow yourselves to hear what we have long been telling you. Harmonise, and your powers will be amplified. Choose not to listen, and discord will shatter you.

'The message is not new,' the cosmos continued. *'It has been sent numerous times before, but many are still not listening, or interpret it in their own fashion and create discord in the process. The message is simple: harmonise with all things and all peoples. That does not mean all must sing in unison. The world is a choir or an orchestra of individuals, who can make a beautiful harmonic sound if they can feel the music.'*

The spiral of light began to fade from the top and appear to plummet back into the earth. Kara felt the message vibrating down the earth's energy lines outwards to travel the world.

*

There was an email from Martin awaiting Kara when she woke later that afternoon. He was clearly desperate to hear what she had to say, and wanted to meet up for dinner that evening. However there was also a text message from Paul on her mobile suggesting the same thing. She pondered her dilemma as she stepped into the shower.

They were all meeting up at eleven tomorrow morning for the photo shoot of Silke and Karl at the new reserve site, followed by the afternoon orchid walk at the Curraghs. Reluctantly, Kara decided to put off Paul until then, feeling disloyal to the man she had come to think of as her soul mate. But Martin had been with her longer on this journey of discovery, and she felt a burning need to discuss everything with him and to help him on his way, just as she had been helped by others.

After hurriedly getting dressed, she sent a text back to Paul asking if he'd mind waiting till tomorrow for dinner. She gave no explanation, hoping he wouldn't delve too deeply, as the situation was rather awkward. She then emailed Martin and told him she would meet him outside his hotel – one of the smaller Victorian boarding houses at the back of Douglas's promenade – at seven-thirty.

By seven-fifteen she was dressed in jeans and a sparkly red top, heading off in her car down to the prom and along Douglas Bay to its northern end, where she could park easily on the road. From there it was short hop to Martin's hotel.

He was waiting outside on the pavement, sniffing the sea air and watching the battling gulls on the rooftop opposite. 'Feeling refreshed?' he asked as she joined him.

'A bit, though still slightly bombed out, like jet-lag. I'm not used to staying up all night.'

'I am. I sometimes have a publishing deadline I have to meet, and sometimes, when I'm visiting my father's relatives in New Mexico, I stay up just to look at the stars.' He cast his eye around the back road full of parked cars and boarding houses. 'So where do you suggest we eat? I'm still on budget-tourist mode, so nothing too flash.'

'Within easy walking distance we've got Chinese, Indian, The Queen's pub or Port Jack Chippy. The choice is yours.'

'Chippy? Is that fish and fries?'

Kara nodded. 'Fish and chips, yes.'

'The traditional British vacation choice. Let's go for that.'

'If you really want, you can try the Manx specialty of chips, cheese and gravy,' Kara suggested, leading him back down to the prom.

'Um, maybe just the fish and chips.'

They had a short walk north, past the tram-horse stables and electric-tram terminus, then crossed the road to a viewpoint above the small rocky promontory of Port Jack. Here they decided to sit on the bench for a while to soak up the flavour of the long sweep of Douglas Bay in the early evening.

A few jet-skis were plying the water, avoiding a fleet of racing dinghies, while on the beach locals and tourists alike were strolling, playing or even testing the water. Bright red Manx flags flew from white flagpoles the length of the prom, and in the distance the municipal sunken gardens added their vibrant colour to the scene. The nearby flax plants growing amongst New Zealand cabbage trees, however, could have made them think they were back in the southern hemisphere.

'It's a shame they don't get sunsets here in Douglas,' Kara said. 'Peel is the place to go in the evening. Sunset City, the locals call it.'

'They get the benefit of dawn here, though,' Martin replied, chasing away a gull that thought they might have chips to steal.

'Speaking of which, I can't wait any longer to hear what happened this morning.'

'Aren't you hungry?' Kara was still having doubts as to whether she ought to tell Martin everything, as Fig and Lambert hadn't said a word to anyone, and Silke had whisked her husband away to bed without revealing anything either.

'Yes, but I'm even hungrier for knowledge at the moment.'

The word 'knowledge' decided her.

'Right. Are you sitting comfortably? Then I'll begin.' Kara tried to think where she should begin. 'You know you said you thought you saw a fuzzy line going into the ground? Well you did. It was an energy line, qi, dragon's breath or whatever you like to call it. A portal even. That's the best way to describe it, I suppose. But only four of us were tuned in to its frequency.'

She paused to draw breath and see how Martin was taking it so far. He nodded encouragingly. 'Go on. Who were the other three?'

'Lambert, Fig and Silke. I thought Rowena might have been more likely to respond than me, but maybe she was the trained one who stayed behind to help us get back.' She saw Martin starting to look confused and got back on track. 'The rest of you started to become shadows when other shadows from another age or dimension appeared, like we were in a transition phase.'

She continued explaining how they had then passed through the transition, had spent the day with the people there then returned to the present to find no time had passed.

'But none of you said anything!' Martin protested. 'Why ever not?'

'It was Lambert. He put his finger to his lips, like it was a secret, then Fig said nothing about what we saw on the video.'

'You're right. She didn't. So why does it have to be secret, and why are you telling me?'

The pestering gull flew back with several mates, standing in a line on the iron railing and eyeing the pair up, as though they might be tasty morsels.

'Shall we head for the chippy?' Kara suggested. 'I'm getting hungry.'

'OK, but I want an answer to that question.'

They crossed back over the road and made the short walk up to the Port Jack shops. They avoided discussing the question while they waited for their takeaway fish and chips. They then walked into nearby

Onchan Pleasure Park and found a park bench to sit on, where they could eat with their fingers out of the paper in true seaside fashion.

'Right. Time's up,' Martin told her. 'What's all this about?'

As she ate the first few chips, Kara tried to think how best to answer Martin's question in detail. 'It's about us: the twelve of us who were on the hill. We're all connected by time and fate.' She popped another chip in her mouth as she considered her next statement. 'Somehow Lambert, Fig, Silke and I went to a different time or dimension. There we met up with twelve people, who were ourselves and you others at another time. There was even a dog that could have been an ancestor of Dolly.'

'You're sure they weren't aliens pretending to be us?' Martin asked in all seriousness.

Kara was quite taken aback by his suggestion. 'I've no idea! I had no reason to think they weren't human, but I suppose it could all have been some kind of mind projection. Or perhaps we're descended from aliens.' She broke off with a laugh. 'Oh for goodness sake, Martin, you've got me all confused now. I'll just have to tell it as I experienced it.'

She began to relate everything that had occurred as Martin sat silently now, absorbing the details.

'I honestly don't know why Lambert indicated we should keep quiet and why Fig didn't say anything,' Kara concluded. 'I can only assume that this whole thing has been kept secret for centuries, and that's what they're used to doing. But I get the distinct impression that now is the time when the secret is ready to be revealed, and that I was told as such, so that's why I'm telling you what happened.' She popped a piece of battered fish into her mouth, and the thought instantly crossed her mind of the dire warnings about ocean fish stocks running out by mid-century.

'I don't seem to be able to do anything now without finding all the interconnections,' she told him. 'Everything we do affects everything else, so what will be the effect of me telling you all this?' She looked at him directly and found her answer. 'You're a journalist. You have the power to influence people. Too many journalists have to toe the editorial line and avoid the real issues. So where do you stand?'

'Me?' he asked innocently. 'I'm a travel writer. I don't have much influence.'

'Oh, but you could,' she replied. 'And I think you intend to branch out, don't you?' She realised she sensed in him a burning drive to make his mark. 'You're going to take this as far as you can go, aren't you?'

He ate a few chips, nodding gently as he chewed, gazing across the rooftops to the Irish Sea beyond. 'You know I saw the lights on the hill. I saw the people too, and today I dreamt about my father's people – the Navajo.' His gaze never shifted from the sea on the horizon. 'The elders spoke to me, like yours have spoken to you. It's like I'm on the way to being connected; something sparked up in me on that hill and I definitely feel in touch with something that wasn't there before. They told me we all have this ability, and now I must use mine.' He finally looked directly at Kara. 'Tell me, who was that me you met in that other time or place? Was I Navajo or European like my mother? What was I like?'

'You seemed more European, but I didn't get to speak to you. You gave me a nice smile, and I somehow got the impression you were the chief stargazer or astronomer.'

A slow smile of recognition spread across his face. 'It was the stars that led me to travel,' he told her. 'As a child I used to watch them in the dark desert sky, and I wanted to follow their path over the horizon to see where they would lead me. That's partly why I wanted to visit the Southern Hemisphere – to see the hidden stars.' He looked quizzically at her again. 'And what were you there?'

Kara absently fed a few chips into her mouth as she struggled to recall anything about Meriel that gave away her role in society. 'It's strange but I never discovered what Meriel did. She was one of the inner-circle, was the partner of Paul's equivalent and took me under her wing there, as did all our other personas. But it was Selena, Silke's counterpart, who showed me how to access the information about trees. I really don't know much about Meriel.'

'So connect with her now and see if you can feel her,' Martin suggested.

'Can I do that?' Kara asked in surprise.

'I don't know. It just occurred to me that you should be able to connect with all knowledge if you put your mind to it somehow.'

Kara laughed. 'Yes, that's the crux of the problem: the "somehow".' Intention. The word flitted across her brain, and she said it out loud. 'Intention. I have to have the intention strongly in my mind. I have to concentrate on it and be disconnected from this time. I'll dream it tonight.'

Martin looked at her in amazement. 'Did you know you were going to say that?'

'No. It just sort of... came out,' Kara told him. 'Like I was repeating somebody's answer.'

The gulls had found them again and began to squawk noisily, jumping up and flapping their wings in an effort to reach the remaining fish and chips in the papers on their laps.

'Pesky birds!' Martin swore at them. 'Sea-rats!'

Kara whistled loudly to counter the hex before explaining: 'You mustn't say that word here. It's bad luck. You have to say sea-longtails.'

He laughed. 'You don't believe that, surely?'

'No, but it becomes a habit. Like greeting the fairies.'

They hurriedly finished their fish and chips then stuffed the papers firmly in a waste-bin, so the gulls couldn't pull them out.

'Let's walk down through Summerhill Glen. The lights should be coming on by now,' Kara suggested. 'Then perhaps we can have a drink at The Queen's pub.'

They began walking up through Onchan Park towards the top end of Summer Hill Road. Martin seemed deep in thought, so Kara left him to muse. By the time they had walked up to Governors Road and past the Lieutenant Governor's residence, hidden behind its high hedge, he was ready to talk.

'Either the fairies are real or they're not. Either what we've been talking about is true, and that somehow we've accessed another time or dimension, or we're living in a fantasy based on all the reading we've done recently. Our dreams could merely be our brains using and processing the information we've read, and not messages from elsewhere. Or...' He paused to indicate a completely new line of thought. 'We're being telepathically contacted by extra-terrestrials, who have some secret agenda of their own and have taken on our identities as ancestors, so they appear less alien to us. In which case, are they friendly or not?' Martin shook his head in despair at too many weird possibilities. 'Do we actually have any tangible proof that what we've experienced is real?' he asked Kara finally.

'I've felt something real, the connection or whatever it is. It only occurs at certain special places, and people most definitely tell me I'm away with the fairies when it happens. I can't be creating that myself, surely?'

They had reached the stone-arched entrance to Summerhill Glen, which led steeply down through woodland to Queens Promenade below. Throughout the glen were frames lit with light bulbs in the form of giant butterflies, animals and even a dinosaur, giving a surreal feel to the place.

They stood in front of a giant bird, hearing the distant roar of the Douglas traffic but alienated from it in a secret, shadowy world. The stream flowing past them had an energy all of its own, and Kara felt her feet tingling. She grabbed hold of Martin's arm.

'Do you feel it?'

'Tingling?'

'Yes,' she breathed. 'It's here too: the connection. Perhaps it's the stream.'

'Let's try then.'

There was a pool of water where the stream became shallower, the lights reflecting on its surface. Remembering Selena's scrying bowl, Kara told Martin: 'Look into the pool. It might help.'

As Kara stared intently at her reflection in the flickering pool, she thought of Meriel. Random thoughts kept popping into her head, and she struggled to clear her mind, staring ever harder at her reflection and blocking out the noise of present day Douglas. Gradually, after a few minutes, the background noise receded, replaced by a ringing in her ears. It was a constant high-pitched tone, its volume rising and falling in waves, and she felt herself swaying gently in the waves. Subtle changes began to take shape in the reflection of her face; her hair darkened and lengthened, her lips became fuller and her eyebrows more arched, but her eyes remained the same, staring back at her from the pool. She was now looking at Meriel, and Meriel's thoughts became hers.

It was like what she had experienced while phoning Paul. But instead of Paul, she was now experiencing Meriel's world through Meriel's senses. And what Kara seemed to have chosen to home in on, was Meriel's relationship with Bran. Unfolding before her eyes was a dimly lit round house, a glowing hearth and a pile of woollen blankets. The aroma of sweet wood smoke filled her nostrils followed by a warm, roast-chicken scent of male flesh, as Bran's smiling face and bare torso loomed over her. It was a moment of such intimacy that Kara's concentration broke. Her stomach lurched, and she abruptly found herself staring again at her own reflection, feeling flushed, aroused and a Peeping Tom.

She breathed deeply and shook her head in amazement, not wanting to let go of the memory of what she had experienced, but feeling she ought to for decency's sake.

She stepped back from the pool and looked towards Martin. He was still standing staring into the pool, motionless and lost to this world. Kara guessed he was like she had been the first few times she made the connection, and wondered whether he would make it back of his own accord, or whether she would have to disturb him to help him back. She decided to wait a bit longer, although she was unsure how long she had been away with the fairies.

Is that what fairies are, she wondered, memories of a long-lost people with mental abilities and skills that had become lost and hidden over time? Or were they a people who possibly still existed and were now trying to consolidate their power again after so many centuries of persecution? Was she one of them without knowing it, or were they gaining access to the modern world by using people such as herself? She sighed out loud in despair that she was only adding to Martin's long list of possibilities as to what this was all about.

Her sigh seemed to reach Martin, who gave a lurch and came back to himself. He looked confused and dazed, so Kara gave him a moment or two to collect his thoughts before asking eagerly: 'Well? What did you see?'

Poor Martin could scarcely contain his excitement. 'I was travelling at high speed through the stars, like something out of Star Trek,' he gabbled to her. 'And then I was positioned above the Earth, looking down, and I could see the continents and everything. I could choose to home in on somewhere and I was there, so I visited home in New Mexico. But then I was over the Andes and the Himalayas, like I was called to the high places. Lastly I was in Turkey, on what seemed like Mt Ararat. The sky was clear and full of stars, some of which were moving.'

'Moving?' Kara asked him. 'How do you mean?'

'Like satellites,' he explained, 'but faster.'

'What do you think that means?'

'Your guess is as good as mine. I could suggest a number of explanations, ranging from meteors to light orbs nearer the ground, to UFOs, to stars changing their positions, to...' He broke off with a shrug. 'Did you see anything?'

Kara found herself blushing. 'Too much. I saw Meriel and Bran – together, if you know what I mean,' she added coyly.

'Wow! Like a pornographic movie, you mean?'

'Hardly pornographic,' Kara protested. 'Just an intimate moment. But why on earth should I have seen that?'

'Oh come on, Kara. It's obvious, isn't it? You saw what you wanted to see: what you want to see happening between you and Paul.'

Kara could hardly deny it. 'So you're saying that was just wishful thinking on my part?'

Martin shrugged eloquently.

'But it was so real!' she protested. 'I was there. I could see, hear and even smell the place.'

'Well then, perhaps you were being told to get on with your life and stop prevaricating. Poor Paul's hardly taken his eyes off you, and you've not had a minute alone together yet.'

'Thanks for being so honest, Martin,' Kara replied somewhat frostily.

'It's the truth, isn't it?' he grinned, amused by her prudishness. 'You don't want to stay a spinster all your life, do you? And if you two are supposed to be an item, like Meriel and Bran, then get on with it.'

Kara had to laugh at his forthrightness. 'It's written in the stars, you mean?'

'You said that, not me.'

'Well, we'll just have to see, won't we?'

'Somehow I don't think you'll be waiting long.' He looked down the path through the glen where the lights twinkled through the branches. 'Now, how far off is that pub you mentioned? After all that space travel, I need a beer.'

'It's not far. Come on then, Buzz Lightyear. To infinity and beyond!'

'You know your kid's movies, don't you?'

'Obviously so do you, if you know what I'm talking about.' She set off down the path, closely followed by Martin.

'Just don't go following any white rabbits!' he muttered loudly enough for her to hear.

CHAPTER TWENTY

Silke and Karl's official photo shoot and brief tour of the new nature reserve was followed by lunch at the nearby, cliff-top Niarbyl café, a popular watering point for tourists, with its view out across towards Northern Ireland. Kara had booked a table for them all except Fig, who was joining Lambert at a meeting with some members of the Native Oak Group that morning. Everybody seemed hungry enough to order a full meal, rather than a quick snack. While Silke and Karl chatted to Vicky Costain about the new reserve, Kara was bombarded by numerous questions from Julia and Henrik relating to island matters. Martin threw in the occasional question too, but Paul seemed engrossed in eating his lunch and looking at the view from the window. The lunch party was going with such a swing, that Kara was sorry to have to break it up, but they had to move on to have time for their orchid walk.

A procession of cars followed Vicky's official truck up the west coast towards Ballaugh and the Curraghs Meadows. At the rear of the convoy Kara was riding with the Drieslers as navigator for them, in case they got separated from the others. It was just as well she did, as the traffic lights at Ballacraine by St John's worked against them, and they were held up for a minute. A horsebox got ahead of them, which proved impossible to pass. Finally it turned right off the TT course at Cronk-y-Voddy and by then Vicky and the others were well out of sight. At Ballaugh Kara told Paul to turn left off the main TT road and head up the lanes to Close Sartfield, the main orchid meadow shown to visitors.

Fig was waiting for them with the others in the car park and, once they were all ready, Kara let Vicky present her usual guided tour.

Despite the official tours finishing the previous day, the Curraghs Meadows were still the promised mass of pink and purple, heath spotted orchids. Dotted amongst them were golden-yellow meadow buttercup and cat's ear, and white and yellow ox-eye daisies. The meadow boundary was marked by the grey-green of the boggy, willow *curragh* and, beyond the trees, rose the central hills clothed in heather, bracken and gorse. Purple and yellow seemed the colours of choice in the Manx landscape.

Henrik and Julia were busy taking video and photos as Vicky began her talk, while Martin just stood transfixed, marvelling at the beauty of the place.

'This land, although it looks natural, is actually carefully managed,' Vicky explained, leading them around the edge of the meadow. 'Where we're standing was a lake thousands of years ago, which gradually filled in with sand and gravels, choking the vegetation and forming peat. Over the last few centuries this peat has been dug up, recreating a few of the wetlands here today. These meadows were reclaimed from the *curragh* by drainage ditches and used for pasture and agriculture, but in the nineteen sixties and seventies the importance of the area as a wetland was recognised. Manx National Heritage now owns a large part of the wet *curragh* area and, since the eighties, we at the Manx Wildlife Trust have acquired half a dozen separate areas of meadow, some of which were under potato and turnip cultivation. We now manage these in the traditional way to maintain the orchid species and other wild flowers you see here.'

Only Martin was too young and unfamiliar with hay meadows to know what that was. 'What do you mean by "the traditional way"?'

Vicky had been about to explain anyway as part of her usual spiel. She spoke directly to Martin, aware that the others in her party were familiar already with the old farming methods.

'We let the wildflowers grow in spring and early summer and, once they have seeded, we cut, dry and remove the hay to feed to stock over the winter. Then we let the Loaghtan sheep in to graze from November to March to keep the turf short, ready for the grass and flowers to grow again in spring.'

Martin nodded appreciatively as he stared out over the purple meadow. 'So many of them. Like stars in the sky.'

'And each of those hundred thousand orchids produces hundreds of thousands of tiny seeds which can't germinate by themselves,' Vicky added. 'Orchids need to grow with a fungus that feeds them initially before the orchid grows leaves.'

As Vicky went on to explain to the group the needs of the orchid, Kara thought about the vast numbers of orchid seeds in that one meadow alone. Martin was right. They were like stars in the sky, each with a potential for life, given the right conditions. Looking up she noticed a hen harrier flying in low towards the willow *curragh* and alerted her visitors to it.

By the time the tour was finished they were ready for afternoon tea at the nearby Wildlife Park. Leaving her holidaying visitors there, Kara returned to the office with Vicky after promising to meet Paul for dinner at seven. As Martin had so rightly reminded her, she and Paul had not been alone together since his arrival on the island, and Kara sensed his growing impatience. She booked a table for two at Bar George, within easy walking distance of her house and Paul's hotel, before buckling down to work for the remainder of the afternoon, trying to concentrate on mundane reports when her head was whirling with fantastic notions.

*

She had chosen Bar George, formerly the church opposite's Sunday school and meeting hall, because it was large and could be noisy. A quieter, more intimate restaurant was not suitable for the conversation she could foresee, although she preferred The Bistro's cosy atmosphere. Next time, she thought as she set off through the narrow back streets of Douglas to meet up with Paul outside the Sefton Hotel on the promenade.

He was standing on the steps outside, waiting for her and watching the evening parade of joggers and dog-walkers along the prom. When he spotted her approaching his smile was so like Bran's in its openness, but warmer and unreserved.

Without hesitation she reached up and kissed him on the lips.

'Well, that's better!' Paul said. 'You were so obviously in "official mode" today that I didn't dare get close to you. Besides, I thought I'd lost you to a younger rival yesterday.'

'Martin, you mean?' she replied, engaging her arm in his and steering him back the way she had just come. 'No. We just had to compare notes on what happened on the hill yesterday morning.'

'Oh?' Paul queried. 'And what exactly did happen on the hill?' He sensed her excitement. 'Did I miss something? Like at the Rollright Stones?' he ventured, her flushed face and sparkling eyes telling him something important was afoot.

'Paul, I can do it! I can cure the oak trees, I know it!'

It had all come out in too much of a rush. She had meant to explain everything slowly and carefully so he would fully understand what had happened, and now she'd blown it.

To her surprise and gratitude, he seemed pleased. 'Really? When did you discover how to do that?'

She was more cautious now. Paul wasn't quite on the same track yet, unlike Martin. She was only too aware of his previous concern in Oxford at her more outlandish statements. As they headed up towards Chester Street and the law courts, she knew she must tell him the truth. But was the truth palatable?

'Paul, you remember what you saw at the Rollright Stones?'

'That strange mist you called the dragon's breath, you mean?'

'Yes. Did you not see that on the hill at dawn yesterday?'

He stopped abruptly and turned her to face him. 'Is that what this is all about: more "faery magick"?'

Kara's heart sank. Too much the scientist, he wasn't going to believe her. But he surprised her.

'Well, yes. I did think I saw something,' he admitted sheepishly, resuming walking. 'But nobody else said anything, so I thought I was mistaken.'

Kara breathed again. 'If you hadn't hurried off, you'd have seen it on Henrik's video. It just wasn't clear enough to persuade disbelievers.'

'Really? And Martin saw it too, didn't he? Is that what you had to discuss with him?'

'He saw a bit more than that, but not nearly as much as Lambert, Fig, Silke and me.'

'Silke? She didn't mention anything.'

'No, she wouldn't have. She, Fig and Lambert seemed to think we should all keep quiet about what happened. But I thought otherwise, and Martin agrees. The time has come when more people should know what there is to know. It is coming out slowly, but people aren't believing it yet.'

'And you think I'm one of those? A disbeliever.'

She looked up at his face and saw interest rather than mockery. 'You can't disbelieve what you don't know about, Paul. Over dinner I'm going to tell you exactly what happened, just as I told Martin yesterday. You can then go and check it out with Silke, if you like, and see if she confirms or denies it. But if she denies it, I won't know where I stand.'

She guided him past the imposing new law courts, adjacent to the white 'wedding cake' House of Keys, the island's parliament building. Crossing over Prospect Hill they were soon at Bar George. The place was half full, the noise of chatter echoing round the stone walls and lofty ceiling. Kara recognised a face or two amongst the clientele, but that was normal on the island. No relationship could be kept secret here. They ordered glasses of wine and their meal at the room-length bar then settled at their table with their drinks.

'So, I'm sitting waiting for an intelligent and beautiful woman to persuade me to join the ranks of the believers in whatever it is they believe,' Paul said. 'But first we must toast the fairies, without whom none of this would have been possible.'

'You're mocking now, Paul,' Kara reprimanded him lightly.

'No I'm not. It's true isn't it?'

He was right. She nodded and raised her glass. 'To Themselves!'

'To Them's elves,' he repeated. 'Who is Them, by the way?'

Kara rolled her eyes in exasperation and had to laugh. 'Let's be serious now.'

'I'll try.'

'No, really.'

'Alright.' Paul composed his expression into one of attentiveness. 'Tell me about the dragon's breath of Old Tynwald Hill.'

Once more Kara launched into her tale of visiting another time, or dimension, inhabited by people just like themselves. She told him about the other Paul and Kara, called Bran and Meriel, and how Selena/Silke had shown her how to access the inner secrets of the oak tree.

'I feel I now have a very strong connection with trees, and I can harness that connection to try to put right what is wrong with them,' she explained.

'Just by intent?'

'No, I think it's more than that. Possibly something to do with replacing the disease with a memory of the tree's healthy state, but I won't be sure until I try. So we've got to go and visit some sick oak trees soon, and see if I can do anything.'

'It might not show straight away. It could take time for the leaves to grow back,' he postulated.

'Possibly. But I feel certain I would know, somehow, that all was well again.'

'And if nothing happened and all this is a figment of your overactive imagination sparked by too much surfing the Internet?'

'Martin and I discussed that very issue, but we're convinced it's real. We both tried to access that other time or place yesterday evening.' Too late she realised she might have to tell Paul what she had seen. 'Martin saw a journey through the stars,' she hurried on, 'which ties in with his other self possibly being their chief astronomer.'

'But couldn't that just be because he knew that, so he saw what he was primed to see?' Paul argued.

'Exactly what we thought, but it was just all too real to be imaginary. We really felt like we were there.' She could see Paul was still dubious and had to concede: 'If Silke, Fig or Lambert won't admit to anything, then I have no evidence.' Her hand abruptly flew to her mouth as she remembered something crucial. 'The vial! I totally forgot about the vial containing the memory-water.'

'That sounds useful,' he quipped.

'No, seriously. Selena gave Fig and me a vial of water each, laced with our memories of our scrying experiences. A bit like homeopathic liquids,' she explained eagerly. 'I'd totally forgotten about it until just now.'

'So where is it then?'

Kara looked blank at first then deep in concentration as she tried to remember what she had done with it. 'It must be in a pocket of the clothes I was wearing. I can't think where else it could be.'

'In your handbag?'

'I had a smaller one with me: an evening bag. It's at home.'

'Then we'll have to go and hunt it out, won't we?'

Suddenly Kara could see where that might lead them and she smiled. From his smile she knew he had the same thought.

Twilight was falling by the time they had walked arm in arm back to Kara's house. The trees on the railway bank below rustled with a light breeze blowing up the river valley. She opened her front door and switched on the hall light.

'Welcome to my pad. Do we begin our search for the vial first, or do I put the kettle on?'

'Kettle on and we can search while it boils. It shouldn't take long. It's either in your clothing or your handbag.'

'Come upstairs, then, and we'll have a look.'

*

The kettle boiled and Kara put two spoons of tea leaves into the pot before filling it with water. While the tea brewed she sliced some wholemeal bread and popped it in the toaster then laid a tray with plates, knives, a jar of Bovril, the toast, butter and an avocado to slice and finally two mugs of tea.

Back upstairs she put the tray on her dressing table and drew her bedroom curtains to let in the daylight.

'Good morning, sleepyhead!' she called cheerily to the figure dozing still in her bed.

Paul stirred and slowly opened his eyes. 'What time is it?'

'Seven. I'm due at a meeting at nine-thirty and I've things to prepare.'

He sat up. 'And I'd better get back to the hotel soon, or my father will start to fret, thinking I've been kidnapped or something.'

'What, on the Isle of Man? Things like that don't happen here.'

'Well, you claim you were spirited away by… whatever it was.'

She handed him the tray and got back into bed next to him. 'It's a shame we couldn't find the vial. Perhaps I dropped it on the way back from their village. The path was rather uneven.'

'Yes, perhaps you did. We'll have to ask Fig if she's still got hers.'

Kara took a sip of tea and began to butter her toast. 'You don't believe me, do you?'

'Not yet,' he admitted. 'But I don't see why I should disbelieve you either. I rather want to believe there's some grand answer to everything. But proof is never given with these great mysteries, is it?'

'Apparently not. But perhaps Selena was showing me how to create my own memory-water. There wasn't much of it in the vial. I'd have soon used it up if I tried pouring it on sick trees, or whatever I'm supposed to do with it.'

'You don't know?'

'No. It'll probably come to me in a dream, how I'm supposed to use it.'

'Ah. Indeed.' He took a bite of toast. 'Nice bread this.' He took another bite. 'I like having breakfast in bed with you. We should do it more often.'

'We will,' she assured him. 'It's written in the stars, according to Martin.'

'What, that you and I are an item together? He told you that?'

She heard an edge of resentment in his voice at Martin's apparent intrusion in their private lives. 'No. He just agreed with me that it was so. According to Meriel, you and I apparently always find each other in whatever life we live, but not necessarily as partners. But this time we most definitely are, she said. And your father and Silke likewise. They were meant to be together.'

'Oh, so my mother had to die first.'

There was nothing Kara could say, and she wished now she hadn't brought up the subject of Karl and Silke to distract him from her mistake in mentioning Martin's name.

'It is intriguing, though,' Paul conceded, seeing his words had upset her. 'It gives some reason for her dying young, if it had to be so in the grand scheme of things.'

Kara smiled her thanks at his generous gesture. 'Maybe there's far more to it than that. Maybe she was needed elsewhere.'

'She had a beautiful soul, my mother. She steered my father through very difficult times.'

'Then perhaps she was needed for other good deeds.'

'Highly likely,' Paul agreed, swigging down the last of his tea. 'Now, who gets to use the bathroom first?'

*

Paul had left her house saying he would organise something for them to do that evening. To her surprise, later that day, she received a text from him saying they were invited, along with his parents, to Lambert's for dinner. Apparently Fig would also be there.

It certainly wasn't going to be the intimate dinner for two that Kara had expected after last night, and she wondered who had initiated the arrangement. At least, she consoled herself, it was a chance to discuss events with the chief protagonists, as well as a further opportunity to get to know Paul's parents better before they returned to Germany.

She knew Martin was busy exploring Ramsey and staying in the north tonight, while Julia and Henrik were doing their own thing from now on. So it was most definitely a gathering of the chosen ones, or so she was starting to think of them, with Paul and Karl in attendance too. She was just grateful that Paul's text message had come after her morning's office planning meeting, as for the remainder of the day she kept hopping up and down from her desk, unable yet again to settle at anything. It seemed to have become a common problem since her New Zealand holiday. Her mind always seemed to be on matters other than her job, especially on such a lovely sunny day as today. She would far rather have been out showing Paul and his parents the island's beauty spots, but she only had a few days of her annual leave remaining, which she wanted to keep available for long weekends 'Across' with him.

That was the main problem with living on an island, she thought looking wistfully out of her window at the sunshine outside: it cost so much and took so long to get across to the mainland. Still, it had its compensations in other ways; it kept the crowds away.

The sun was still shining brightly when she tidied her desk at the end of the afternoon, and she felt reluctant to drive straight home to her dark house. It was on days like this, when she had been stuck in the office all day, that she took the five-minute drive up to Glen Helen for some fresh air and exercise. She parked among several other cars and briskly walked her usual trail around the glen, crossing the little bridge at the top and ending up at the wishing chair.

Sitting down on the cold stone seat, she wondered whether she was taking a risk being here on her own. Last time she had needed Dolly's help to get back to the here and now. But since her scrying experience in Summerhill Glen, when she had managed to cut the connection, she felt she had more control. And now she had the very strong feeling she needed another encounter to prepare herself for this evening in some way.

She tried to empty her mind and tune in to whatever there was, but all she heard was the bubbling stream and the rustling of the beech leaves.

Trees. When it had happened before she had been standing behind the tall beech tree by the wishing chair, not sitting on the chair. Jumping up, she moved across the path to stand behind the silver-barked tree on the bank of the stream. Laying her palm against the smooth trunk, she looked up into the beech's lofty heights and immediately felt the now familiar tingling sensation and a buzzing in her ears, as the trunk seemed to melt and ripple upwards, carrying her with it, like she was riding on the back of a silver dragon.

It was her journey again; up into the branches, down the twigs and into the leaves she went, carried by water as vapour then sap, feeling the health of the tree glowing and vibrating around her. This time, as she flowed down to ground level at the ends of the roots, she imagined herself stepping up out of the soil to stand next to the tree, successfully breaking the connection.

'You're well,' she told the beech tree. 'There's nothing wrong with you. But you've shown me how to experience the healthy resonance of your water, and that I can carry that memory with me for the others. Thank you.'

She took her hand from the beech tree and looked around. There was nobody in sight, fortunately, to have seen her talking to the tree, and she even began to feel a little foolish as she wandered slowly back to her car, enjoying the beauty of the late afternoon in the glen.

Memory-water, consecrated water, holy water, homeopathy. The theme ran through her mind as she drove back to Douglas.

CHAPTER TWENTY-ONE

Lambert's Edwardian villa nestled in the coastal hills north of Peel. Far across the sparkling sea to the west loomed the dark mass of Northern Ireland.

'Those are the Mountains of Mourne,' Kara pointed out to Paul and his parents as they approached the front door. 'Visibility's good today.'

'Very brooding,' Silke remarked, tugging on the old-fashioned bell-pull to announce their arrival.

Lambert must have heard their car draw up, as he immediately opened the door and welcomed them all into his elegant home. The house oozed *art nouveau* from every door handle and balustrade. Organic forms erupted from stained-glass windows on the stair half-landing, and a large, wooden 'Green Man' plaque was stationed on guard duty in the entrance hallway. Kara stood staring at the Green Man in fascination, trying to fathom out how he managed two contrasting expressions at one and the same time. He appeared to smile benevolently down on welcome visitors but also showed a wild gleam in his eye that would ward off unwelcome ones. She eventually decided that his left eye was friendly while his right eye was the scary one.

Fig was staying with Lambert now, having moved on from Rowena's. She joined him in greeting the new arrivals then led them all through the hall to a back door. Outside was a spacious terrace, warmed by the evening sun.

'Aren't we lucky with the weather this evening!' Fig declared, directing Karl to the nearest chair: a wicker, peacock-tail throne. 'I never thought that cloud would clear up, but it has, just in time for us. Like magic!' she laughed.

They heard another car pull up at the front of the house, and soon after Lambert appeared on the terrace with Martin in tow.

'I thought you were supposed to be in Ramsey!' Kara exclaimed on seeing him.

Martin grinned. 'I was, but I got the call to come here. It seemed important, so I came.' He stood gazing out at the view for a moment, displaying the back of his T-shirt to those seated on the terrace. Kara recognised the T-shirt from the MWT shop. It portrayed a coyote howling at the moon, and seemed to indicate Martin was beginning to connect more to his Navajo ancestry.

Fig was dressed for the occasion in a floating concoction of turquoise and brown floral cheesecloth, which seemed to date from the seventies. Silke too seemed to be competing in the hippie-throwback fashion parade, wearing a colourfully embroidered smock and smart jeans. Kara half expected Lambert to join in the theme and sport a printed-cotton caftan, but he was soberly dressed in his usual outfit of tweed jacket and brown trousers.

While their hosts poured out some of Fig's special drink concoction for everybody, Paul spoke in Kara's ear. 'This wasn't my idea, in case you were wondering. I was wanting a romantic dinner for two, but Silke got a call from Lambert and had arranged this for us all before I could have a say.'

'Not to worry. This seems sort of providential, doesn't it? We wanted to ask this lot some questions, and here we are. Very convenient, isn't it? It's as if they knew, or need to talk it over themselves.'

'We do,' Lambert spoke out, as if he had overheard her, which she felt sure he hadn't. He sat down in a large wicker chair matching Karl's and appeared to call the meeting to order. Martin hurriedly took his seat in the circle.

'We asked you here today, Martin, Kara and Paul,' Lambert addressed them, 'as we decided that things are moving far more rapidly than we anticipated. You, Kara, have made unprecedented progress in opening your mind, and you, Martin of the Navajo, are also now well on the way.' He adjusted his gaze. 'Paul, you are still in the very early stages yet, but your connection now with Kara will most likely bring rapid advancement in your abilities.'

'So this is all real?' Paul asked. 'The four of you did experience something on the hill?'

Silke spoke up. 'It was the first time for all four of us that we made such a strong connection. We needed all twelve of us in our group for our mutual energies to reach out at the time and place decided for us. Until recently we were not certain who all the twelve-group members were. Lambert, Fig and Rowena knew each other initially, of course, but they were convinced that Bill Paget and Melissa Brown were part of their group until our New Zealand tour. At that point Fig and I found our connection through Kara, and when Kara announced who was coming for the Midsummer's Eve gathering, Lambert knew we had our twelve.'

'You're right,' Martin interrupted. 'I just knew I had to come here.' He smiled ruefully at the thought of Fate controlling his actions. 'So I was kind of a back-up generator to help get you folks across.'

'In a manner of speaking, yes,' Lambert nodded.

'But what about the other eight who didn't make it across to wherever it was you went? Where does that leave us?' Paul wanted to know.

'With room to grow.' It was the first time Karl had spoken. 'Like myself,' he added. 'I've known for some years now that Silke was special, apart from the fact I married her, of course. But I've never been able to experience anything that she does. I put it down to my lack of spiritual interest. I just do the Qi-Gong exercises like she tells me, and keep fit and active under her direction, but I feel no real ability to go further myself. You, Paul, on the other hand, have got your mother's feel for spiritual matters. You've already experienced something, and now you and Kara are to work together as a team, or so I gather from Silke.'

'Is nothing secret?' Paul muttered, though he was patently pleased his father approved.

They all laughed, guessing the reason for his embarrassment. Lambert clapped his hands briefly to regain everybody's attention. 'I think some of us have questions we want to ask of each other, so let's press on. Fig? You particularly wanted to ask Kara something?'

'Yes. Thank you, Lambert.' Fig spoke directly now to Kara. 'We both had a similar experience with Selena, who gave us a glass vial containing water to bring back with us, but I don't have mine, and I want to know if you have yours.'

'No, I don't, and that's exactly what I wanted to ask you. But this afternoon I think I worked it out.' There were grunts of interest all round, and Kara launched into the account of her experience in Glen Helen by the wishing chair. 'When I travelled through the tree,' she concluded, 'I knew I hadn't literally been in the tree, only my energy had, so it was likely only our energy, astral selves or however you care to explain it, had travelled to wherever, or whenever, Selena and the others were. So we couldn't bring back anything tangible with us. Only knowledge. And that's what was in the vial – knowledge contained in water.'

There were mutterings of agreement from the others as she went on: 'Water can somehow be given a memory, as can crystal, and our bodies are largely water, holding the genetic memory of generations. The tree I visited was healthy, and I need to capture that memory of health and take it to the sick trees to retune them back to health.' She turned to Paul. 'That's what we're going to try out with the oaks,' she reminded him.

He was trying his best to look convinced, but underneath there was still Paul the scientist with a deep level of scepticism. He had yet to feel the connection, she patiently reminded herself.

Fig was not holding back however. 'Wonderful!' she burst out. 'And my work will concentrate on homeopathy and plant extracts, just as I was shown in my scrying. Specific plants have specific vibration levels that retune sick cells to a healthy vibration.' She turned to Paul, sensing his scepticism just as Kara had. 'It's a bit like when two people, who are sitting near each other and who are in empathy with one another, in other words are 'on one another's wavelength', find their heart rhythms start to coincide. Their heartbeats synchronise as their hearts' electro-magnetic fields, which are apple-shaped by the way, connect. Isn't that lovely?' She took a much-needed breath. 'Similarly, in homeopathy a plant's energy empowers the water with its particular vibration level, even when it's been diluted so there's hardly a trace of the plant in it.' She saw Paul begin to nod his comprehension and spoke again to the assembly. 'I could write a book now about what I learnt that day, except I can't possibly provide any credible references!'

Martin butted in. 'I developed a link with the stars in my scrying. I'm still trying to work out what it means though, so I don't think I downloaded all the knowledge yet. Perhaps I need to read up on quantum entanglement and see where that gets me. I might understand things a bit more then.'

'They're trying to tell you which star system we all came from,' Paul suggested in jest, but the others just nodded. He fell silent, casting a glance at his father, who smiled and gave a wink of support to his son, as if to say 'learn to live with it'.

Kara sensed Paul's unease and hurriedly moved the discussion on. 'Silke, can I ask you what you learnt?'

'Certainly. I was shown the most effective ways to make connection with the other dimensions, for that is what they are. We're surrounded by energies and beings who are eager to help us, but we can't sense them in our dimension until we reach the right resonance, or until they decide to reveal themselves to us.' She turned to her husband and stepson. 'You can both be helped to tune in, if you wish. But I'm particularly keen to try out what I've discovered with our rehabilitating drug addicts at our Hereford centre. Sound therapy is going to be on the agenda, making use of Tibetan singing bowls tuned to specific frequencies, and there are certain types of choral music I must look into. I think it might help them find a new focus to their lives.'

Martin's ears perked up. 'I think that's what I'm supposed to do too. I feel a sudden urge to learn the ancient Navajo chants and dances. Going back to the stars was like going back to my roots.' His eyes began to shine with enthusiasm, and he seemed to come to a momentous decision. 'If you don't mind, Silke, I'd like to study with you then join the Navajo rejuvenation movement that's already growing back home. I want to help my greater family reconnect both with their past and with the cosmos, so that they have more of a future.'

'It would be a pleasure, Martin. I might even set up a study centre for anybody else who's interested in developing healing skills. I feel that is my new future.' Silke too seemed ablaze with newfound zeal. 'I'm just wondering how Julia, Henrik, Tina and Matt might fit into all of this, as they are obviously part of our twelve-group.'

She looked across at Kara. 'As Fig intimated earlier, you seem to be the keystone to our group. Eight of us met when we booked the same holiday or were in New Zealand at the same time. That was the critical turning point that got us all together. But Tina and Matt came in with you, and everybody else linked up by coming here to the Isle of Man to see the orchids at a particular time. You brought us all together in the end. I don't think it would have happened without you, Kara.'

'And all because I saw a fairy in Doubtful Sound,' Kara declared in amazement. 'It's proved to be a life-changing moment.'

'And like Silke,' Lambert told her, 'you must pass on your skills when you've practised them here on the oaks. You've been thinking of the kauri trees in New Zealand, haven't you?'

'Yes,' she admitted, past being surprised at anything now. 'The Maori already send blessings and prayers to much of the natural world, so I only need to find a way to share this and pass on the knowledge, unless they know it already, of course. None of this information is new, so we were told. Only lost to us.'

'Perhaps we'll go back there on our honeymoon,' Paul said. A look of dismay overcame him and he quickly turned to Kara and reached for her hand. 'I'm sorry. I totally got ahead of myself. For some strange reason I thought I'd already proposed, and you'd said "yes".'

'Probably because I'd already thought it,' she beamed. 'You're tuning in nicely, Paul,' she added with a kiss of his hand in hers.

'Does that count as an official engagement announcement?' Fig asked eagerly, reaching for her bottle of 'Syrup of Fig's' to replenish their glasses.

Kara and Paul looked at each other and saw agreement written on each other's face.

'Yes,' Paul declared. 'I suppose it does. And it's going to necessitate a lot of changes to our lives and places of work. I'm not risking another marriage by having different ideals and aspirations from my partner,' he told Kara firmly, before adding in all seriousness: 'I feel that I too have been kissed by the dragon's breath and want to learn more.'

'So be it,' Lambert moved, raising his glass.

BIBLIOGRAPHY

Over recent years I have read many books, magazine articles and websites which prompted the writing of this book. I have only listed those books I have made reference to, or that are of particular relevance. The websites I consulted are simply too numerous to mention in a work of fiction. My grateful thanks go to all those authors out there who inspired me.

Books

Bourne, Edmund J: *Global Shift*, Noetic Books, Institute of Noetic Sciences, 2008

Bratman, Dr. Steve: *Complementary & Alternative Health: The Scientific Verdict on What Really Works*, Collins, 2007

Cooper, Primrose: *The Healing Power of Light*, Piatkus, 2000.

Cowan, James: *Fairy Folk Tales of the Maori*, Whitcomb and Tombs Ltd, 1925

Dubbeldam, Andree: *Wild Flowers of Mann*, Lily Publications Ltd, 2004

Ellis, Peter Berresford: *A Brief History of the Druids*, Robinson, 2002

Foxwood, Orion: *The Tree of Enchantment*, Red Wheel/Weiser Books, 2008

Frantzis, Bruce: *The Chi Revolution*, Blue Snake Books, 2008

Gardner, Laurence: *Realm of the Ring Lords*, Element 2004

Gardner, Laurence: *Lost Secrets of the Sacred Ark*, Element, 2003

Imbrogno, Philip: *Interdimensional Universe*, Llewellyn Publications, 2008

Miller, Hamish and Broadhurst, Paul: *The Sun and the Serpent*, Pendragon Press, 1998

Miller, Hamish and Brailsford, Barry: *In Search of the Southern Serpent*, Penwith Press and StonePrint Press, 2006

McTaggart, Lynne: *The Field*, Element, 2003

McTaggart, Lynne: *The Intention Experiment*, Element 2008

Michell, John: *The Sacred Center: The Ancient Art of Locating Sanctuaries*, Inner Traditions, 2009

Morton, Chris and Thomas, Ceri Louise: *The Mystery of the Crystal Skulls*, Element, 1997

Quest, Penelope: *Reiki for Life*, Piatkus, 2009

Randles, Jenny: *Supernatural Isle of Man*, Robert Hale, 2006

Rickard, Bob and Michell, John: *Unexplained Phenomena*, Rough Guides, 2000

Webster, Richard: *Dowsing for Beginners*, Llewellyn Publications, 2008

Magazines

New Dawn: Editor, David Jones, published by New Gnosis Communications International Pty Ltd, www.newdawnmagazine.com

Nexus: Editor, Duncan M Roads, Publisher Lee Brogan, www.nexusmagazine.com

Uncensored: Editor, Jonathan Eisen, Publisher Brian Jewell, www.uncensored.co.nz